SINÉAD O'HART

SKYBORN

LITTLE TIGER

LONDON

PROLOGUE

A watchful girl stood before the walls of a silent city. She knew those walls as well as she knew her mother's face, but while her mother was tawny-cheeked and quick to smile, the walls were crumbling in some places and covered with ivy in others. Their ancient red-hued stone was the colour of well-rubbed copper, so different from the grey, sparkling rock the people of the nearby town had used to build their houses and streets. So much thicker and stronger and *older*. The girl lived in the town and the town lived in the shadow of the city, and as far as the girl was concerned, these things had always been.

The girl's mother, like all the mothers of the town, had warned her since the moment she could walk that the city behind the walls was out of bounds. Now those warnings reverberated in her ears like a heartbeat, so clearly that she paused for a moment to listen – but there was nothing on the wind besides her own fears.

She shut her eyes as her mama's voice rolled through her one last time. "We don't go near there! Ester, keep *out*!" The terror in the words made the girl tremble, but she pushed the fear away. *What does Mama know*, she told herself. *Mama's afraid of her own shadow.*

Ester glanced at the piece of torn-off paper in her hand – a hastily completed map of the silent walls which she'd made in secret – and began to run. She folded the map and slid it into her pocket as she charged through the long grass. Lifting her gaze to focus on the walls, she tightened her lips in determination.

Her older brother Bastjan had once told her there was a way in, a way *through*, a crack worn by time in the massive stone barrier, and that if she could only find it, the mysteries that lay beyond the walls would be hers to understand. He'd spent years looking for it, to no avail, and now he'd never have another chance. When she and Mama had heard the news about the fishing boats lost on their way back to Grand Harbour, Ester had given herself one full month to grieve, another to get angry, and then another to find the way through the wall.

She'd crept out whenever she got the chance, night or day, to make her map, and finally here she was. Nothing could bring her brother back but she was willing to try anything that might come close. She could feel him with her in every step, his excitement mingled with her own.

And now she stood beneath the walls, staring up.

Ester feared many things – the dark; the sea, which had taken both her father and her beloved Bastjan; the loneliness which consumed her, sometimes, in the heart of the night. But one thing she did not fear was heights. She dreamed of flying. Every naming-day she wished, so hard, to be given wings. Wings that would carry her on the wind above Melita so that she could see the whole of her island and its scattering of islets, ones that would take her high enough to watch the continent of Afrik stretch out before her like a never-ending tapestry, ones that would bring her around the world.

Mama had often told her such things did not exist – "And anyway," she'd say, resignation veiling her dark eyes, "if they did, who'd waste them on a *girl*?" – but all that did was make Ester more determined that one day she'd soar. People would know her name. Everyone would remember her – the girl who flew.

A bird took off a hundred feet overhead and Ester's heart thundered. She closed her eyes for a moment and imagined it – *flight!* – and then without another thought, she was off. Taking a firm hold of the nearest ivy branch, Ester began to pull herself up.

Go on! Bastjan whispered, inside her head. *Go and find your wings!*

Stories about the city had been told for generations, though nobody had actually been inside it since Ester's great-grandfather's time. The Silent City behind its gateless, impenetrable walls. Home of the Slipskins, beings who could change their shape, slip their skin to become something else – things that flew or breathed fire or swam through the ocean, bringing ruin far and wide. Hunters had long ago run every last Slipskin down, leaving the Silent City truly silent – or so they said – but Ester knew that couldn't be true. She couldn't *allow* it to be true.

Legend had it that the city sank for a thousand miles beneath the earth, that it had roots deeper than the island of Melita itself, and that the Slipskins lived on the fish and flotsam that washed up through its heart. Tales were told at every hearth about how the Slipskins flew from the city on moonless nights, stealing away sleepless children from all across the island. Ester had often sat in her window with a candle burning on those nights, waiting and hoping, but she'd never seen a single thing.

Yet, she still believed. It would have been unthinkable not to. Bastjan had believed too, with everything he'd had, but belief hadn't been enough. When the water came to claim him, he'd remained a human boy. *If only he'd found a way in, perhaps he could have learned how to do it, how to slip his skin, and maybe...* But Ester couldn't finish the thought.

She gritted her teeth as she pulled herself up, higher and higher. The ivy was beginning to thin. Ester used her strong fingers, digging them into the stone like tendrils. Her skin tore and bled, her arms and hands ached, her legs trembled with the strain. She wished with all her heart she'd taken off her shoes – the soles were third-hand and well-worn, but they were still too thick for her to feel for footholds.

Then, to her left, perhaps ten feet overhead, she saw something that made her breath catch. *A crack!* She clung on, blinking hard and trying to focus her eyes. There it was – a fissure in the wall, which looked *just* wide enough for her to squeeze through. It was tucked out of sight behind the ivy and Ester knew it wasn't visible from the ground. She knew, because this was the first time she'd seen it.

You were right, Bastjan, she thought, her limbs trembling. *You were right!* She ducked her head against her upper arm, her eyes squeezed tight; then, sucking the sweat from her top lip, she looked up and began to move crab-like across the wall, feeling for and testing every handhold and foothold. The wall crumbled at her touch and every breath she took tasted like dust. One slip and Ester knew it would be a quick trip to the ground.

Soon, she was able to reach into the base of the crack and use the strength of her arms to pull herself up. She braced her knee against one side of the gap as she pushed her head and upper body through, anchoring herself with her elbows, and then—

A flock of bats, disturbed from their rest by the scrambling girl, exploded past her face. Ester shrieked, but somehow she clung to the wall until the bats had gone. She trembled, panic washing over her in waves, and suddenly she was wracked with pain – her grazed and bloodied knuckles, her trembling knees, her strained muscles, her broken heart – and she knew she had only a matter of moments before she'd lose her grip and fall.

Look, Bastjan whispered in her ear. *It's all before you, Ester. Our dream. Look!*

Ester opened her eyes.

The Silent City was spread out beneath her, though it looked like no city Ester could have imagined. Trees sprouted between mossy piles of stone, each gigantic block lying tumbled like a half-played game. Here and there Ester could see huge, jagged cracks, half obscured by undergrowth, which led into unfathomable darkness. In the centre was a pool, glinting in the sun. It looked as though the whole place had fallen through a hole in the earth and the wall had been placed around it so that people might forget it was ever there.

And nowhere could she see, or hear, the faintest hint of movement. The Silent City was well named – it was quieter than a grave in this huge, abandoned place.

Ester hung on the wall for longer than she could bear, her muscles cramping and growing sore, as she searched the city below. Her eyes filled with tears and she simply let them fall. *There's nothing here,* she told herself. *There's nothing here, Bastjan. Nothing that could have saved you. Nothing that will save me. Nothing—*

Without warning the wall beneath her gave way, crumbling into powder. Before she had time to draw breath to scream, she was falling back the way she'd climbed – until a pair of thin dark arms reached through the crack to grab her around the right wrist.

Instinctively, Ester lunged for the arms with her other hand, flailing for a foothold at the same time. The hands that held her were strong despite their size, and as Ester stared up, she saw a bare shoulder and a small, dark-eyed face, with unkempt hair and a jaw set with effort. The rest of the person – a child, perhaps a girl, Ester thought, much younger than her – was naked but for a few rags, and they were braced against the inside of the wall, their legs bearing most of the burden.

Ester felt faint. "Help!" she wheezed.

The child chirped and twittered at Ester, their intelligent black eyes staring into her own, but whatever they were trying to say was lost. If they were speaking a language, it wasn't one Ester knew.

Ester felt her grip on the child start to slip. Her sweaty

fingers were seconds away from losing their hold completely, and then her hand began to slide. In desperation she clung to the only thing she could feel – some sort of woven bracelet wrapped around the child's arm, coiling between wrist and elbow like a braid.

The child's eyes widened and their mouth opened in a horrified shriek. Ester just had time to see a mouthful of unnaturally sharp teeth before the bracelet came undone beneath her weight. The child let go of her other wrist, making a futile grab for the bracelet clutched in Ester's hand, but it was too late – Ester was falling, dropping from the wall like a stunned bird, and then she knew no more.

"Ester? *Ester!*" The young man's voice cut through the dusk. Light from his lantern fell on the bruised, scratched face of the unconscious girl, and he stood straight, holding the light high. He cupped his free hand around his mouth. "She's here! I've found her!"

He placed his lantern on the ground as he checked the child for signs of life. She was breathing and none of her limbs appeared to be lying awkwardly. As he bent to pick her up he saw she was holding a woven strap made from what looked like multi-coloured strands of fine hair. The man frowned as he released it from her fingers and tucked it into her pocket, wondering if she'd been using it to climb, somehow.

"Best not let your mother know you were disobeying her, child," he whispered to her. "Let her think you tripped and fell. Let her think anything but that you were up on that wall." He glanced up at its bulk overhead, feeling a chill run through him.

"Nikola!" The cry came from behind him and the man turned. Ester's mother came tearing over the grass, her lantern bobbing in her hand. He stood, taking the lantern from her as she fell to her knees by Ester's side.

After a moment she turned to look up at Nikola, her cheeks shining with tears. "She's alive," the woman whispered.

Nikola gave a relieved nod. "Let's get her home, Mrs Manduca. Doctor Farrugia is already on his way."

In the next few moments the rest of the search party arrived and the stretcher they'd thought to bring was put to good use. Ester was carried back to her village, the bracelet hidden in her pocket. The next day, once she'd fully woken, she would find the bracelet and hide it, along with her map, in a special enamelled box her father had given her after a particularly successful fishing trip. There it would stay for the next twenty years, until almost everyone had forgotten about it.

Almost everyone, except the Slipskin child, whose

keening cry of loss and grief would become, in time, the part of local lore that every mother would whisper to their children on stormy nights, when the wind howled.

CHAPTER ONE
TWENTY YEARS LATER

"*Whoop*-ah," murmured the hidden boy, holding a candied walnut high. It glistened in the slice of lamplight coming through the boards above him as he spun it in his grubby fingers. "An' here she goes! Sailin' through the sky, ladies and gents, sure as you like. Ain't nothin' our gal Wilma the Walnut can't do. Flyin' trapeze? You got it! Dancin' on the high wire? A breeze, to Wilma."

The boy pushed himself up on one elbow, his voice dropping to a threatening whisper. "But what's this? A beast from the deep, with wide-open jaws? It *is*, my friends, an' it looks hungry! Run! Save yerselves! It's too late for Wilma..." With this, he flicked the unfortunate walnut into his mouth, happily crunching it for a moment or two before swallowing. He licked his lips and continued. "Not to worry, folks, she went the way she would've wanted.

An' luckily enough, here's 'er brother Wally, ready to take 'er place."

He flopped back down into the dust, rummaging casually through the striped bag containing the nuts. He'd pilfered it moments before from Franco the clown's wagon, and he knew he'd have plenty of time to hide the evidence before tonight's show was over. The last act was about to begin, and he had at least half an hour before he was expected back in the ring to take his final bow. His fingers closed around another sticky nut and he pulled it free.

The boy had many hiding places around this circus ring, each of them with their own particular charms. This one, right beneath the ringside seating, gave him an ant's-eye view of things, but allowed him to smell the sweat and sawdust, and to hear the lifting lilt of the music. There was also the added benefit of the occasional treat landing nearby – a coin or a sweet slipping from the pocket of an unwary punter overhead – but they were becoming rarer and rarer these days, both punters and pockets. Tonight's audience was thin.

He pressed his eye to a hole in one of the planks and looked around as he crunched his final walnut. There were a lot of empty seats, particularly in the more expensive tiers. *No takers fer the boxes tonight at all,* he thought, looking at the plush velvet cushions and roped-off sides. Everything was damp and lacklustre, a bit like the night outside the tent. The rain hammering on the canvas was almost loud enough to drown out the ringmaster's voice – almost, but not quite.

"And now, ladies and gentlemen, boys and girls," came that very voice, one that seemed to pull an invisible thread in the chest of every performer under this roof. The boy drew up his knees and angled himself to better see Cyrus Quinn, the man on whom this entire show depended. The ringmaster wore his golden jacket tonight, its fabric gleaming in the spotlights, and his polished top hat shone almost as brightly as his shoes.

"Our time together is almost done. But let there be no mourning – no, ladies and gents! For what you have experienced this evening, here in this ring, is magic beyond compare. You have seen lions!" The ringmaster cracked his whip and there was a burst of fire from behind him, causing a lady or two in the audience to shriek, followed by a sputtering of embarrassed laughter. The ringmaster smiled indulgently before continuing. "Tigers!" Another whip crack, another explosion of fire. "Elephants from the Land of Kings!" The third and final crack, and the last of the explosions.

"You have seen knife throwers and contortionists, wire walkers and prancing dogs, a man so strong he could move the earth itself, given a long enough lever and a place to stand!" The boy smiled at this, imagining the eye-rolling that the strongman, his friend Crake, was probably doing somewhere backstage at these words.

"And now, ladies and gentlemen, boys and girls, *friends*, it is time to close our show with an act none of you will forget." The ringmaster's voice dropped slightly as he continued and every ear beneath the tent strained to hear. "The woman you are about to meet has performed before khans and emperors, sultans and doges, kings and queens. Her glittering career has taken her from the streets of Moskva in the Empire of the Rus to the palaces of Constantinople – and tonight she is here, my friends, to display to you the skill for which she has become renowned."

The ringmaster paused to take in his audience, his smile wide, and in a louder voice, he carried on. "In the aerial hoop, she is unparalleled; her talent makes gravity weep. She dances through the air as though wings sprouted from her back." Somewhere close by the circus drums began to roll as the ringmaster's patter reached its crescendo. The boy had heard this a hundred times or more, but he still found himself holding his breath, his heart pounding with excitement. He spared a glance at the audience. They looked rapt, their eyes following the ringmaster as he strode around the ring. Whatever else you might want to say about Cyrus Quinn, he was a ringmaster to the core, and he knew how to hold a crowd.

Quinn stopped and held out his arms, looking from side

to side. The boy was close enough to see the glitter in his black eyes, the shine on his pomaded moustache and hair, which spilled from beneath his hat in a dark cascade, and the glint of his strong white teeth. "Ladies and gentlemen, I am proud to present ... *Annabella Sicorina, the Flying Girl!*"

The audience's applause was thunderous, given how few of them were left, as a young woman in a sparkling red costume bounded into the centre of the ring. Her hair was piled in chestnut curls on top of her head, her lips and cheeks were painted scarlet, and as she took a bow to acknowledge the crowd, a large silver hoop was lowered until it hovered right behind her. Without looking, she hopped backwards into it, landing with practised precision just as the cymbals crashed, and the applause grew as the hoop began to rise.

The boy closed his eyes, not sure he could watch any more. His excitement faded and he let the sounds of the circus drift into the back of his mind. *Annabella Sicorina,* he thought, chewing on the inside of his lip. *This must be the fifth one we've 'ad now.* They never lasted long, these young women the ringmaster booked to perform not under their own name, but under the assumed persona of an aerialist he'd invented years before, an aerialist with an incredible talent – the Flying Girl.

Ain't none of 'em a patch on my mum, he thought,

blinking away his sudden tears. She had been the first Annabella, the one who had made their circus a success. His mum was gone now, but Annabella lived on. None of the performers who assumed the name had ever quite reached the heights of the original, and the circus's fortunes had begun to slide too.

Eventually, the boy looked up. The act was progressing well, he thought – tonight's Annabella was better than some he'd seen. She was graceful in her movements, the hoop swinging smoothly as she spun around inside it, hanging from one leg as she reached out to her audience. Applause sputtered, here and there, but the boy was dismayed to see several people getting to their feet.

Walkouts, he thought, his lip curling. *They'll be lookin' fer their money back, no doubt.* The act they were getting wasn't the one they might have been expecting, the one his mother had made famous. The death-defying, headline-grabbing Dance of the Snowflakes. It wasn't performed any more and the boy doubted it ever would be again.

The boy felt sorry for the woman in the hoop. She had to be able to see what was going on beneath her, but still she controlled her movements perfectly, the suspended ring spinning gently as she flowed from pose to pose. Finally, the ring was slowly lowered as the music crashed to an end. With one last perfect tumble, 'Annabella' dropped from her hoop to land in the sawdust of the circus ring, and she took her final bow to thin, disinterested applause.

He could see the smile fixed on her face as she looked around. Then he spotted the ringmaster. Quinn strode across the ring to stand beside her, raising her arm in the air as they bowed together – but the boy's attention was held by something the ringmaster had in his other arm. Something small and wrapped in a sparkling silver shawl. At the sight of it his face began to itch and his scratching fingernails came away clotted with the thick green face paint of his own act, the all-tumbling, all-bouncing Runner Beans. His stomach rolled, as though he were spinning in mid-air.

The circus music grew louder, the tune changing to one every performer knew – the melody which signalled the end of the show. Tonight, a weight seemed to keep the boy tethered to the dusty floor, and even as he watched the curtain to the backstage area twitch aside as his fellow performers streamed through it and out into the ring to take their final bows, still he couldn't move.

That silver shawl. The boy's heart raced as he looked at it and he swallowed back sudden fear. *He can't be goin' to ask her to do the Dance*, he thought, even though he knew the shawl, and its contents, could mean nothing else.

The performers bowed, each in their turn. The music surged. Luella, the oldest and most placid lioness, was led around the ring, licking her chops, and Mammoth – the circus's only elephant – was brought out for a final trumpet.

The applause died away, the last of the crowd trickled out into the rain and finally the tent was empty but for Quinn and 'Annabella'. The boy held his breath and listened, afraid to move in case he gave himself away.

"What's the problem, eh?" the woman said, trying to break Quinn's grip around her wrist. "You can't tell me that act wasn't perfect."

"It was perfect – but it wasn't enough," Quinn replied. He shook free the silver-wrapped thing with his other hand and the boy saw her body stiffen. He watched, trembling, as the ringmaster held up something that looked like a baby, but wasn't. It was a doll, frighteningly lifelike, which had been made years before to replace him in his mother's act once he'd grown too big and she could no longer be sure that when she threw him, high above the circus ring, that she could catch him again.

"What *is* that?" the woman said, her voice tinged with disgust.

"Look, Rosie. You saw the audience tonight," Quinn began, his voice tight and urgent. "It doesn't matter how much you bring to your act, you ain't going to hold the whole tent unless you give 'em what they want." He brandished the doll. It was dressed in a tiny silver leotard, a sparkling band around its head. "And what they want is *this*."

"I told you," the woman replied. *Rosie*, the boy thought,

barely committing the name to memory. Next week, there would probably be a new performer in her place. "I *ain't* doin' that act. Not only is it the worst luck, tryin' to recreate another performer's trick, but you know I can't do it. I can't pull it off, Mr Quinn! And then where'll we be?"

Cyrus Quinn's face grew grim. He released Rosie's hand and stroked his beard, which fell almost to his waistband. "The Dance of the Snowflakes is the only thing that's going to save this circus," he said. "I implore you. Please. Give it a try." He placed the doll into Rosie's arms, but she held it away from herself, staring down at the lifeless face with horror.

"Your *wife* –" Rosie began, looking back up at the ringmaster – "was crazy to even try this act. It's no wonder she fell, Mr Quinn. It's no wonder she's dead. I ain't havin' no part of it, sir. No part. An' you can take this back." Rosie flung the doll to the floor, its loosely articulated limbs flopping wildly as it landed. "Next thing you'll be askin' me to take your son up with me too, just like your wife did when he was nothin' bigger than that puppet there on the ground."

The boy's heart thudded painfully hard at these words and he screwed his eyes shut.

"That *boy* is not my son," Quinn growled, "as you well know. And if you're refusing my offer, you can consider your employment here terminated."

"You can consider my wagon empty as of an hour from now, in that case," Rosie retorted. "There's nothin' that could convince me to stay another night here, Mr Quinn. I'll take my leave of you an' I'll expect my wages in my hand before I go. Good luck finding another headline act to match the one I just gave you."

The boy opened his eyes again. Cyrus Quinn stood alone in the centre of the circus ring, rubbing his forehead with one hand. Rosie had disappeared. As the boy watched, Quinn dropped into a crouch, picking up the discarded doll. With a sigh, he retrieved the shawl and got to his feet. Then he strode out of the ring into the darkness beyond the reach of the spotlights. Faintly, the boy heard the ringmaster shout an order at someone unseen and the sound sent a jolt through him.

Quickly and quietly, the boy crept out of his hiding place and made his way to the side of the circus tent, where he'd loosened one of the ropes just enough to make space for him to come and go as he pleased. He ducked beneath the canvas and vanished out into the night, hoping he'd make it back to his wagon before anyone could summon him to face the wrath of Cyrus Quinn.

Chapter
Two

The boy had just finished scrubbing off the last of his green face paint when the door to his wagon was pulled open and a very irritable, and preposterously large, man made his way up the steps. Cornelius Crake was so heavy that the wagon dipped as he clambered inside, pulling the door closed behind him. Then he used one thick finger to flip the latch and lock it.

The boy watched as the strongman trod past him and up the wagon's central aisle, his width filling the gap. Crake sat on his creaking bed, tucked lengthways across the end of the wagon beneath the only window. He hung his lantern on its hook and, without a word, lifted one foot to the other knee and began to unlace his hobnailed boots.

The boy threw his washcloth into the basin, letting it soak for a moment before starting to wring it out. He could just about see Crake reflected in the mirror, his thick beard still in two large braids, the way he wore it for performances. The strongman had begun muttering to himself as he pulled ferociously at his bootlaces.

"Not bothered about inspections tonight then, eh?" the boy said mildly, jerking his head towards the door. Performers were always supposed to leave their wagons unlocked and flouting this rule was likely to get your wages docked.

The strongman looked up and met his eyes in the mirror. "Cyrus Quinn can go and take a runnin' jump," he said. "If there's to be an inspection this evenin', after all that's been said to us, then he won't have to worry about lettin' people go. We'll be walkin' out in droves all by ourselves, mark my words."

The boy hung the damp cloth on its nail and turned to his wagon-mate. "That bad, was it?"

Crake's expression brightened. "You skipped it, then," he said, a note of admiration in his voice.

The boy grinned. "Nothin' I ain't heard before."

The big man's face darkened again. "Not like this, son," he harrumphed, pulling off his boot. He wiggled his toes and the largest one popped out through his stocking. Crake sighed with relief before swapping one foot for the other. "He was like a rat in a bag tonight. Told us we'll all get our marchin' orders unless we can find a new showstopper. Half rations for the next month, no extras, no nothin'.

Some o' the crew are already makin' plans to hit the road. We'll be lucky if we have enough to put on our next show." He looked up. "An' he gave Rosie the sack," the strongman said, in a quieter voice.

The boy sighed, glancing over at the wall above his bunk. The boards were covered with pictures, carefully snipped from newspapers and circus handbills, which he had pasted there over the years. Some were faded and yellowing and others were still bright, but each of them showed Annabella Sicorina, the Flying Girl. In no two did 'Annabella' have the same face.

His gaze drifted to the pictures closest to his pillow. These were the oldest, drawn while his mother was playing the role of Annabella, and the closest he had to an image of her. They showed a beautiful young woman, her hair dark, flying on a trapeze, and her tiny baby – a tiny baby that was pinwheeling through the air, free-falling with a wide grin on its chubby face, waiting to drop into its mother's outstretched arms. He didn't remember it, but he knew this had been the original Dance of the Snowflakes – his very first act in the circus which had been his home since he was six months old.

He looked back at Crake. The strongman regarded him with cool, patient curiosity as he yanked on his bootlaces. "She wouldn't do Mum's act," the boy said, and Crake's eyes widened. "He showed 'er the doll, but she wasn't 'avin' any of it."

"Can't say I blame her." Crake grunted as the knot finally came undone. A moment later the second boot fell free, hitting the floor with a thump, and the strongman bent to line them up neatly and tuck them beneath his bunk, military-fashion. Crake's legend in the circus was that, once upon a time, he'd been a soldier in a foreign, far-off army. There was even talk that he had a metal plate in his chest where he'd been grievously wounded, years before. Sometimes the boy could believe it was all true, though Crake was famed for his gentleness.

The wagon door began to rattle, as though someone was trying to open it. After a few seconds, when it became clear that it was locked, there was an indignant knock. "Hey!" called a voice. "C'mon. It's only me."

"Jericho," sighed Crake, leaning forwards to reach into a cupboard. He pulled out a heavy iron kettle, setting it on the gas-flame hob. "Let him in, will you?"

As Crake busied himself filling the kettle from their water jug and lighting the hob, the boy opened the door outwards into the night. There, as Crake had said, loomed Jericho, the circus's chief tumbler. His perfectly smooth head shone in the light of the lantern he held in his hand, and he smiled at the boy.

"Bastjan," he greeted him, and the boy gave the tumbler a grin. His mother had named him after her brother, long lost to the sea – or so the story went. The ringmaster usually chose to refer to Bastjan, when he spoke to him at all, as 'that boy' or 'that thing', so he liked hearing the sound of his name when it was spoken with kindness. Every time, it was like an echo of his mother's voice.

"Jericho," Bastjan replied, standing to one side to let the tall man enter the wagon. He pulled the door closed and, without needing to be told, took up a seat on the floor. Jericho settled himself on Bastjan's bunk. The tumbler set down his lantern, looking awkwardly between Crake and Bastjan as though he had a thistle in his mouth.

"Spit it out, will you," Crake grumbled, the gas jet hissing beside him.

"It's the boss," Jericho said, glancing apologetically at Bastjan. "He wants to see the boy."

Bastjan felt something settle in his stomach like cold lead. His mouth dropped open. "Me? But – what've *I* done?"

"Nothin', little man, nothin' that I know of. He jus' wants to talk, is all." Jericho's words were like music and he smiled at Bastjan in a comforting way.

Bastjan turned to Crake. "He can't get rid of me. Can 'e?"

Crake snorted, shifting his bristly red moustache from side to side. "That fella would sell his own grandmother for the price of a saucepan," he said, in a dark tone. "I'd put nothin' past him."

Bastjan swallowed hard. "Thanks," he croaked.

"Arragh, you know what I mean," Crake said irritably. "You're his family, aren't you? Or the closest thing to it? So I'm sure you're probably the safest out of all of us." He gave Bastjan a look that was unexpectedly soft. "If there's anythin' left here worth stayin' for, after tonight," he added quietly.

"You're the only family I got, here or anyplace else," Bastjan said, meeting Crake's eye. There was silence in the room for a moment or two, and then Crake coughed and looked away.

"Will you get out of it now, and stop with your nonsense," the strongman muttered, just as the kettle began to whistle.

"You want me to walk with you, little man?" Jericho asked, but Bastjan knew what he'd really come to Crake's wagon for: hot whiskey – or, in Jericho's case, hot rum – and a game of cards. Jericho was already reaching into his jacket pocket for his well-thumbed deck and the hip-flask of what he called 'Louisiana's finest', which reminded him of his home across the ocean, and Crake had pulled out the low table, ready for their game. The boy shook his head.

"'Sall right. I know the way." He gave Jericho a quick grin.

"Don't be there till you're back," Crake muttered, pouring hot water into two mugs. "And if I hear about

26

you gallivantin', you'll have questions to answer in the mornin'."

"I'll be quick as I can, Crake," Bastjan sighed, pulling on his jumper. It was misshapen, holed around one elbow and an indeterminate colour, but it was warm. He opened the door and just as he was about to step out, Crake called his name. Bastjan turned to see the strongman lift a lantern down from the wall.

"Take a light, lad," he said, holding it out.

Bastjan reached for it before slipping out into the night, leaving the warmth of the wagon behind. He breathed in, looking around at the encamped circus as his breath escaped again in a white cloud. Jericho's faithful whippet, Biscuit, was curled up on the bottom step of the wagon stairs and Bastjan bent to give him a quick pat. The dog rewarded him with a gentle lick on the palm of his hand.

To his left, the empty big top reared into the night, its lights extinguished and its flags flickering in the gentle breeze; to his right were the animal enclosures, the occasional muffled *roar* letting him know the lions were, most likely, receiving their bedtime snack. All around, parked in a large, rough semicircle, were the performers' wagons, all varying in size and shape and colour, but each as familiar to Bastjan as the one he lived in.

The one belonging to Ana and Carmen, the sisters from Iberia who tumbled and did horse tricks alongside Jericho, had a light outside its door; beside it was the arch-roofed wagon where Magnus Ólafsson lived. Magnus was billed as 'the Icelandic Giant', despite, in reality, being merely a very tall Norwegian. But that was the way of it in circus life; very few people were what they seemed, and that was what drew most of them to perform beneath the big top. Once you were in the ring, you could be anyone.

With a thoughtful sigh, Bastjan stepped down into the churned-up mud, pulling up the neck of his jumper against the drizzling rain. He knew which wagon was the ringmaster's, but anyone with half a brain would have been able to work it out. Quinn's wagon was the largest by far, the only wagon Bastjan had ever seen with two floors. The upper one had a large window with an ornate balcony in front of it. Directly below this was a decoratively carved door, complete with a bell.

Bastjan gathered in a breath, put his lantern, along with his foot, on to the wagon's lowest step, and jangled the long bell cord. Then he hopped back down into the mud, biting his lip nervously as he waited for the ringmaster to answer. It didn't take long.

CHAPTER
THREE

"Come in, come on," Quinn said, before he'd even finished opening the door. "Lots to talk about, you and me. Pull up a pew." He stood back and Bastjan hopped up the steps, nodding a greeting as he passed his boss. *An' my stepdad,* he reminded himself, hardly able to believe it. His mother hadn't been married to Cyrus Quinn long before she'd had her accident, but it was a fact that they had exchanged vows. Bastjan found it difficult to imagine.

The ringmaster's wagon was, some said, the closest thing to a house. Bastjan had never been inside a house, and so he had no idea if this was true, but he never grew tired of looking at its interior – though of course there was rarely any joy to be had in being summoned before Cyrus Quinn. As he walked into the wagon, Bastjan tried not to stare at the latticed windows and the gleaming staircase and all the *rooms*. There was space in here for five families and yet Quinn had it all to himself.

"Now. If you're quite finished gawping, you an' me have business to attend to," the ringmaster said, striding past Bastjan and bumping his shoulder on the way. The boy stumbled momentarily before following him through a brightly lit doorway, which was standing open. Inside was a most remarkable room lined with heavy bookshelves, floor to ceiling. A desk made of dark wood was bolted to the centre of the floor with a tall chair behind it and two rather more modest ones in front. The ringmaster settled himself in the large chair and gestured for Bastjan to sit before him. The boy pulled himself up on to the hard seat, fighting the urge to swing his legs as the ringmaster sorted through a pile of papers on his desk.

Cyrus Quinn's beard was braided, as he preferred to wear it when he was out of the ring. His eyes were so dark that you could barely see the pupils. Most of his fingers bore gold rings and his fingernails were clean. His jacket was slung over the arm of his chair and he sat before Bastjan in a white shirt which was past its best, the sleeves rolled up to reveal his thick tanned forearms. His hair, which hung in curls beneath his top hat while he was in the circus ring, was scraped up into a knot on the top of his head, and the kohl around his eyes was smudged. Anyone who had seen him in his finery during the show would be hard pressed to believe this was the same man – only his sharp eyes and his strong white teeth remained the same.

Some people thought him handsome, but nobody who knew him well.

"Right, then," the ringmaster finally said, once the stack of paperwork was sorted to his satisfaction. He sat back in his chair, placing his elbows on the armrests and tapping one finger on his chin. "Let's talk, shall we, about your role in this circus."

Bastjan blinked. Absentmindedly he scratched at his hairline, and despite the scrubbing he'd given his face earlier, his fingernails came away green. He wiped them on his trousers, hoping the ringmaster hadn't seen. "My … role?"

"You're wasted as a simple floor performer," the ringmaster said. "Hopping around, gurning for laughs. I could hire ten kids who could do that." He sat forwards a little, fixing Bastjan with a look. "But a boy with a lineage like yours is made for the air."

"Sorry?" Bastjan said, frowning.

"Your mother," the ringmaster continued, and the words were like a bell ringing in Bastjan's ear. "Your mother, rest her soul. My original and best Annabella." Quinn's eyes softened momentarily at the memory. "She was born to fly, you know. Always climbin', never able to sit still. She used to wish she had wings, she told me –

an' when she was performin', you'd think she had. Such a talent." The ringmaster's gaze sharpened again. "When you were born, she told me how she put a name on you. 'My little Skyborn', she'd say, as if it was the name you liked performin' under. No wonder you took to it so well while you were still bottle-fed, eh?"

Quinn paused. Bastjan wondered if he could hear the thunking heartbeat inside his chest. "So what I propose is this: we get you tested on the high wire, see how you are, check whether your mum's talent has somehow passed down to you. If it hasn't, no harm done. If it has, I've got a new headline act without spendin' a penny." The ringmaster picked up a sheet of paper and sighed as he looked at it, before crumpling it up. "And goodness knows I need to stop spendin' 'em," he muttered, tossing the ball of paper to the floor.

"An' what if I say no?" Bastjan said, after a moment.

"Then I guess I'm countin' the miles between here an' the nearest orphanage, an' wonderin' whether it's worth the journey."

Bastjan felt his lips compress. He stared at Quinn, who raised one jet-black eyebrow.

"Knew you'd see sense," the ringmaster said in a reasonable tone. "And here. To sweeten the deal, so to speak, I've got this for you." He pushed at something beneath the table and Bastjan looked down to see a chest come sliding towards him, propelled by the toe of the ringmaster's boot. It was made of dark wood, bound with brass bands. Its corners and edges were bashed as though it had been dropped from a height.

"This was hers. Your mother's. Nobody's looked inside since she passed. I'm betting her old costumes are in it, maybe some dried up face paint. You might even find a love letter or two, perhaps addressed to your dearly departed dad." Bastjan blinked away from the chest and his eyes found the ringmaster's; they glittered now with a strange light, one that was colder than before. "Whatever's in it is yours, but only if you go up on the wire like I'm askin' you."

Bastjan felt something huge swelling inside him, like a whale turning over in the sea. "You've 'ad it all this time? This … treasure box?"

The ringmaster snorted. "Treasure," he said. "I hardly think so. An' who cares how long? I only discovered it the other day, doin' a bit of a clear-out."

Bastjan looked down at the chest again. It felt like his nose was filling up with glue, and his eyes burned, but he kept breathing as though nothing was wrong. *All this time*, he thought. *An' it's been right 'ere. I've bin stickin' pictures on my wall, an' this was right 'ere…*

"Have a look now, take whatever you can carry," the ringmaster said. Bastjan flinched as the man stood up.

"I'll have someone bring the rest to Crake's wagon tomorrow." Quinn walked around the desk, then dropped to his haunches to meet Bastjan's eye. "An' I'm assumin' we have a deal."

Bastjan forced himself to give a single nod and then the ringmaster got to his feet. "Excellent," he said. "Now if you'll excuse me, I've got somethin' I need to dispose of."

He bent to lift something into his arms – and Bastjan saw it was the doll, still wrapped in its shawl. Quinn curled his lip at it as he strode out of the room and then out of the wagon.

As soon as the ringmaster's footsteps faded into silence, Bastjan slid down off the chair to sit, cross-legged, in front of his mother's chest. The hasp had no padlock keeping it secure. He ran his fingertips over it briefly, before pulling it up and opening the lid with a groan and creak of its long-unused hinges.

For a moment, all he could see were piles of clothing, thrown haphazardly in. Some were crusted with old dirt and face paint; some were ripped and ragged. Others looked to be as new as the day they were made. There were corsets and dance shoes, rope-walking slippers and a pair of trapeze boots, and finally – right at the bottom, shoved into a corner – he saw a large, flat rectangular box with an enamelled lid. He reached into the chest and pulled out the box, feeling the weight of it in his hand.

The box gleamed in the light of the lamps, the wood black and shining, and the pattern on the lid was of a leaping fish surrounded by colourful waves. Bastjan's fingers quivered as he examined it, his eyes widening as he took in every detail – and then he heard the ringmaster's rapid steps as he came striding back into his wagon.

Bastjan shoved the enamelled box beneath his jumper. He leaped to his feet as the ringmaster entered the room, hoping it wouldn't come crashing to the floor.

"Anythin' worth keepin'?" Quinn said, nodding at the open chest.

"All of it," Bastjan said tightly, and the ringmaster winked at him.

"Just teasin', boy," he said. "Run along now. Get to bed. You're goin' to start trainin' with Nanette, first thing tomorrow. She's comin' out of retirement to give me an aerial act for a week or two, until you're ready, an' until then you'll be pullin' double duty. Your floor routine with the rest of the Beans will carry on as normal, and as soon as you can do it, you'll be airborne. See you in the mornin'. Right?"

He took hold of Bastjan's shoulder and ushered him out. Just as he reached to pull open the door, he leaned down to mutter in the boy's ear. "An' don't forget – if you muck up, or get cold feet, or, heaven forfend, have an *accident* out there tomorrow, your mum's things get chucked on the nearest bonfire. Do we understand each other?"

Bastjan stared up at him for a long moment. Then, he nodded.

"Good boy. Clever boy. Out you go, then," the ringmaster said, closing the wagon door firmly in Bastjan's face. When Bastjan turned to make his way down the steps, he noticed the lamp that Crake had given him was sitting forlornly where he'd left it, its flame gone out, dark as a forgotten memory.

Chapter
Four

The rain had stopped, leaving behind a cold night. Bastjan's breath plumed whitely as he looked around the deserted camp. The campfire was low and there were no gatherings of friends between wagons, no instruments being passed from hand to hand, no singsongs or arguments or laughter. It was as though the ringmaster's bad mood had sucked the life out of the circus, at least for tonight. He felt for the box beneath his jumper and hopped down from the bottom step of Quinn's wagon, his boots landing in the mud with a squelch, and then he began to walk. There weren't many places to think in the circus, but Bastjan knew there was one quiet spot. His feet trudged on, making for the animal enclosures.

The cages housing the animals were set out in two wide lines, their wagons well spaced and surrounded with piles of fresh straw. Their handlers patrolled day and night, but Bastjan was known to them all. The only greeting any of them gave him was a distracted nod as he passed by, until eventually he found a patch of ground beside the circus's largest animal wagon – the one belonging to Mammoth.

Even though he saw him almost every day, the elephant's size still made the boy hold his breath in amazement. He looked up at Mammoth's huge bulk as the elephant explored the top of his cage with his trunk, his tail swishing lazily as he shifted his immense weight from side to side. Bastjan watched his ears twitch and wondered if the elephant knew he was here – or if he knew Bastjan existed at all. Perhaps all the people in Mammoth's life were just specks and he was simply waiting for the day he could squish them all flat.

Not for the first time, Bastjan noticed that no matter how big Mammoth's cage was, it never seemed quite big enough. He glanced at the elephant's front foot, the one on the far side of the cage. A metal shackle was attached to it, with a short chain anchoring the animal to a post driven into the ground outside his wagon. It was one of the first jobs they had to do whenever the circus moved to a new place. Bastjan could hear the *thud-thud-thud* of the post being hammered into position if he closed his eyes and thought about it, but he didn't like to think about it much.

He settled into the straw and fumbled inside his jumper

for his mother's box. He ran his fingers around the pattern on the lid once again. It was so fine – the most beautiful thing he had ever seen. *An' it was Mum's*, he thought, the words painful.

He tried to open the lid, but the box was locked tight. The keyhole was tiny – too small to see clearly – and he wondered if there was a key for it. "Should I even open it? What d'you reckon, Mammoth?" He glanced up at the elephant, who twitched his ears again and flicked his tail, but had no other wisdom to impart.

"An' he's makin' me go up," Bastjan whispered, stroking the lid of the box. "I haven't been up since you fell, Mum. I don't even remember what it feels like." He closed his eyes and tried to imagine it – the height, the lights, the concentration. The fear.

And the thrill. Flight!

He opened his eyes just in time to see Mammoth lifting his tail. Bastjan, knowing what was coming, braced himself, watching carefully to make sure none of Mammoth's droppings escaped from the cage. He slipped the box back beneath his jumper and pulled himself to his feet.

"A pleasure, as always," he whispered to the elephant. Bastjan reached out his arm, stretching into the cage, and then a noise caught his ear. *Ahyuk, ahyuk.* The sharp retort of a man clearing his throat. Hubert, one of the animal handlers, had a habit of doing that every few minutes, as though something immovable was stuck just behind his tongue. A few cages down, Bastjan saw the handler's tall shape moving in the shadows as he checked on one of the lions. Soon, he'd be here. Bastjan wanted to be gone before that happened – he didn't fancy answering any questions about what he was up to.

With one last look at Mammoth, Bastjan slipped out between two cages into the open air. He took in a deep breath as he walked.

The camp was still quiet, but Bastjan knew he had nowhere else to go now but home. He wondered whether Jericho and Crake's card game was over yet. Sleeping through it could be hard, particularly if the game was going against one of the men, but Bastjan didn't think he'd be able to sleep tonight anyway. His head was too full of thoughts about the morning.

He walked towards his wagon, trudging as quickly as he could through the mud. Just as he reached the middle of the camp, a door opened to his right, spilling a rich yellow glow out into the night. Bastjan glanced towards it, squinting; a shape was moving against the light, pouring wastewater from a pitcher out on to the ground. Then the shape noticed him.

"*Querido*," said a gentle voice, and Bastjan's face relaxed into a smile.

"Evenin', Ana," he whispered.

The woman gestured for him to come nearer, and as he did so Ana perched on the top step of her wagon, setting the empty pitcher on the step below. She wrapped herself in her shawl and patted the space beside her, where Bastjan settled. Ana was warm and she smelled of lemon-scented soap.

"You're out late, *niño*," she said. "Is everything all right?"

Bastjan thought about how to answer. "'Spose," he finally decided, and Ana gave a chuckle.

"When I have a problem, I am lucky," Ana said, her brown eyes shining into Bastjan's. "I have my sister Carmen, who listens to everything I need to tell her. If you have a problem, you know I will listen."

Bastjan gripped the box through his jumper, suddenly feeling unsure. "I'm … it's all right, Ana," he said. "I was just thinkin' about my mum, that's all."

Ana nudged him gently. "Ah, yes. I remember her, but not well. She passed a few months after Carmen and I joined the circus. You were so small then, *querido*. You became everyone's boy."

Bastjan gave Ana a quick smile. "I miss 'er," he said, and misery lurched in his chest again.

Ana freed an arm from her shawl and wrapped it round his narrow shoulders. "You know something? Next time you miss her, come visit Carmen and me." She jerked her head towards the open door. "This used to be your mama's wagon. This is where you and she lived, when you were tiny. Did you know?"

Bastjan's eyes went wide. "No," he said. "Really?"

Ana nodded. "Yes! I think of your mama often. When I look in the mirror, when I step on the squeaky board at night and wake my sister, when I watch the stars shine through my window, I wonder – is this what Ester saw, or felt, or heard? And then I pray for her, *querido*, and blow a kiss to the sky."

Bastjan quivered. Something deep inside him felt like it was being squeezed – not painfully, exactly, but it wasn't something he knew how to understand. "Thanks," he managed to whisper. *Ester*, he thought, closing the name like a pearl inside a shell. *My mother*. As rarely as he heard his own name, he heard his mother's even less.

"It is no problem," Ana answered. "And remember, come any time. Carmen and me, we would love to have you. We will have a party, just for you – *una fiesta!* But for now, you should go back to Mr Crake. We do not want him stomping over here and shaking his big old silly beard all over the place – *ay! Dios mío!*" Ana tickled him, and Bastjan gave her as wide a grin as he could manage.

"G'night," he said, getting to his feet.

Ana reached out and pulled him close. She kissed his cheek and whispered into his ear. "Goodnight, *querido*. Sweet dreams."

Bastjan hopped down from the step. Giving Ana a final wave, he began to walk away. She lingered in the doorway of her wagon, in the shadows, watching until Bastjan reached his own door before going inside.

As Bastjan neared his own wagon he knew the card game was over – Biscuit was gone, and all that seeped out beneath the door was the muffled sound of gentle, regular snoring and the glow of a damped-down lantern. He opened the door and crept inside, closing it behind him as quietly as he could.

Slipping the box from beneath his jumper, he took one quick look before putting it silently under his pillow. Then, he got into his night things. He washed his hands and rubbed his teeth down with a clean finger. Before he slid into his narrow bed, he reached out to the low card table between his bunk and Crake's, where the lantern had been left sitting, and put out the light.

He reached up to the pictures on his wall, running his fingers over them. He didn't need to see to know which one was which; he knew them by touch. Here was the one where his mother – or an artist's impression of her – walked the high wire while balancing on top of a large wooden globe; there was the one where she sat on the swing like a lady from a painting, surrounded by flowers. And here, the picture of them together, dressed in matching costumes, spinning through the air as though they were held together with invisible string, his mother and him…

Bastjan's stomach lurched as he jerked out of the doze he'd slipped into, his chest tight with panic and cold sweat standing out on his forehead. He opened his eyes, blinking into the darkness. *A dream*, he told himself. *Jus' a dream.*

Crake snorted as he turned over in his bunk and Bastjan tried to calm his thundering heart. *I was fallin'*, he thought. Some of the thready tendrils of his dream still lingered, hanging in the air like smoke. *Fallin' from somewhere high. An' there was somethin' in my hand.*

But when he opened his tightly clenched fist, it was empty.

CHAPTER FIVE

"Didn't have a chance to ask you last night, young fella," Crake said, pulling the curtains open with a *whish*. The sound of his voice brought Bastjan fully awake. Instinctively, he slid his hand beneath his pillow; his fingers met with the corner of his mother's box and he relaxed. "What had the boss man to say to you?"

Bastjan pushed himself up on his elbows to stare at his friend. Crake's nightshirt and cap were worn and faded, and his reddish-tinged, mostly grey hair stuck out around his head and face like he was caught in a stiff breeze. "He wants me to go up," he said.

"No," Crake breathed, his cheeks paling. "You must've got the wrong end of the stick, lad. You must have!"

Bastjan sighed and slipped his legs out of bed. He perched on the edge of his bunk, staring at his toes.

"No joy, Crake. It's what 'e said."

Crake threw back his blankets and sat forwards. "But you've not been airborne since… Since you know when."

Since my mum died. "Yeah," Bastjan said miserably.

Crake's expression softened. "Well. Yer mother was born to it and that's a fact. So if you're anything like her – and I reckon you are – then you'll probably be a natural."

Bastjan looked at his friend. "Was she really that good? Somethin' to see, I mean?" *Ester*, he thought, feeling the name glowing inside him, somewhere deep and private.

Crake gave a quick smile, but there was sadness in it. "It was like she had a touch of somethin' otherworldly about her," he said. "Never seen anythin' like it, lad." Crake paused and looked Bastjan in the eyes. "But more important than that, she was part of this troupe and that means she's my family, blood and bone. To the grave." He blinked hard. "And so are you."

Bastjan slid off his bunk and ran the three steps to Crake's bed, launching himself into the huge man's arms. The tears came hot and fast, and without warning.

"Now, now," Crake murmured. "There's no need for that." The big man held Bastjan tightly for five long breaths and then placed him gently on the ground.

"He gave me somethin'," Bastjan said, rubbing his wet face on his sleeve. "Last night. To make me go up." He turned towards his bunk and lifted the pillow. The box lay on the plain white sheet, its dark wooden casing made even more striking by the daylight. Its enamelled pattern gleamed.

"Well, I'll be," Crake said.

"It was Mum's," Bastjan said. "I can't open it."

Crake's hands were already outstretched and Bastjan placed the box into them.

"A whole chest o' stuff, Crake. Outfits an' shoes an' face paint an' all sorts, and 'e *had* it. All this time." Bastjan's rage felt like an ember glowing deep down, just waiting for a puff of air to blow it into life. "He should've given it to me."

"He should have, that and more," Crake murmured, turning the box over and over in his large hands.

"There's a keyhole," Bastjan said. "Smaller'n any key I ever saw."

Crake squinted. "There is an' all. And you're right. Looks like a pin would fit into it."

"A pin," Bastjan whispered. "D'you think we could pick—"

A loud knock rattled the wagon's front door and Crake almost dropped the box. "Glory," he muttered, shoving it back into Bastjan's hands. Quickly, Bastjan pushed it under the pillow again.

Bastjan heard faint knocks falling on the other wagon doors as the circus was roused for practice. Even more faint were the whistles that sounded around the camp as the roustabouts passed messages to one another in the code only they fully understood, the roustie code that kept the big top up and the lights lit and the camp running smoothly.

Crake heaved himself off his bed. "After practice, we'll have another look. All right?"

Bastjan nodded and Crake began to search through the drawers beneath his bunk. As the strongman pulled out leotard after leotard, sniffing them or checking them for rips, Bastjan dropped his gaze to his own bed. The box was impossible to see beneath the pillow, and it wasn't likely that anyone would poke about the wagon while they were gone, but something about leaving it unguarded made Bastjan uneasy. He knew there was no time to look for a better hiding place – they had to get to the ring.

A couple of minutes later, Bastjan was hopping out of the wagon pulling on a plimsoll as he went while Crake strode across the campground, his oiled beard in its two thick braids resplendent in the morning light.

"Come on, lad!" the strongman called. "I'm not missin' me kippers on account o' you." Bastjan followed Crake to the mess tent. Word had spread fast about his debut on the wire. Everywhere Bastjan looked he saw interested eyes, some kind and some merely curious, watching him pass.

Then, as he was halfway through his first kipper, he

heard a voice. "She'll be looking after you, sonny," it said, and Bastjan turned to see Zenobia, the Painted Lady, leaning down to whisper in his ear. She pulled her fringed shawl tighter around herself as she met his eye. "Never you fear."

Bastjan looked away from Zenobia's face, but his eye was caught by one of her many tattoos – barely a patch on her skin was left untouched by the artists' ink. This particular tattoo showed a grinning skull wearing a hat made out of bones – possibly the skeleton's own – and something about it made him cough on his breakfast.

"That's enough, Lady Z," Crake said, wiping his greasy mouth. "Leave the lad be."

"I meant no harm, I'm sure," Zenobia replied, straightening up.

"That's as may be," Crake said, getting to his feet. He ushered Bastjan up, and the boy followed him. "Good day to you now."

Bastjan trotted after Crake. The strongman had already reached the door of the mess tent and knocked it aside as he strode through – Bastjan almost had to run to keep up. "What did she mean?" he asked. "Lady Z, Crake. What was she on about?"

"Superstitious old bat," Crake muttered. "Ignore her, son."

"Is she talkin' about Mum?" Bastjan said, and Crake

stopped. Bastjan stopped too and the strongman crouched to look him in the eye.

"Up on that wire, don't worry about anyone or anythin' but yerself," Crake said. "Those who came before you and those who'll come after – let them go." He waved one hand, as though swatting away a fly. "An' don't let anyone make you believe you can't do it – most of all yerself." Crake prodded Bastjan in the chest with one thick finger, making the boy stagger backwards a step.

Crake's knees clicked loudly as he straightened his legs and he muttered an oath under his breath as he began to walk. Bastjan followed, and minutes later, they stood at the edge of the circus ring, staring up at the trapeze and high-wire apparatus overhead. Without the audience, the space beneath the tent echoed strangely. It seemed much bigger and less comforting than usual, and Bastjan clenched his fists as he tried to imagine himself on the wire, forty feet in the air.

"Come on, then! Chop chop!" Cyrus Quinn whacked aside a flap of canvas as he strode into the ring. "Let's see what you've got!" His gaze fell on Bastjan for the briefest moment, and then he was gone, taking up his usual spot on the ringside barrier to keep an eye on proceedings.

As Quinn barked instructions at Ana and Carmen, who were practising their floor routine, Bastjan looked up at Crake. "I won't say good luck, lad," Crake said. "You won't need it. Trust yerself." Bastjan's eye was caught by the approach of a short older lady, dressed in a faded practice leotard. "An' listen to Nanette," Crake added, nodding at the woman. Crake pinched Bastjan's cheek, very gently, before moving off towards his own rehearsal area.

"Ready?" Bastjan turned to Nanette van Hemel, the circus's most experienced aerialist, as she spoke. He nodded and the woman gave him a kind smile. "We'll start with a low wire until you find your feet."

The low wire was still further off the ground than Bastjan was tall, and falling from it to the sawdust below was deeply unpleasant – and very frustrating.

"Come *on!*" he growled, after his fourth tumble to the ground.

"It takes time, Bastjan," Nanette said. Her eyes never left him for a moment. "Remember what I told you, now. Arms out and don't look down. Keep those knees bent. *Slide* your foot forwards. Feel the wire. And stand up straight, boy. No slouching. That's it!" Bastjan focused on the pole opposite, where his wire was anchored, and tried to let it run alongside his big toe, as Nanette had shown him. His right foot felt like it was cramping, and every muscle ached, but he kept going.

He tried not to look at the ringside barrier, where Quinn was sitting.

"Pay no heed to that man," Nanette said, her voice low.

"Even your mother had to learn. Nobody walks the wire without training."

Bastjan wobbled. "Did you train my mum?"

Nanette heaved a sigh. "She was an artist before I ever met her, that girl. Such a loss." She leaned close as Bastjan crouched low on the wire. "But I'll bet she was no good on her first day, either," Nanette said, her eyes twinkling.

Bastjan grinned at her before slowly rising into a standing position again. He was over halfway to the other side and he felt his determination roar. *I'm gonna touch that pole.* He focused his gaze on the spot where his wire was tied off and everything faded into the background – even Nanette's voice. All he could feel was the bite of the wire along his soles and the pull in his muscles as his body sought to keep him balanced, and all he could hear was his own calm and steady breathing.

Then, a few feet from the pole, he couldn't resist the urge any longer. Tucking in his head, he flipped into a forward roll, feeling the crunch of the wire as his spine travelled along it. In the blink of an eye he was on his feet again – and the pole was right in front of his nose. He slapped it in triumph and his head exploded with sound. Nanette was cheering, Jericho, Ana and Carmen were clapping, and from somewhere not too far away he could hear Crake shouting "That's my boy!" Bastjan glanced at the ringmaster. Quinn's lips were tight, his dark eyes intense, and the boy looked away.

Nanette jogged to his side, her yellow curls bouncing. Her eyes shone with pride. "I think it's time to try a little height," she said, reaching to help him down.

CHAPTER
SIX

Bastjan stood on the platform high above the circus ring, his soft-soled leather shoes making his toes sweat. Before him stretched the wire, disappearing into the distance, taut and steady. Unbreakable.

Then, out of nowhere, the sense of falling that had woken him in the night washed over him again. He had to shut his eyes, planting his feet wide on the platform to keep himself upright. Nanette was somewhere on the other side, watching his every move, and he didn't want to let her down.

When he was ready, Bastjan opened his eyes and stared at the wire again. He took a breath, looked up, steadied himself – and then he slid his right foot out, feeling the wire grip his sole. Somehow, it felt as though there was already a groove worn in his foot, as though the wire had been holding him up for years. It gave him strength.

Taking the second step was always the hardest part, but Bastjan did it. He glided further along the wire, his strong and agile feet finding the correct position as though they remembered it. Keeping his back straight and his knees slightly bent, his arms held out to either side and his weight centred over his leading leg, Bastjan focused his gaze on the far-side platform and allowed himself a smile. *Three more steps*, he told himself, *an' I'll try a trick.*

Those three steps brought him almost to the wire's midpoint. Taking a deep breath, his heart racing in his chest, he ran through the moves in his mind. Then, his breath held, he rotated his back foot and began to turn his torso, remembering to keep his arms steady. In the next breath, he'd completed his trick – and now he was facing back towards the platform he'd started from.

There was a sudden flash of bright white sequins and a half-formed figure appeared before him on the wire. He saw a raised arm with elegant fingers outstretched, the shine of a spotlight on a wide smile and a leap into the dark. He blinked. The person and the sequins were gone, as though they'd never been, and Bastjan realized they were a memory. *Dark hair*, he thought, trying to clear his mind. *Dark hair, an' brown eyes, just like Mum's...* His breath began to stick and he wobbled on the wire, his arms trembling. Steadying his weight-bearing leg, he found his balance and moved again.

"Is that all you've got?"

The voice was loud and large, as though the person who'd spoken was standing right behind him, and Bastjan felt his body contract in shock. Then he made the mistake of glancing down. The ringmaster was standing beneath the wire, his hands on his hips, and even from this height Bastjan was sure he could see the scorn on the man's face. He looked at the platform again – it was so close, just out of reach – but the ringmaster's mocking shout had ruined any chance he had of making it back. The boy let himself slip, his body calm and his limbs relaxed, and he bounced to safety in the huge net which was strung beneath the wire.

"That net won't be there when you're performing," the ringmaster snapped, his voice carrying around the ring.

Bastjan made his way to the edge of the net and sat there for a moment or two, his feet dangling, as he fought to catch his breath. The sparkling light he'd seen on the wire still danced behind his eyelids and his narrow chest started to labour, his ribcage billowing in and out. The *whoop* as the air left his lungs could be heard throughout the tent.

Jericho jogged up to him, his face shining with sweat and his eyes clouded with concern. "What is it?" he asked, placing a hand on the boy's arm.

"It's – nothin'," Bastjan panted. "Just – *whoop* – not

used to it, is all."

"Not used to it, my be-hind," Jericho said, frowning. "You sound like you're breathin' through a reed."

"It's fine," Bastjan insisted, trying to squash down his panic. His chest felt like Mammoth was standing on it. He'd never felt like this before, not even during the toughest routines with the Runner Beans.

"Mr Jericho!" the ringmaster shouted. "If you're *quite* ready."

"Sir, I think the boy needs a doctor," Jericho called. Horrified, Bastjan clutched his arm. Needing a doctor was one step away from being thrown out like last week's scraps.

"No!" he croaked. "Jericho, I'm fine!"

"You're makin' him perform where his mama lost her life," Jericho continued, his voice rising. "Don't you think that's a bad idea?"

"I've had a lot of bad ideas," the ringmaster called. "But putting that boy on the wire wasn't one of them. P'raps I need to thin out my floor performers, Mr J. What do you think? Do you fancy a change of scenery, eh? I'm sure there's work down the shipyard for a clever fella like you."

Jericho swallowed. "No, sir."

"Didn't quite catch that," the ringmaster shouted, cupping one hand behind his ear.

"No, sir!" Jericho called.

"Then get back to your job," Quinn said, jerking

his thumb towards the rest of the tumblers. Ana and Carmen were standing together, shooting angry looks at the ringmaster. Ana raised her fingers in a tiny wave to Bastjan, and he tried to take heart from the gesture as Jericho turned to him with sorrowful eyes. Then he was gone, loping easily over the floor, long-limbed and loose.

Within a minute or two he, Carmen and Ana had resumed their routine and Bastjan, his body quivering with the effort of breathing, rolled himself out of the safety net. He landed gracefully on the floor and began the walk to the ladder without being asked. High above on the far-side trapeze platform, Nanette watched.

Bastjan's next try was a disaster: halfway through a jump he lost his nerve and spun out. For a horrible second the world whirled and then he felt the pain of the wire against his inner thigh. He bent his leg and reached up to grab the wire with both hands, his heart thudding and his breath squeaking. Finally, he got the strength to pull himself right side up, where he shuffled backwards to the platform. He sat there for several long moments, his leg throbbing and his head pounding and his lungs sticking to themselves inside his chest.

"Again! You worthless *thing*!" the ringmaster shouted from below.

Bastjan stood, ignoring the agony in his thigh, and took his position. He blinked back his tears and raised his arms over his head, imagining the surging music, and waited for the cue nobody else could hear. Then he bounded on to the wire, landing lightly, feeling the spring at his ankles and the looseness in his knees and thinking about nothing except the next move, the next trick, the next jump—

He landed on his wrists and one gave way beneath him with a painful twang. Then he was falling, despondently, into the net.

"I don't know who the bigger fool is here," the ringmaster said, his full-chested voice carrying around the ring. Bastjan sat in the net with his head in his hands, hating his every squeaking breath, desperately trying to open his lungs. "You, or *me*, for ever believing you could deliver. Your mother could do these routines with her eyes shut! She could've done them with three limbs strapped behind her back!"

He paused to spit in the dust. "And, what's worse, the *least* of the aerialists who came after her could have done better than the *performance* you've just given." He stared up at Nanette as he said this, his eyes glittering with fury. "And I'm about to put you on as my headline act?" He shook his head. "I might as well just put this whole place up for sale, lock, stock and flaming barrel, and leave it at that."

He turned and stalked out of the tent, yelling at anyone unfortunate enough to get in his way. Finally, there was silence beneath the canvas – a silence broken only by Bastjan's mournful *whoops*, his chest sticking and squeaking as it rose and fell.

"Come on, son," Crake rumbled, his words low in the quiet tent, once they were all sure Quinn was gone. He helped Bastjan down from the net. "You've earned a rest."

CHAPTER
SEVEN

Bastjan took his place in line as the circus band kicked off a familiar melody, the one which alerted him and the other young tumblers to get ready to enter the ring. They each had their faces painted green, and their costumes were a matching shade with gold trim running up and down the arms and legs. Nobody really knew any more what they were supposed to be – the spirits of spring, some said. Peas in a pod, said others. But mostly their act went by the name of—

"The Runner Beans!" announced a strange voice, and the spotlight swung to the curtain behind which Bastjan and the others were standing. Bastjan frowned as they began to run into the ring.

"Where's Quinn?" he whispered to the girl next to him. She shrugged and kept moving, her broad smile as plastered on to her face as the thick layer of paint. The children took their places, settling into the routine that they'd known by heart for as long as many of them could remember, and Bastjan tried to look around.

One of the rousties – the one with the loudest voice, it seemed – was dressed as the ringmaster this evening. He was a tall dark-skinned man without a trace of beard, and he looked exceedingly strange in Quinn's circus outfit, mostly because it didn't fit him anywhere. *But where's the ringmaster gone?* Quinn never trusted the evening show to an understudy; something important was keeping him away from the tent.

"Oi!" hissed one of the other tumblers into Bastjan's ear. "Get your head in the ring!"

Bastjan turned to find he was out of position. He took a leap, reaching up to be ready to catch the smallest of the troupe as she came spinning through the air. He and four of the other Beans, the eldest of the group, then took their run-ups to the springboards and launched skywards, tucking and rolling with ease and landing like cats on the far side of the ring. The audience responded with a ripple of short-lived applause.

Bastjan ran through the rest of the act as though he were an automaton, barely thinking about the movements of his body, and then it was over. He and the others jogged through the curtain to backstage, where Gustav and Lily, the knife throwers, were preparing to go on.

"Lily," said Bastjan breathlessly. The woman glanced down at him, her eyes focused on the routine inside her head. She blinked and looked at him properly, her blue eyes shining as she smiled.

"All right, little bean," she replied.

"Where's Quinn?" Bastjan coughed, wiping his sweaty forehead on his sleeve. The green paint smeared, but he didn't care.

Lily shrugged. "Search me, sweetheart. Off into Oxford on business, I heard." Behind the curtain the music surged and Lily looked towards the ring. Her husband, Gustav, gave her a nod and reached out his hand for hers. "Wish us luck, then," Lily said.

"Luck," Bastjan replied, and the woman ruffled his hair. Then they were gone.

Bastjan perched on the nearest haybale. He hadn't seen the ringmaster since his terrible rehearsal that morning. *Maybe he's gone lookin' fer an orphanage to stick me in*, he thought, and his chest clenched again.

He looked around the performers' space, the secret domain behind the curtain that nobody but his circus family could see. It was haphazard – full of scenery and equipment, sandbags and props, coils of rope and lengths of chain and old coal sacks – but it was home. Bastjan's heart gave a painful lurch. This wasn't much, but it was his. And he didn't want Cyrus Quinn, or anyone, taking it away. *'Specially not now I've gone up on the wire*, he thought. Despite his failure during rehearsal, all he could think about was going up again. When he closed his eyes, he could see the flash of sparkling light, the hand reaching towards him, and he longed to see it one more time.

"There y'are," came a voice he knew, and Crake's shadow fell over him. The strongman was scarlet-cheeked and sweaty, his mighty beard looking a little frayed. Bastjan budged over as the strongman sat beside him. On one of Crake's biceps there was a tattoo Bastjan had always loved to look at – blue sea surrounding a scattering of green islands and a three-coloured flag waving at the top. This was Hibernia, Crake's homeland – but he only spoke of it when he'd had one too many whiskies.

"D'you ever miss it?" Bastjan asked, looking away from the tattoo and meeting Crake's eye. "Home, I mean."

"The ache never leaves me," Crake replied. "But most of it is below water now." Bastjan frowned questioningly and Crake explained. "The sea's a hungry beast, these days. Past few years, it's been gettin' greedier and greedier, risin' higher and higher and takin' more of the land into itself. Hibernia was one island, once, and now it's many; only the highest hills remain above water. That's why most of her people have had to leave, an' find other places to settle."

Bastjan blinked. "Why? I mean, why's the sea doin' that?"

The strongman shrugged. "Nobody really knows. Somethin' to do with glaciers, or icebergs, meltin' or somesuch. I read about it in a newspaper a few years back."

Bastjan shook away his curiosity and focused on his other question. "Where's the ringmaster, Crake?"

The strongman sucked at his top lip. "Gone into the city," he replied. "Probably to pick up his post, that sort of thing. Pay a few bills, if there's anythin' to pay 'em with. Why d'you want to know?"

"Never mind," Bastjan said, closing his eyes. Suddenly, he felt exhausted – but then, like a far-off spark of light in a dark night sky, he remembered his mother's box, still lying beneath his pillow, and it was like someone had prodded him with a sharp stick. He looked up at Crake.

"Been a long day for you, eh," Crake said gently. "I'm off to rustle up a drop of hot water. D'you want to head back to the wagon and I'll bring you some?"

Bastjan shook his head. "I jus' need a lie-down, I think," he said, stretching. "I'll wash later."

"Right you are," Crake said. But as Bastjan got to his feet, the strongman gripped his arm. He spoke to the boy in a low voice. "If you feel the need to do any embroidery, or anythin' like that, remember there'll be pins in my mendin' kit. Y'know where that is?"

Bastjan looked at his wagon-mate with a guileless expression. "Sounds easy to find."

"Good lad," Crake said, straightening up.

Bastjan grinned up at his friend and they went their separate ways. Hurrying out through the performers' exit, he kept his eyes peeled for rousties. There were a few standing around the campfire and he kept going as quickly as he dared, hoping he didn't look like he was in a suspicious rush to get back to his wagon.

He pulled the door closed behind him and, taking a leaf out of Crake's book, he flipped the latch closed, feeling quite daring as he did so. He lifted the glass on the oil lamp and lit the wick, and then got to his knees beside his bed. His hand crept beneath his pillow, and his fingers felt for the box. For one breath-stopping second, he couldn't find it – then there it was, its dark wooden case cool and smooth to the touch. He pulled it out into the light. The enamelled fish danced, its jewel-like eye blinking greenly as he tilted the box this way and that.

Bastjan tucked the box into the crook of one arm and sat on the floor, his legs crossed. Facing his bed was the low, narrow cupboard where Crake kept almost everything he owned.

It didn't take him long to find the mending kit – a length of canvas with a multitude of small pockets, each of them a perfect size for a pair of scissors or a crochet hook or a spool of thread. In one there was a small pincushion bristling with silver pinheads. Bastjan carefully took one out and, settling himself cross-legged on the floor with the box in his lap, he set to work. The pin jiggled around inside the lock to no effect, slipping between his sweaty fingers, until finally it felt as though he'd found an edge, deep inside the lock – an edge that moved.

Then the pin snapped, jabbing Bastjan in the thumb. He hissed a word Crake would have cuffed him round the ear for and stuck his wounded thumb in his mouth. Once it had stopped bleeding he pulled out another pin and tried again – but exactly the same thing happened. He shoved Crake's pincushion back into his mending kit, kicked the cupboard door shut and flopped on to his bunk with the locked box clutched to his chest.

I ain't goin' to break it open. But I got to see what's inside.

His thoughts turned to his mother's trunk, which still sat in the ringmaster's wagon. Bastjan knew there was no chance he'd be able to get to it until Quinn decided he could have it – *which*, he thought with a sigh, *will prob'ly never happen*. He wondered whether the key would even be in there – if it were him, he knew he would have found somewhere better to hide it. Somewhere private, somewhere only he knew about.

Somewhere in my wagon, Bastjan realized, his eyes slowly widening.

CHAPTER
EIGHT

Bastjan scurried between the wagons, bolting from one to the next as soon as he was sure the coast was clear. Besides the occasional roustie and the noises from the animals, all was quiet, and Bastjan soon found himself in front of Ana and Carmen's wagon without – he hoped – having been spotted by anyone.

He hopped up the steps, pausing to take one last glance around. Then he opened the door and made his way in, slipping off his muddy plimsolls at the threshold. Placing his still-glowing oil lamp on the floor, Bastjan closed the door.

The wagon was slightly larger than the one he shared with Crake, with a pair of beds side by side, a narrow gap between them. Beneath the window at the far end Ana and Carmen had a window box, which they'd made into a seat, and their curtains were thin but cheerful. Over each bed were three shelves crammed with all manner of knick-knacks, from books to perfume bottles to mysterious pots which looked to be filled with gloop of some sort or other. After glancing into one, which was sitting open, Bastjan quickly left the others alone.

Just inside the door, on the left-hand wall, was a small stove with narrow shelves built over it, shaped to accommodate the wagon's curved roof. They were packed with cups and plates and cooking pots – and, Bastjan discovered with a small smile, a glass jar of caramels. Facing the stove, tucked on the other side of the wagon door, was a washstand with an age-spotted oval mirror over it.

Bastjan took a deep breath. He was no stranger to this wagon – usually, his visits were unofficial ones, as Ana and Carmen always managed to have a stash of the best sweets in the circus – but he found himself looking at everything differently now. He thought about how strange it was that this had been his first home. His mother had checked her make-up in that mirror and she'd slept in one of those bunks. Here, his mother had fed and changed and nursed him, soothed him to sleep, played with him... *An' then brought me out to fling me around on the trapeze.* The thought was sudden and darting, painful and poisonous, and Bastjan flinched away from it.

"Weren't her fault," he whispered to himself. Dust motes danced in the air, disturbed by his breath. "He would've made 'er do it. I know it."

He looked around one more time. He didn't have long before the show came to an end. Ana and Carmen probably wouldn't mind him being here, but he wanted to find the key before they found him. They'd only distract him with stories and tickles, and he'd never find the key then.

The key. He chewed on the inside of his lip. *Where are you hidin'?*

Bastjan lowered himself on to the right-hand bunk. The mattress sagged beneath his weight and something about the squeaking springs made a memory bloom in his mind. *This was my bed,* he thought, the knowledge settling inside him. The memory acted like a magnet, drawing others to it, and he let them come. *An' the sound of the springs used to make Mum laugh. We made up a song to go with it, didn't we?*

He closed his eyes again and saw her singing to him in a low voice, her eyes bright in the light of a lantern and her smile wide. Then his memory shifted a little. Bastjan saw his mother sitting at the washstand with a pen and a pot of ink, writing. She looked up and saw him, raising one ink-stained finger to her lips as though to shush him back to sleep, and then the memory faded.

Bastjan opened his eyes and headed over to the washstand. He pulled out the stool tucked beneath and sat on it. He wasn't quite tall enough to see his reflection in the speckled mirror so he got to his knees and stretched – and there he was. Brown eyes, dark shock of hair, thoughtful expression.

He looked at the mirror, imagining his mother's face in it instead of his own. His gaze hopped along the clasps holding the glass in place and he ran his fingers across them, one by one.

Then he noticed one of the metal clasps seemed slightly smoother than the others, as though worn by someone's touch. It was barely noticeable, not unless you were really looking. The moment Bastjan put his finger to it, the clasp began to move – and along with it, so did all the other clasps, like they were connected by some unseen mechanism.

In his mind's eye he could see his mother, one evening after she thought he'd gone to sleep, perhaps the same evening he'd seen her writing. He'd been tucked up in bed, drowsily watching as she sat by the mirror brushing her hair and quietly humming him a lullaby. Then she'd put down her brush. She'd kept humming, but she'd glanced behind her as though to check there was nobody watching, and then she'd turned back to the mirror and pushed at this secret clasp, just as he was doing now.

The clasps slipped off the edge of the mirror and the glass oval popped forwards a fraction, inviting him to pull it open. Bastjan chewed his lip so hard he tasted blood – but he wiggled his fingers around behind the glass.

The mirror pivoted on a secret hinge, opening up to

reveal a shallow hidden compartment behind the glass, cut into the wood. The hollow was about the length of his hand, and barely deep enough to be there at all. But it *was* there, and inside it was an old sheet of paper folded up tightly into a neat, narrow rectangle.

Bastjan took it out with shaking fingers and pulled the paper open. It was covered with drawings and diagrams, and none of it made any sense, but that hardly mattered. Bastjan barely noticed the fading loops and curls of his mother's long-ago handwriting – he couldn't have read it, anyway. He'd never learned to read, nor had anyone ever taken the time to teach him.

Sitting in the middle of the paper, in one of the folds, lay a tiny silver key. Embedded in its shaft was a miniature fish, enamelled like the lid of the box it surely opened.

Bastjan didn't know how long he spent sitting before the mirror with his mother's secrets spread out on the washstand table. His eyes skipped from one to the other – the tiny key and the paper covered in stick-figure drawings and dense scribbles – and his chest felt as though someone had scraped it out with a knife. He was as raw inside as a peeled apple.

Through the window, his eye was caught by the crowd leaving the circus tent. Lanterns bobbed in the growing dusk and even from here the sound of the band could be heard. The performance was over – which meant he had to get out. Ana and Carmen could be back any moment.

He popped the mirror into place again and gathered his mother's things together as quickly and carefully as he could. Then, slipping them into his pocket, he picked up his lamp and hurried out of the wagon, pausing barely long enough to stick his feet into his plimsolls.

He fell into his own wagon, strangely out of breath. He felt like he'd been running for miles, even though all he'd done was cross the campground. Dropping to his knees, he placed the lantern beside his bed and pulled the box from underneath the pillow. Then he took his hand out of his pocket and carefully unwrapped the paper. The neat folds his mother had made were less sharp now, but all that mattered to him was the key. He picked it up between two fingertips and fitted it into the tiny lock. It turned. With a barely perceptible *click*, the enamelled box popped open and Bastjan lifted the lid with unsteady fingers.

The box was lined in black velvet. Curled inside was something that looked like a bracelet; Bastjan frowned as he pulled it out gently, watching it unspool. It was woven out of hair, he saw, and the clasps were made from something white. *Bone*, he thought with a shudder. *Or teeth*. Something about the object made his skin crawl and his head begin to pound. He quickly dropped it on to his bedspread and kept digging through the contents of the box.

There were pebbles – some with holes in them, others without – and shells, and an old feather that was, by now, mostly skeletal. There were some coins, large and flat and brown, which Bastjan didn't recognize. He saw an old key, far bigger than the one which fitted into the lock of the box. It looked like the key to a house, but Bastjan had no idea whose. And at the very bottom of the box, tucked neatly away, was a notebook, its pages thin and yellowing.

Bastjan pulled out the book, wishing he could read it. He frowned, concentrating, determined to learn what he could from the book anyway. He opened it, the spine crackling through lack of use, and turned the first page.

He saw a picture drawn in slightly faded blue ink; it reminded him of Crake's tattoo. There were several irregular shapes, like islands, and the spaces between the shapes were mostly filled with closely drawn lines going up and down like waves. These lines were occasionally broken to accommodate a sketch of some sort of sea creature. One of the sea creatures looked like a monstrous fish; another had a multitude of legs and one huge, round eye. The largest shape – or island – looked vaguely like a teardrop, with a wiggly bay at one end like a tail. A group of smaller islands speckled the sea around it, like babies following a parent. A circular shape at the top of the page was criss-crossed with four arrows, pointing in opposite directions.

A compass, Bastjan guessed.

He continued flicking through the notebook. It was packed with words, so many that it made Bastjan's head spin, but every few pages there was a drawing. A stick-figure sketch of a woman with dark hair and a man wearing a black suit came first, each with names printed beneath. Then, a few pages later, a house. And then a page that made him pause.

Bastjan flattened out the notebook on his knees to have a closer look. Etched into the page with frantic scratches of the pen was a terrifying sketch – a creature, like a child but also unlike one. The arms and legs were too long, the face too narrow, the teeth too sharp… And then he spotted the narrow band wrapped around the creature's arm – a narrow band that had the same unusual clasp as the one in his mother's box.

He glanced at the bracelet, which he'd left lying on his bed, and picked it up again. Letting the woven hair thread through his fingers, he began to wonder how something which might have belonged to the creature in the picture, whoever or whatever it was, had ended up among his mother's things. A few moments later, a thudding, bright-red pain began behind his eyes and his head filled with a sound like distant screaming, the agony in it so palpable that it made his heart race and his skin pucker into gooseflesh. The stink of burning filled his nostrils and he was overcome with fear and the desperate need to run…

He grimaced, his eyes closing of their own accord, and fumbled the bracelet back into the box. Almost instantly, everything ebbed away. As his pulse began to slow, Bastjan opened his eyes and stared at the bracelet. *Memories?* His brain thudded at the impossible thought. *Did that thing put memories in my 'ead, memories that ain't mine?*

A gentle knock sounded on the door. Before he could hide his mother's belongings, the top half of the door was pulled open a crack and Crake peered through.

"All well, lad?" he asked.

Bastjan hesitated, wondering when – or how – to start telling Crake what he'd just experienced, but the strongman was distracted. Crake glanced over his shoulder, looking troubled, and then met Bastjan's eye.

"We need you at the tent. The boss has called a gatherin'." Crake sighed. "And he has a head on him like a hammer, so you'd better hurry."

Bastjan simply nodded. *Ain't no point tryin' to talk about somethin' that don't make no sense, anyway.* He quickly gathered up his mother's treasures and replaced the box, his lips pressed tight with worry. *I'm comin' back fer you before Quinn sends me away*, he told it, before settling the pillow over it once more. Then, together, he and Crake slipped out into the evening.

CHAPTER NINE

"This isn't right!" a voice was calling as Bastjan and Crake entered the big top. It belonged to Zenobia, her tattoos mostly covered by her shawl, and her dyed red hair hidden beneath a headwrap. "You can't cancel shows, Mr Quinn! It brings bad luck!"

There was a rumble of agreement among the performers. Magnus Ólafsson was pacing along the back of the crowd. Ana and Carmen sat at the front, their faces twin pictures of concern. Gustav and Lily were perched on a pile of straw, looking thunderous. Nanette sat on the ground beside them and Jericho stood with his arms folded, glowering at the ringmaster. Christabel, the dog trainer, perched on a haybale nearby, looking awkward without the cloud of wagging tails that normally surrounded her. The other members of the Runner Beans were dotted between the adults, their attention mostly elsewhere.

"I've got to tell you, Lady Z, if you think we don't already have bad luck around here, you've not been paying attention," the ringmaster replied. "I hope to *change* that bad luck, but I need you all behind me to do that."

"You don't come from performing people," said Atwood, a fire juggler. His son Clement stood beside him, holding a still-smoking firestick from their act. "With respect, Mr Quinn, we do. My father, Solomon Ebele, inherited his flying circus from his mother Ihuoma, an' he was its ringmaster until the storm that brought down his fleet of airships in the Gulf of Guinea. I served under him nearly twenty years." Atwood paused for a moment before continuing. "We have traditions, sir – customs. Asking us to break faith with them is like asking us to leave some of our family behind. It's too much."

The ringmaster stared around at his troupe, sucking hard on his teeth as he took them all in. "Tradition, you say," he began. "*Customs.*" He met Atwood's eye and the fire juggler looked away. "I'll give you customs, my friends. Or, rather, things you might be accustomed *to*. Like eating. And working. And gettin' *paid* for your work." He reached into the pocket of his waistcoat and drew out a piece of paper.

"This here's a letter," he announced, "which I had the good fortune of receiving earlier this evening in Oxford.

It's no joke, trying to maintain correspondence with your friends and relations while you're on the road in this line of work, as I'm sure I don't have to tell any of you. But Oxford is one place where mail is held for me, and whenever I'm within travelling distance of that fine place I go and collect it. This letter concerns all of you, so listen up." Quinn shook the letter open and held it at arm's length. He cleared his throat and began to read.

"*My dear sir,* et cetera, et cetera, *I write in connection with your circus, of which I have heard some concerning reports of late, and to make inquiries after one of your former employees. I hope you will indulge me a question or two. I, like all who admired her, was very sad to hear of the loss of your star performer, Miss Ester Manduca*—" at this, Bastjan stiffened. Crake placed one warm, heavy hand on his shoulder as Quinn continued speaking.

"*It pains me that your fine establishment has suffered such a downturn since her demise. In order to secure not only the future of the Quinn Family Circus, but also the individual futures of each and every artist and worker relying upon you, I am willing to forward you the sum of*— Well," Quinn said, breaking off and looking back up at his troupe. "The finer ins and outs of it won't interest you." He paused as he folded the letter again and tucked it back into his pocket. "Suffice it to say, this gentleman has offered to save our hides. He's investing significant funds, in exchange for one or two favours on our end. One of those favours is our immediate departure for St Wycombe. So we leave tonight. I've telegrammed ahead. It's all arranged."

There was a moment's pause and then the tent erupted with noise.

"What favours?" Crake bellowed. He wasn't the only one asking that question. Bastjan looked around at his fellow performers, the fear and uncertainty on their faces making him nervous. He'd always assumed the circus would just *be* – that it would run and run forever. But now it seemed that things weren't as solid as he'd thought.

Quinn called for attention, his arms raised in an attempt to quell the noise. Eventually, the crowd began to settle, but the ringmaster waited until there was perfect silence before he spoke again.

"You talked to me earlier about tradition," he began, his voice low and dangerous, like something preparing to pounce. "You spoke about customs. I'm here trying to save the roof over your heads – over *all* your heads – and this is how you greet me on my return? What about the custom of respectin' your ringmaster, eh? The tradition of followin' his lead, pullin' together as a team?"

He stopped, rubbing his sweaty face with one broad hand. "I need *all* of you in your wagons by nightfall, an' on the road by midnight. Our sponsor has a business trip overseas comin' up in the next few days and he wants to see us in action before he sets off. So we're goin' to meet him in a place that suits him, which happens to be St Wycombe. And here's the rest of it." He relaxed his stance, folding his arms. "In order to mark this new era in the history of our circus, we'll hold a Grand Parade when we reach the town, to announce our arrival in style. Just like the good old days." He fixed a mirthless smile on his face, his lips drawn thin. "Perhaps that'll be traditional enough for you."

Surprised murmuring greeted this pronouncement, and the ringmaster rolled his shoulders and began to pace back and forth as he waited for the troupe to finish their discussions.

"What's a Grand Parade?" Bastjan whispered to Crake.

"We haven't done one in years – not since you were tiny and your mother's act was new, if I'm rememberin' right," the strongman replied. "As he says, they're another performin' tradition – you'd announce your arrival with a parade, maybe, or if you had a particularly impressive headline act you'd put one on to get the crowds in." Crake paused. "But tradition also says that whatever happens durin' the parade dictates the fortunes of the circus – so if somethin' goes wrong, then the circus is doomed."

"But if everythin' goes well, then it's good news?" Bastjan said.

Crake raised his eyebrows. "Somehow, nobody ever looks at it that way."

"We accept," Zenobia finally said, in a clear voice, straightening her shoulders and standing tall. "And we thank you for respecting the ways of the performing people, Mr Quinn. We'll do a Grand Parade, in the hope that it will bring good luck to all of us."

"But one thing," rumbled Atwood. "Who is this mysterious benefactor, sir? And what else does he want in return for his money?"

"His name's Bauer," the ringmaster replied. "And if you want to keep yourself and your family warm and fed, that's all you need to know about him, Atwood. As to what he wants in return for his money?" The ringmaster looked away and Bastjan flinched. He was sure that Quinn's eyes had fallen on him, gimlet-sharp, for a too-long moment, before returning to Atwood. "That's for me to worry about."

Bastjan watched as Quinn turned to speak to someone else. He was sure he hadn't imagined the strange look the ringmaster had given him a moment before – and he couldn't shake his fear that Quinn was trying to find a way to make good on his threat to leave him behind. *Whatever you're plannin'*, he thought, *you can forget it. I'm goin' to become the most amazin' high-wire act ever and then you'll never be able to be rid o' me.* Something inside him roared as the ringmaster walked away into the shadows. *This is* my *circus, Cyrus Quinn – an' you* ain't *takin' it from me!*

CHAPTER
TEN

In the shadows of a coal-dark railway tunnel, it was a quarter past midnight – and someone was wide awake.

Or *two* someones, if you counted the dog.

"Come on, Wares," came a whisper. Wares the dog, his tongue hanging out at a jaunty angle, trotted along after the young girl who'd spoken. Both of them kept well away from the tracks as they walked, because – as the girl had learned quickly on joining the gang she was now attempting to flee – nobody lasted long in the Tunnellers if they couldn't keep clear of the rails. As she hurried along, the girl found herself glad of Wares's company even if, technically, he wasn't *her* dog. He belonged to everyone and no one, having followed one of the other kids back to the tunnels one evening after a day spent singing for pennies on a street corner. Mrs Palmer, the woman who ran the gang, had never liked him; he'd been given his name, Wares, because Mrs P kept asking "Where's the dog?" if she was in the mood to kick something. So, the girl supposed, it was no great surprise that the little dog would take the first chance he got to leave it all behind – though she hoped he wouldn't abandon her as readily as he'd turned his tail on the Tunnellers.

The girl was carrying a stolen lamp, along with several other things she'd lifted from Mrs Palmer's private stash, way back in the dark tunnel. She wished she could stop for a moment and light it, but she was too close to the gang's hideout. Instead, she was relying on the occasional faint gaslight on the tunnel wall to keep her from twisting her ankle. At least at this hour there were no trains to contend with – but there was an ever-present risk of railway workers doing who-knew-what in the quiet after-hours.

"Come on, Alice," the girl muttered to herself, shaking away the shadows. "Don't tell me you're afraid of the dark."

Alice knew she couldn't risk being caught. Not only because it would land her right back at her grandfather's door, but also because it would endanger all the children she'd left behind, sleeping in a side-chamber, huddled around the gang's only other light. Mrs Palmer herself was out for the night, something so rare that Alice had never known it to happen before in all her months as part of the gang. If what the others said was true, Mrs P wouldn't return until late the next morning, probably the worse for wear after a night spent drinking with others of her ilk. Alice was hopeful she'd be gone long before the woman even noticed her absence.

Alice shuddered, blinking hard in the darkness to drive the image of Mrs P's chalk-white face from her mind. Mrs P, when she was in the mood for it, doted on some of the children, particularly the younger ones, allowing them to call her 'mother'. Then, when her mood turned, as it inevitably did, she'd beat those same children for daring to show her affection. It hadn't taken Alice long to realize a burning hatred for her and she'd been plotting escape ever since. But for so many of the other children in the gang, right beside Mrs P was where they wanted to be – they'd never known anything else.

As to what she planned to do when she reached the tunnel's end, Alice had no idea. It would be better, she reasoned, to stay away from the trains. The Tunnellers lived and worked along the railway, begging and singing and doing odd jobs for pence, as well as picking the occasional pocket, all the way between Oxford and Paddington station in London. Alice hoped that by steering clear of the tracks she'd stay out of their way for long enough to be forgotten about.

But she's not going to forget a girl who steals. Alice slipped her hand into her secret pocket and ran a fingertip over its contents – some old costume jewellery, a fistful of largely worthless coins, and a large gold ring, a memento from a long-ago wedding, possibly even Mrs Palmer's own, though Alice had never heard any mention of a Mr Palmer. Alice was planning to pawn the ring at her first opportunity, hoping Mrs Palmer had treasured it for a reason. *It'll be enough to get me started.* But, Alice realized, also enough to put Mrs Palmer on her trail. One thing Mrs P couldn't abide was thievery, but only when someone was stealing from her. Stealing things from other people was how the Tunnellers kept food in their own bellies, and grog in Mrs Palmer's.

"And that's not even considering how I'm going to feed *you*," Alice whispered to Wares. He trotted along ahead of her, sniffing at anything that was remotely suspicious-looking, damp, or furry with mould, and cocking his leg against the tunnel wall every few hundred yards. For the first time in too long, Alice felt the beginnings of a grin tickling her face as she watched him.

Up ahead, the tunnel was coming to an end. Her lungs ached for fresh air and her eyes for the light of the lamp. She picked up her pace, hoping not to trip – not now, not in the last few feet before freedom – and then she was out.

She fell to her knees, placing the lamp on the ground, and dug her fingers through the gravel by the track as she breathed. Wares licked her cheek. She picked the wriggling dog up in one arm and got to her feet. *Well, Grandfather*, she thought. *What do you think of me now?* Part of her almost wished he were here, just so she could see his face, but she knew there was no chance of that. Alice had run to the tunnels because she knew her grandfather would never, *could* never, think of looking for her there.

Beside her rose the embankment next to the railway line. She let Wares make his own way up and she scrambled after him, grabbing handfuls of grass to pull herself to the top. She took stock of her surroundings. There was a wide road, with tall, dark-windowed houses on the far side. The pavement running along in front of the houses was dotted with gaslights. Oxford and her grandfather's house, with its quiet, polished corridors, its locked doors and its frowning disapproval, was to her right; to her left lay the unknown. *So*, Alice told herself, *that only leaves me with one choice.* She looked down the dark empty road to her left, wondering how far she could get on foot before daybreak.

Suddenly, Wares began to growl.

"Shush, silly," Alice whispered, but the dog ignored her. He was looking towards the city, his body poised to attack – and then Alice saw what the dog had smelled. *Something's coming!*

She dropped to the ground, scrambling down a few feet to hang precariously off the top of the embankment. In her haste she dropped the lamp; it rolled to the bottom and landed with a *smash* beside the railway line. Wares gave a sharp bark. Alice looked back towards the road and her mouth dropped open in surprise. She pulled Wares close as they watched.

Horses, some wearing plumes, pulling the biggest and most impressive carriages and wagons she'd ever seen – and there were so many of them. They kept coming, the caravan of wagons continuing for what felt like miles.

Finally, like a smoke-puffing dragon, a huge steam engine brought up the rear of the procession. It was pulling a long trailer with high sides, and as it passed, Alice read the words *Quinn Family Circus* painted on it in letters three-feet tall. It lumbered slowly along after the rest of the procession, and Alice's pulse quickened. The trailer was moving slowly enough for her to catch up with it – if she was brave enough.

With Wares at her heels, she pulled herself up on to the road just as the steam engine passed by. The trailer might have had high sides, but it was open at the back, and sticking out were several huge rolls of canvas and tarpaulin, some with wide red stripes. *The big top!* Alice marvelled at it, her eyes wide. Grandfather had brought her to the circus once, years before, back when she still thought he loved her, but she pushed that memory away.

Her eye was caught by a light coming on in the window of one of the tall houses on the far side of the road. Perhaps a child had woken in the night, disturbed by the sound of the passing circus. The curtain in the window twitched, and Alice realized someone was about to look out into the night. That someone might also see her. She was a good way from her grandfather's house, but he knew everyone – and she doubted there was a single soul in the whole city who'd forget her face. *I can't take the chance they might recognize me*, she told herself. *Go, now!*

Alice hurried after the slow-moving trailer and lifted Wares on to it. Then, using a strap attached to one of the canvas rolls, she hauled herself up, finding a place to hide among the pieces of the downed big top. And as they rolled away from the only life she'd ever known – first with her grandfather, and then with Mrs P – Alice breathed a huge sigh of relief.

Chapter
Eleven

The order for pegs-up had come just before midnight, as the ringmaster had instructed, and the circus convoy rolled through Oxford and away. Bastjan kneeled on Crake's bunk, his elbows on the window ledge and his chin resting in his palms, and watched their slow progress through the open window.

Nothing in the circus felt right tonight. Spirits were low and tempers high. There'd been a fight between Clement and Lady Zenobia about the placement of their wagons in the convoy, and Magnus Ólafsson had taken to his wagon with a flagon of beer, which meant he wouldn't re-emerge for a day or two. Questions about the mysterious money man were on everyone's lips, and Bastjan couldn't forget how the ringmaster had looked at him when he'd mentioned the new sponsor earlier. As if that wasn't enough, there was the issue of the strange bracelet in his mother's box. Every time his thoughts even skirted it, he felt his fear spiking – along with his curiosity.

At least there was one mystery that he could get some help with. He turned away from the window, pulling it closed. The half-door at the far end of the wagon was open and Bastjan could see Crake's shoulder as he sat outside on the porch, the horse's reins in his great hands. Bastjan slid off the bunk and reached beneath his pillow to take his mother's notebook out of her box. He tucked it into the waistband of his trousers as he made his way to the door. Crake greeted him with a good-natured grunt.

"How far 'ave we come?" Bastjan asked. Goodness knew what time it was. The moon was high and the stars were up, and even Crake had a scarf on to muffle against the cool night air.

"Fifteen, maybe twenty miles, I'd say," Crake answered. "Should be there by first light, with any luck." He harrumphed. "Not that we've been havin' much of that, of late."

Bastjan reached out to unlatch the half-door and Crake shifted a little to make room for him. "Gotta ask you somethin'," Bastjan said, keeping his voice quiet as he pulled himself up.

"Somethin' so important that it has to be discussed in the heart of the night, when all good boys should be in bed," Crake said. A smile danced over his lips as he threw his young friend a sidelong glance.

"Yes," Bastjan replied, his face set and serious. He pulled the notebook free and Crake's grin faded. The strongman looped the horse's reins around the wooden railing in front of him and held out his hands. The horse, accustomed to following the wagon in front, simply kept on plodding as Bastjan handed over the book.

Crake took one look at its cover, illuminated by the wagon's swinging lantern, and stared at Bastjan. "Your mother's," he whispered. "You got the box open, then?"

Bastjan unfolded his fingers. The key lay in his palm. Crake's eyes widened as he stared at it.

"I got to know what it says, Crake," Bastjan said.

The big man cleared his throat. "I'm years out of practice, lad," he said, in a small voice. He carefully laid the notebook down on his knee and opened it with the tips of two fingers. He squinted at the page with the drawing of the island on it for a moment, holding the book at arm's length and then bringing it right up to his nose. "No good," he proclaimed. "I'm goin' to need me goggles."

Bastjan went back into the wagon, searching through Crake's cupboard until he found the wire-rimmed, thick-lensed glasses which Crake had discovered one evening after a performance and afterwards kept for his own. He brought them out to the strongman, who took them from him with grave dignity before settling them on the end of his nose.

"Now," Crake muttered, peering at the book again over the rim of the purloined spectacles. "Me-li-ta," he read, sounding out the syllables of the unfamiliar word written beneath the hand-drawn map. "An' the rest of it, I can't read. I'm sorry, son."

"Please, Crake," Bastjan begged. "Try!"

Crake turned, blinking at him over the top of his glasses. "It's not in English, lad. The rest of the words are in a language I don't know." He sighed, flipping through the pages. "Ah. Now here's somethin' I can understand," he said, as the book fell open at the page with the stick figures drawn on it. "Mama," Crake read. "And this here says 'Nikola'."

"Who're they, then?" Bastjan asked.

"Well. If your mam drew this, as I'm sure she did," Crake said gently, "then this lady here –" he jabbed at the page – "is your grandmother. I'm not sure who this Nikola chap is, but he must've been someone who meant somethin' to your mam, I s'pose."

My grandmother. Bastjan gazed at the drawing for several long minutes, taking in the pencil marks sketching out the woman's headscarf, her dark eyes, her long dress.

Crake began to flick through the notebook from the back. Bastjan frowned, wondering what he was doing.

All the pages seemed to be entirely blank. Finally, the strongman flattened it out to reveal a torn-off page from a different book – a printed book – folded into a tight square and jammed in against the notebook's spine.

"Hah," Crake said. "I thought I felt somethin' back there. Here we are."

Bastjan reached in and pulled the loose sheet free. He unfolded it and, together, the man and the boy stared at the page. Bastjan's scalp prickled as he looked.

"Now there's a sight," Crake said.

The page, its torn edge ragged and uneven, bore a drawing of a creature which was half woman and half something else – something with a scaly body from the chest down, short, lizard-like legs and small feet with three red-tipped claws. From behind her rose a tail which was poised to strike. She had human arms and a human face, and her hair fell in thick golden waves which turned, eventually, into streams of water. She stared out at them with an angry gaze.

"I can't read what it says," Crake said, running one thick finger along the words printed beneath the picture. "Meta-somethin'. Makes no sense."

"Crake, look," Bastjan said, pointing to the top corner of the page, over the lizard-lady's head. "That word. Ain't it the same as the one my mum wrote?"

Crake blinked. "Begob," he said. "You're right. Melita."

They looked at one other in confusion. "A place," Bastjan finally said, his expression clearing. "The island."

"Her home, lad," Crake said gently.

They turned back to the page in Bastjan's hand. Above the word 'Melita' was a drawing of something Bastjan couldn't describe. It looked like a gigantic hole in the earth surrounded by a high wall, drawn as though the viewer had a bird's-eye view of it. A sheer cliff leading down to the sea was pressed against one of its sides, and in the centre of the enclosed space was a beast, one with arms and a humanlike head, but the body of a fish. *Part human, an' part animal, jus' like the lizard-lady*, Bastjan thought. *An' like the thing my mum drew.*

They turned the page over, but all they could see on the other side were more drawings of nightmarish creatures, including one which gave Bastjan a cold shiver down his spine – a huge, tentacled thing with a wide-open beak, thrashing in water and destroying a ship in the process.

"Let's just put it back," he said, yanking the notebook from Crake's hands. As he did so, two narrow white pieces of card slid from between the pages and landed in the boy's lap. A thin night breeze threatened to blow them away and Bastjan slapped his hand down to catch them before they vanished into the dark. They were covered in words printed in thick black type.

"Tickets," Crake said, taking one. "Well, now. This here's

a third-class ticket on a ZepLiner, leaving from Isle of Dogs Airship Station in London, heading for the city of Mdina, on the island of Melita, for one adult. And the other –" he peered at it, still held carefully in Bastjan's fingers – "is the same, except for a child." Crake blinked, meeting Bastjan's eye. "And they're one way."

"What's that mean?" Bastjan whispered.

"It means she wanted to go home, son," Crake said. "An' she wasn't comin' back."

"Mum," Bastjan whispered. "She bought 'em, right?"

Crake ran his finger gently over the dates of travel printed on the ticket in his hand. "Right before she died, by the looks of it. An' she never got to use 'em."

Just as Bastjan opened his mouth to tell Crake about his mother's bracelet, and the other things he'd found in the box, a jolt rocked the wagon on its springs.

"Whoa!" Crake called, reaching out to pull the reins free as Bastjan scrambled to grab the notebook, the loose sheet and the tickets. He lost his balance and pitched sideways, his hands too full to break his fall – and then he felt Crake's fingers wrap securely around his arm, hauling him back on to the seat.

"All right, lad?" Crake said, holding the reins with one hand as he settled Bastjan with the other. He squinted into the darkness. "We must've rolled over a rock. I'll have to pay better attention to this road or we'll be on our ears before too long."

Bastjan caught his breath. He looked down at the things in his hands. Luckily, nothing had fluttered off into the night.

"Go on to bed, boy," Crake said to Bastjan. "Take these with you and keep 'em out of sight. I'll stay out here and try to keep old Betsy from turning us over."

"Crake…" Bastjan began, but the strongman was focused on the road.

"It'll have to wait till mornin', son," Crake said, his tone firm. "I've enough to be doin' now. Off you go an' rest. It's a big day ahead."

Bastjan sighed, getting to his feet. He took his mother's things and went back into the wagon, closing the door behind him. But he had no intention of going to sleep; his head was thudding with everything it was trying to contain. He hurried to the window, swishing the thin curtain closed. Then he turned up the flickering gaslight and sat cross-legged on his bed, his mother's notebook on his knee. Opening it, he flicked to the page with the creature his mother had drawn, the one with the band around its wrist. There was a link between this drawing and everything else he'd discovered, but no matter how hard Bastjan twisted his brain, the answer wouldn't fall out.

And then, with a jerk, he remembered the bracelet and the power it seemed to have.

Bastjan pulled out the box from beneath his pillow. It was still unlocked, and he lifted the lid carefully, as though afraid something was about to jump out and bite him. The bracelet sat at the top of the box, curled in on itself like it was sleeping. Gently, he pulled it out. Its touch on his skin was soft, like cool silk; the threads that made it up were many-coloured, some of them gleaming in the lamplight, golden strands among the black. It was beautiful, but the fang-like clasps still made his stomach churn.

Closing his fist around the bracelet, Bastjan shut his eyes. He pushed away the noises of the circus – the clip-clopping of hooves, the distant whistle of the steam engine, the shouts of the rousties, the occasional burst of song – and tried to focus. *Come on*, he thought, setting his jaw. *Do it again! I'm ready this time – I ain't afraid. Do it!*

And then a face burst into his mind – a thin face, young and scared, one with fine golden-brown hair on its cheeks and down its neck as well as on top of its head, where the hair was long and matted and thick. A face with a wide-open, screaming mouth filled with sharp teeth; a face with eyes that were too wide and too hungry, their golden pupils slit like a cat's. In the next breath it felt like he was falling, and the face grew smaller and smaller above him until finally it vanished into the dark.

CHAPTER
TWELVE

Morning light trickled greyly through the wagon curtains, tickling Bastjan's eyelids until they opened. Straightaway, he knew they were in a new place. Everything smelled different and the noises coming through his window were unfamiliar. Voices shouting, horses whinnying, the rumble of cartwheels on cobblestones, and somewhere the clack and whistle of a train.

His head pounded as he sat up. There was something in his hand and he was surprised to find it was the bracelet – he must have fallen asleep still holding it. Feeling around beneath his pillow with his free hand, Bastjan yanked out the box and deposited the bracelet inside. His chest felt tight as he slid the box back into its hiding place.

He sat on the edge of his bunk, trying to shake away his dreams. But some fragment of them lingered around him as though it didn't want to leave – as though it had finally found the warm place it was looking for and wanted to make itself at home. He forced in a few deep breaths, trying not to remember the face he'd seen in his dream – if it had been a dream. *A memory*, he told himself, feeling sure he was right. A thought needled at him: were the memories trapped in the bracelet his mother's? He could hardly bear its touch, but something inside him needed to know.

Bastjan padded to the washstand and grimaced at his sunken-eyed reflection. Then, balancing on one leg even as the wagon tipped and dipped over rough ground, he pulled himself into his Runner Bean costume, ready for the Grand Parade. Carrying his plimsolls in his hand, he unlatched the wagon door and went outside. The morning was crisp and bright, and the freshness of the air finally began to clear his thoughts.

Stop bein' such a baby! Bastjan told himself. *Believin' in fairy tales an' monsters, an' lettin' dreams get the better of you. You got bigger things to worry about.*

Crake's eyes were small and red-rimmed beneath the brim of his hat as he took in their surroundings. Bastjan plopped down on the bench beside him and pulled on his plimsolls, one by one.

"Mornin'," Crake grumbled, before clicking the horse on gently. "I know, girleen. I know you've pulled my rickety old bones the whole night long. But you'll be able to rest soon."

"Where are we, then?" Bastjan said. Close-packed houses lined the narrow street, with warrens of lanes and alleys breaking off at every junction. To their right soared a huge church, and just ahead arched an impressive stone structure – a railway bridge, Bastjan realized, watching a plume of steam pass over it at speed. He didn't like cities, or even towns like this one, the tall, overhanging buildings made him feel crowded and locked in, and it seemed too easy to get lost.

"Comin' into St Wycombe," Crake replied, glancing around. "Though it's changed a bit since I was last here."

Bastjan pulled his knees up to his chin. "How d'you know this place?"

Crake shrugged. "Been through it once or twice. This is far from the most direct road to London, but the old ways are underwater now. You spend long enough in the travellin' life, an' you get to know every road and byroad, lad. Now –" he handed the reins to Bastjan – "let me go an' get into me fightin' gear."

Bastjan felt nervous as he guided the horse through the unfamiliar streets, but they were midway through the convoy so all they had to do was follow the rolling trail of the wagon in front. Soon, they took a turn to the left, clopping up a narrower road, before turning again and passing over a bridge. The railway lines shone below them, and Bastjan squinted at the large, forbidding building not far from the tracks. *It looks like a prison*, he thought. *Or a work'ouse*. He suppressed a shudder and looked away.

Just as the wagons approached the gates to a huge park and the convoy began to slow, Crake emerged. He was dressed in his showtime clothes, his beard in its two great plaits, his red hair slicked back and pinned unwillingly down around his ears. He stood in the doorway and left Bastjan to drive, placing one reassuring hand on the boy's shoulder.

Somewhere behind them, the band began to play, a bright and heart-gladdening tune, and Bastjan noticed faces looking in their direction. Some were curious; most were smiling.

Moments later, they entered a wide thoroughfare with parkland all around. The ringmaster led the way, his magnificent wagon emblazoned with the circus name in gold letters already beginning to draw a crowd. The other wagons took their accustomed places, pulling to a halt in a large semicircle with the ringmaster's wagon at the top, and the band marched into the centre, playing with gusto.

Crake leaped down from the wagon before it had quite finished moving, leaving Bastjan to roll it into position. When that was done, Bastjan hopped down from his perch. He watched as the crowd started to gather at the open end of the semicircle. Children pushed to the front and a cluster of them took up residence around the hissing steam engine, which had pulled to a halt a few moments before with a sharp *toot* on its whistle.

The rousties were trickling through the camp, smoothly swapping out tired horses with fresh ones and beginning to lay out the perimeter fence. The animal wagons were being re-hitched, ready to roll out, and Bastjan watched as three rousties walked the length of the trailer which had carried the circus tent all the way from Oxford, checking for damage.

As the men reached the halfway point, something at the end of the trailer caught Bastjan's eye and he blinked. He frowned, staring harder, as a girl jumped down from the end of the trailer. She was covered in grime, but as she turned her head to look behind her Bastjan saw a rust-red birthmark on her face, like a splodge of faded paint, almost covering one cheek and trailing down her neck.

The girl turned back to the trailer to grab a small, nondescript dog, which she tucked under one arm. Then she and the dog melted into the crowd – and just in time too, as in the next breath the three rousties arrived at the end of the trailer and began to haul out the rolls of canvas, ready to reassemble the big top.

Bastjan watched the space in the crowd where the girl had vanished and jogged towards Crake. "Breakfast's goin' to have to wait, eh, son," the strongman muttered as he drew near.

From behind them came the stilt walkers, their impossibly long legs swishing gently in the morning air, and the circus band struck up once more. The ringmaster, in his full regalia, stepped into position at the head of the band, and then, with one swoop of his metal-tipped cane, he summoned his performers into formation behind him. Like soldiers behind their general, the members of the Quinn Family Circus filed out into the morning sunshine and the Grand Parade began.

Alice's every instinct was telling her to stay away from the crowd, but something else – maybe her memories of the magical days when she was new to living with her grandfather, when they did things together, and before he'd started ignoring her unless there was a doctor in the room – was forcing her to stay. She pushed through the crowd, jostling like everyone else for the best position. The stilt walkers had passed overhead moments before, scattering flyers like leaves in their wake, and the band was probably half a mile away, though its music could still be heard.

"Look at *that*, Wares," she gasped as a fire breather looked skywards and blew, the flame exploding from his lips as though he were a dragon. Alice felt herself grinning, and everywhere she looked all she saw were shining eyes and smiles. *Nobody's looking at me*, she realized. *Nobody cares about my face – not here.* The next act to pass was equally entrancing

– four shining horses, their coats like polished pearl and manes that seemed made of rainbows, and two dark-haired, beautiful women doing acrobatic tricks on their backs.

After the horse ladies came six richly dressed animal handlers, sinewy, quick-eyed men, whistling and calling to one another as they walked. Each of them was holding a long pole and Alice grimaced to see their sharp-spiked tops. Between the men, utterly uninterested in the crowd, plodded the largest creature Alice had ever seen. She'd never been so close to an elephant before and the sight stole her breath. Its tusks were hung with garlands and on its head it wore a crown. Behind its blinker, the animal's eye was wet and sad – and then it was gone.

A sound caught her ear and Alice stepped back as a tumbler came spilling up the path, inches from where she stood – a tall, muscular man in a sparkling red costume, he was bald as an egg and wore dramatic make-up, made more so by the darkness of his skin. He was so close that she could hear his controlled breathing and smell his greasepaint. Then he too was gone, his legs flying over his head one moment and his entire body bouncing along on one hand the next.

Alice felt her heart skitter in her chest at the beauty of it. There, a pale woman covered in bright tattoos, her dress cut scandalously low at the back; here, a huge man on the back of a slow-moving float with his beard in two red braids, each as thick as one of Alice's legs, holding an anvil in each hand. As his float passed by, he lifted the anvils into the air to resounding applause. Then there was a display of acrobatics by a troupe of children, each of them dressed in green. They ran, jumping and spinning in mid-air, landing on one another's shoulders for long enough to draw applause before tumbling to earth once more.

One passing wagon looked ordinary enough until, at a shout from a man nearby, its sides dropped to reveal a pair of prowling tigers held in a cage, its bars a little too far apart for comfort. Alice, along with everyone else nearby, gasped in fright; Wares bared his teeth and yapped fearlessly at the bigger of the tigers, who gave him a laconic growl.

Next came a group of clowns, their face paint as garish as their clothes, followed by jugglers and knife throwers and a woman, her hair in faded yellow curls, who sat inside a large silver ring suspended from a tall metal arch, looking down upon them all with an inscrutable expression.

Alice had grabbed one of the flyers as they'd fallen from the hands of the stilt walkers and now she took the chance to look at it properly. It showed a rearing horse wearing a plume, a woman in a sparkling costume which looked, Alice thought, rather uncomfortable, and a growling lion with one great paw raised – all of them standing inside a gaily painted ring.

She glanced back up at the passing parade. It was almost

over now. A line of trotting miniature ponies brought up the rear, each with glittering harnesses and plumes on their heads. After them, all Alice could see was the dust of the path and the running children playing in the circus's wake, fired up with imagination after what they'd seen. Around her, the crowd began to grow restless, drifting away in clumps, and she realized two things: her opportunities to stay out of sight were vanishing, and so were her chances to put the rest of her half-thought-out plan into action. Her tummy rumbled unexpectedly and she sighed. *And I need to find something to eat too.*

Alice slipped her hand into her inside pocket, feeling for the trinkets and the ring she'd stolen from Mrs Palmer. *Come on*, she told herself. *You've got enough to make it to London.* But something was sticking her feet to the ground. The circus music lingered in her head, and Oxford with its domes and spires and silent squares seemed a million miles away. *He'll never think to look for me here*, she told herself, her grandfather's face floating in her mind's eye. *I could be safe, for a while.*

Alice glanced at the parked wagons and the men busily moving between them, and her gaze landed on a wagon with a half-door – the bottom part of which was swinging slightly open.

And then, before she could allow her second thoughts to drown out her first, she made her move.

CHAPTER
THIRTEEN

Bastjan had just shovelled a forkload of fried egg into his mouth when the ringmaster appeared in his peripheral vision. In his hurry to chew and swallow he began to cough, finally spluttering down his mouthful of breakfast with a swig of hot tea. Quinn pulled up a stool next to him and watched, with barely controlled patience, as he tried to get his breath back.

"Good work out there this morning," the ringmaster said, at last. "You and the rest of the kids." Quinn paused, scratching at his beard. "But the patron's here, ahead of schedule. He wants to take a walk around the camp, have a look at the big top, and he wants to watch you rehearse."

Bastjan stared into Quinn's eyes. There was something in them which was even more frightening than his anger – *hope*. Trust, even. Quinn gave a cautious, tight smile and clenched his fist nervously.

"*Me?* What's 'e want to watch me for?"

Quinn waved a hand. "He was a fan of your mum's, apparently. I told him you were part of the troupe now and he was fascinated to hear it. So you an' Nanette have got to put on something a bit special today during practice. Right?"

"Right," Bastjan mumbled.

"Good lad. Good lad," Quinn said, clapping him on the shoulder.

The ringmaster got to his feet and looked around the crowded mess tent, raising his voice as he kept speaking. Every face turned to him. "Our benefactor has arrived early. I know this throws us out a bit, but I need you all at your best. Is that understood? He'll be present for rehearsal; he may even stay for tonight's performance, if his business doesn't take him back to London. Either way, we've got to perform like the queen herself was sittin' down among us. There'll be no matinee performance today, which leaves some of you free to rest, and others to train." He looked down at Bastjan. "After breakfast, we'll see you in the ring."

As soon as Quinn was gone, Bastjan turned back to his food. The eggs now seemed to swim in a bath of grease and his toast had gone cold. His stomach turned at the sight of it.

"Let's get you ready, then," said Crake, his words

muffled as he crunched down his last morsel of bacon. Bastjan glanced at his friend.

"I'm not my mum," he whispered, looking at Crake with worried eyes.

"Nobody will ever be," Crake said, getting to his feet. "And all you can do is your best, lad. Come on, now. Chin up."

They walked side by side back to the wagon, and Bastjan was so deep in thought that he didn't notice the bottom of their half-door was slightly open until he put his foot on to the steps. His heart froze.

"Crake," he gasped. He turned to the strongman, who'd gone pale.

"I mustn't have latched it after me earlier, before the parade," Crake said. "It'll be all right, son."

But Bastjan was gone, up the steps in a flash and through the door. He raced to his bunk and thunked down on both knees, shoving his hands beneath the mattress – and finally, his head fell forwards on to his blankets.

"Is it … is everythin' all right?" Crake sounded like he was a hundred miles away, through the rushing in Bastjan's ears.

"It's there," he said. "Mum's box is there, an' her book. No one's took 'em."

The wagon dipped beneath Crake's weight as he climbed in. "Why would they, son?" he said, as gently as he could. He sat on the bed beside the quaking boy, patting his head awkwardly.

Bastjan looked up, the weight of everything on his mind finally growing too heavy to bear. "I need to tell you somethin', Crake," he began. "About Mum's things. It's not just a box of old tat. It's—"

But Bastjan was interrupted by an unexpected sound – a sneeze, which someone had desperately been trying to hold in. It was followed by a scrabbling noise, like claws on wood, somewhere inside the wagon.

Bastjan's eyes widened and his shock was mirrored on Crake's face. The strongman pushed himself up off the bunk, standing between Bastjan and the wagon's open door like a wall. "Show yerself!" he shouted, his hands curling into two great fists.

There was a muffled *thump* from Crake's cupboard. Bastjan pulled open the door and there, folded up behind the kettle, the contraband half-empty bottle of whiskey and Crake's squeezebox was a person with two bright eyes, a shock of raggedy dark hair and a deep red birthmark on one cheek. Tucked, somehow, against her body was a small, friendly-looking dog, his tongue lolloping out and one ear poking up inquisitively.

"It's *you!*" Bastjan said, his mouth falling open.

The girl blew a stray lock of hair out of her eyes and frowned at him. "What do you mean, 'it's you'? I've never seen you before in my life."

"I saw you earlier. You chose some humdinger of a hidin' place, didn't ya? If one of those rolls of tarp had moved, you'd've bin squashed flat." He made a rude-sounding noise to indicate what being squashed flat might have sounded like.

"Yes. Well. I'll count my blessings," she replied, raising her eyebrows.

"Come on out of there, child," Crake said. "Let's see what we're goin' to do with you."

"Nobody," said the girl, sounding strained, "is going to do *anything* with me, thank you very much." Bastjan moved aside as a leg, wearing a scuffed boot, popped out of the cupboard, quickly followed by another. Next, the girl shuffled forwards on her bottom, plopping out on to the floor in a most undignified manner. She pulled her head free, her dog still clutched tight to her chest, and looked from Bastjan to Crake and then back again, her green eyes wary. Crake sat on Bastjan's bunk, making it creak beneath his weight, and gazed thoughtfully at their uninvited guest.

"I din't think folk actually *did* it, y'know," Bastjan said, after a minute.

"Did what?" the girl replied, frowning.

"Ran away to the circus." Bastjan gave her a grin.

"I'm not running *away*," the girl said, putting her dog on the floor. He began, cheerfully, to sniff his way around, and Crake watched him with a careful eye. "Not really. I'm running *to* something. I just don't know what, yet."

Bastjan shrugged. "Sounds about right. Here, you ain't some sort of princess, are ya? Only, you talk like one." He pursed his lips, pulling his face into a snooty scowl. Crake tapped him smartly on the back of the head, just enough to get his face to pop back into its usual shape.

"Oi!" Bastjan said, staring up at his friend. "What was that for?"

"Remindin' you to keep yer nose where it belongs," Crake replied. "Now. What can we call you, lass?"

"Alice," the girl replied, before wincing, as though she'd thought better of giving her real name. Bastjan raised his eyebrows at her, amused, and Alice stuck her tongue out at him.

"You got a family name, Alice?"

The girl glanced up at Crake. "Just Alice will do."

"Just Alice," Crake said, with a nod. "An' who's this fine young fella here?" He reached out to rub the dog on the top of his shining head.

"His name's Wares. And all we need is a place to stay for a day or two." She tightened her lips. "Well, a week. No more than that, I promise."

"We'd best pass you by the ringmaster," Crake said. "Mr Quinn, to you. He'll probably want to—"

"No," Alice said, her face paling. "No, please. I have

to stay hidden."

Crake and Bastjan shared a look. "Are you in trouble, lass?" the strongman asked kindly.

Alice sucked on her lips, her gaze flicking between Bastjan and Crake. "I just don't want to be found," she finally said.

Crake exhaled heavily. "Right," he said. "It's not something I like – and I want to make clear you won't be a captive here, you can come and go as you please—"

"Yes, yes, that's fine," Alice said eagerly. "Thank you."

"I amn't agreeing to a thing yet," Crake said, raising his shaggy eyebrows. "If we're to split our rations three ways, we want to know what we're gettin' into."

"Splittin' rations?" Bastjan said, staring at Crake incredulously.

The girl shoved her hand into an inner coat pocket. "I have … I've got some money. Some things you can sell?" She pulled her hand out and sitting in her palm was a tarnished gold ring, some coins and a lump of lint. Bastjan reached out to touch the ring and Crake cleared his throat meaningfully.

"What?" Bastjan said, but Crake made no reply. Bastjan dropped his hand again, muttering to himself.

"We don't need payin', child," he said. "Just some questions answered. Firstly, will keepin' you with us put us in any danger?"

Alice blinked. "No," she finally answered, though she didn't sound sure.

"Will it put *you* in any danger?"

The girl shook her head, but this time her "No" sounded even less certain.

"Do you promise to do what you're told?"

Alice bristled. "Well, I don't know if I can promise that," she said stiffly.

Crake harrumphed quietly. "I'm assuming you're not here to rob us, or you'd have done it and made off by now," he said.

"There's nothing worth taking, anyway," Alice answered, without thinking. "I mean … there doesn't *look* like there's anything worth taking."

Bastjan hissed. "I *knew* it," he said. "Mum's things – she's been through 'em! Her book was in the box when I left it earlier, an' it ain't now – it's just shoved in beside it."

"All right, yes, I found the key," Alice said, holding up her hands. "I had a look in the box. But I didn't take a thing, you can check."

"You looked in my *smalls* drawer?" Bastjan asked, his voice a squeak. "Crake, she looked in my smalls drawer! I was hidin' the key there," he protested.

"I was looking for something to eat," Alice said hotly. "You'd have done the same."

"Ain't *no* chance you'd catch me lookin' through no

girl's—" Bastjan began.

"All right! Enough, the pair of you," Crake bellowed. "It don't matter who saw whose smalls, let's just get back to the important stuff here."

Alice coughed politely. "I'm sorry," she said, looking at Bastjan. "I didn't mean to pry. But I thought the box was pretty. And then when I found the book, it was so interesting that I had to look. Everything's still there, though. I promise."

Bastjan sniffed. "I'm interested in it, an' all. Shame we can't read most of it," he said.

The girl blinked in confusion. "Why not?"

Bastjan looked at her. "In another language, in't it?"

"Not all of it," Alice replied. "Didn't you check the last few entries?"

Crake's mouth dropped open. "What are you sayin', lass?"

Alice looked up at them, confused. "I'm saying, there are pages and pages in that book, all written in English."

CHAPTER
FOURTEEN

Bastjan stared at his mother's notebook, which lay open in his lap. On one side of him, Alice peered at the slanted, elaborate handwriting and on the other, Crake did the same.

"I can't make anythin' of it, son," Crake said, blinking and frowning. "It might be in English but the way it's written has my eyes in a knot."

"I can read it," Alice said. "Or some of it, at least. She talks a lot about her baby. That's you, isn't it?" She looked at Bastjan. "You're her son."

Bastjan nodded. "Yeah."

"What happened to her?" Alice asked gently.

"An accident," Bastjan said, running his hand over the page. "She fell."

"I'm sorry," Alice said quietly. "My mum's gone too.

And my dad."

Outside, a whistle blew, and Crake and Bastjan both leaped at the sound of it, looking towards the door.

"That's the five-minute warnin'. We've got to get to the ring," Crake said, slipping off his glasses and sliding them on to a shelf. He turned to face Alice. "I know you want to stay out of the way, but I don't really want to leave you here on your own, girleen."

"You could come with us," Bastjan said, closing the notebook. "We'll get you in backstage, no problem. There're tons of spots around the ring where you can watch us practisin', all of 'em well hid."

"I don't know," said Alice. Her long hair hung down over her birthmarked cheek and she tucked it back behind her ears. Her jaw was set, defiant and proud, as she stared at Bastjan and Crake as though expecting them to challenge her to a fight. "It's not like I blend in."

"I noticed your firemark," Crake said, his tone respectful. He looked Alice in the eye. "It's a good thing, in the circus."

Alice let her hair fall back over her face, her fingers trembling. "Really? Well. That's unexpected." Wares gave her other cheek a lick and the girl smiled, briefly and sadly, down at the dog. "Why is it good?" Alice finally said, her voice tight. "My – whatever you called it. The mark. Why is it good?"

Crake thought for a moment before answering. "It's a mark of power, given to the best among us – or so they say." He raised his eyebrows thoughtfully. "Certainly nothin' to be ashamed of, not round here anyways."

"I wish everyone thought so," Alice muttered.

"Listen," Crake said, getting to his feet. "If ever you're goin' to blend in anywhere, it'll be in a circus. There's odder'n you here, believe me. So come with us an' we'll put you somewhere where you'll get the best view. It'll be somethin' to keep you out of mischief for an hour or so. What do you say?"

Alice glanced at Bastjan, who smiled at her. "All right," she said, returning the smile and looking gratefully up at Crake. "When you put it like that."

They got to their feet. Bastjan started to slide his mother's box back into its hiding place, but Alice put a hand on his arm. "I could bring it with me," she said. "Keep it safe for you while you're rehearsing."

Bastjan frowned. "Why would you do that?"

"It's important to you, isn't it? Anyone can tell that. And if you're worried about it being found – well, it's already *been* found. The next person to find it mightn't want to give it back."

"She's got a point, son," Crake said, with a shrug.

"I'll take care of it. I promise," Alice said.

"You already know there's nothin' in it worth stealin',"

119

Bastjan said, looking back at her.

"I won't—"

"No money, nothin' valuable," Bastjan continued.

"I wouldn't—"

"An' if anythin' happens to it, I swear—"

"*Nothing* will happen to it," Alice said, looking between him and Crake. "Listen. I haven't been completely honest with you."

She licked her lips nervously and closed her eyes. "There *is* someone after me – a woman, named Mrs Palmer. She's ... she's not someone you really want on your tail. I need to stay away from her. And if I'm trusting you both to keep me hidden, and if I have nothing to give you, then the best way for me to pay you back is to take care of this box." She opened her eyes again. "I'm not going to run – why would I? Mrs P would be on me in a heartbeat." She looked beseechingly at Bastjan. "Plus without me, you can't read what's in the notebook and it might be important. I want to help."

"Does this Mrs Palmer know you're here?" Crake asked, looking serious. Alice shook her head.

Another whistle sounded outside, sharp and commanding. Bastjan and Crake shared a look, and then Bastjan turned to Alice.

"That's the last whistle. We've got to go." He handed her the box and she took it with a grateful, surprised grin.

"C'mon. Let's get you hid, an' then we can get on with the show."

Bastjan took a deep breath. So many thoughts were swirling around inside his head that he felt like it was going to spin right off his shoulders and fly out of the big top, straight through the hole where the king pole passed through the canvas roof. He looked up, seeing the circle of blue sky, and shook out his limbs. Nanette had started his rehearsal on the low wire and he was about to begin his fifth attempt to make it all the way across.

"You can do it, Bastjan," came Nanette's gentle voice. "Come on."

Bastjan nodded, raising his arms. Nanette lifted him high enough for him to land lightly on the wire and he found his balance instantly. He began to walk, standing tall, his shoulders relaxed and his arms held out like he was a bird poised for flight.

The curtain leading from the performers' area was suddenly pulled aside and Bastjan's focus wavered. Two men came into the ring – one was Cyrus Quinn, in his shirtsleeves, his hair and beard braided; the other was a stranger. He was a full head shorter than the ringmaster and dressed in a smart suit. He had a long coat draped over one arm and his face was strangely pale, like something which had been left in the dark too long.

"Here we are," Bastjan heard Quinn say. "This is the act you were interested in, sir, Ester's boy. If you'd care to take a seat, Mr Bauer?"

The stranger *tsked* irritably. "It's *Dr* Bauer, Mr Quinn. I have explained this already." His voice was low, but somehow it carried throughout the tent.

"Apologies, sir, apologies," Quinn said, ushering Bauer to the stalls. They climbed the steps to sit midway up, where the stranger could get a clear view of the entire ring.

Bastjan took one step after another, concentrating on the bite of the wire. He turned a careful cartwheel at the end and pivoted on one foot to change direction, before beginning the return journey. He glanced to the side; the ringmaster had appeared at the ringside barrier and Bastjan felt the weight of his presence. He placed his foot and then risked a look up into the stalls. Dr Bauer's distant, moon-white gaze was unsettling enough to make him look away instantly.

"Good work," Quinn called, too loudly for Bastjan's benefit alone. "Keep it up."

Bastjan reached the end of the wire and leaped down, landing neatly in the sawdust of the ring. Nanette gave him a quick, satisfied nod and the boy walked to the water butt. He pulled out the dipper and took a drink, watching the ringmaster approaching from the corner of his eye. When he could avoid it no longer, Bastjan turned to face him.

"Are you ready?" Quinn asked.

Nanette looked at Bastjan and the boy nodded. She gave the ringmaster a level stare. "With the net," she said. After a breath's pause, the ringmaster whistled his rousties into action.

Nanette and Bastjan jogged to the trapeze platform. As soon as they were in position, Nanette signalled to the roustie controlling the ropes and he released the sandbag which acted as their counterweight. Up they went, fast as a thought. They made the platform secure at the top, where the hoop had been tied off and was waiting for them. Far below, a team of rousties were running around the ring, chaining the safety net in place. Bastjan's ears were primed for their whistle, the signal to let them know it was ready.

"While we're waiting –" Nanette stretched her muscles as she spoke – "just listen. You're going to be fine, Bastjan. Nobody is expecting you to be your mother." Bastjan quivered at her words. "Do some basic moves, whatever you can manage, and do them as well as you can. And that will be good enough." Nanette bent to place one hand against Bastjan's cheek. "It's just like the swing you're used to with the Runner Beans." She grimaced. "Well. It's near enough like it. If you can manage that swing, you can manage this. Believe me." Bastjan closed his eyes against the whirling in his belly. The swing he used as part of his tumbling act was suspended ten feet off the ground. This hoop was three times as high.

The signal came, making Bastjan jump and open his eyes. Nanette grasped the hoop, pulling free its mooring rope, and held it steady while Bastjan sat into it. Finally, he gave the nod to say he was ready – and Nanette released her grip.

The hoop swung gracefully across the roof space and Bastjan allowed himself one full swoop to get the feel of it. Then, on the return leg, he leaned backwards, gathering speed as he went. He started with a simple trick – turning around in the hoop – and, his confidence growing, he stood and balanced on one leg, holding on with one hand while he raised the other above his head, imagining the applause from below.

He swung back into a sitting position, his legs dangling casually, and then he let his hands slide along the cool metal as he dropped his body out of the hoop, keeping his legs bent tight around it. At the apex of the next swing, once his heart had stopped hopping in his chest, he let go of the hoop and allowed his arms to swing freely.

He was tumbling through the air, spinning in his sequinned costume with his legs and arms spread, shining like a star – or a snowflake. That was the name of the act, of course. The Dance of the Snowflakes. From nowhere, out of the darkness, came a slender hand, its grip strong as it caught him. Then he was being bundled against his mother, their costumes locking together with specially made hooks. Her fingers fumbled a little as they settled him safely and then they were off, sweeping across the roof space with the spotlight on them making them sparkle so brightly that every eye beneath the big top could see them fly. The applause was deafening. He looked up; there was his mother's smiling face, sweaty and shining in the lights, strands of her hair sticking to her forehead, and her heart inside her beating, beating, beating...

Bastjan jerked out of his dream-memory, throwing the hoop's momentum off. His chest felt as if it was full of mud, suddenly – hot mud, thick and choking, and he couldn't catch his breath. The hoop began to wobble dangerously and he lost his nerve. He pulled himself up into a sitting position again and coughed, pleading with his lungs to open up.

"*Whoop*," he croaked, cold sweat standing out on his forehead. "*Whoop*." He glanced at the platform; even from here, he could see the concern on Nanette's face. She readied herself to catch the hoop the next time he got close enough.

As Bastjan reached the platform and the comfort of Nanette's solid arms, he looked down. The ringmaster was standing with his hands on his hips, staring up at him.

"*Whoop*," came his breath once more, fighting its way through his neck and into his lungs. "Nanette, I – *whoop*

125

– I gotta get down."

"Yes, you do," the woman agreed, signalling to the roustie. He dropped the platform and a moment later they were on the ground. Bastjan fell to his knees on the sawdust floor and fought for breath. A shadow loomed over him and he looked up to see Quinn standing there with his eyes wide and his teeth gritted.

He crouched beside the trembling boy, grabbing him beneath the chin. "Get back up there," the ringmaster hissed. "Get up there *now* or this whole circus will be on the skids."

"*Whoop*," Bastjan replied. "I … I can't."

Quinn's eyes bulged. He leaned closer, increasing his grip on Bastjan's chin until it became agonizing. "Didn't you hear me, you ignorant lump? Get up there now or feel the back of my hand!"

Bastjan tried to breathe. His eyes filled with hot tears. "I tol' you," he gasped. "*Whoop*. I can't."

Quinn hauled in two or three deep breaths through flared nostrils, until finally he spoke again. "You *can't*? More like you won't! What's the use of 'avin' an 'igh-wire boy who can't even catch 'is breath, eh? I should sell you, I should! You're not worth the food I pay for!" The ringmaster's face reddened and Bastjan's heart beat faster as he heard Quinn's true accent, his true self, begin to creep through his ringmaster persona.

"I'm sorry! I – *whoop* – I'm sorry, Dad! I'm doin' me best!" The tears he'd been trying to keep inside finally spilled over. *Dad.* Quinn wasn't his dad. Bastjan had never known his father – all he knew was he'd been a roustie from another circus. But somehow, in his desperation, Bastjan tried to remind the ringmaster that he was also his stepfather. It had never done him any good before, but he prayed it would help now.

His prayers weren't answered. "Your best ain't good enough," Quinn growled. "Yer nothin' but a clod! Yer mother'd die all over again, this time out o' shame, if she could see you now!" He scrubbed his hands through his hair, pulling the top of his braid loose. "You stupid *thing*, I wish I'd left you in the poorhouse!"

Bastjan closed his eyes and sobbed, his mind filling with the memory that had made him lose his balance – his mother's beautiful smile, the pride in her eyes, the joy she felt in flight. The sound of her beating heart.

"Mr Quinn," came Nanette's voice, sharp as a whip. "That's quite enough, sir."

Quinn looked up at her. "You stay out of it, you old has-been," he snapped. "God knows why I keep you around."

Nanette dropped to one knee, her arm going round Bastjan's shoulders. "Because before you lost your heart to this poor boy's mother, I was the finest aerialist you'd ever seen," she told him calmly. "And now that she's gone before her time, I'm *still* the best aerialist you've got. So —" the woman shrugged – "take it or leave it." She glanced up at the stalls. "Oh, and you might like to know your *benefactor* has done a runner."

Quinn swore, turning to look at the seat where Dr Bauer had been. Nanette was right; the man with the strangely pale face was gone.

CHAPTER
FIFTEEN

Wares stuck close to Alice's heels as they crept out of the big top. They'd been hiding behind a haybale when a man had come striding through the performers' area – a pale man with sideways-slicked hair, carrying his coat over one arm. In his wake he left a strange smell. It was more like the *absence* of a smell, like a wave of cold air which seemed to surround and trail behind him. He'd walked right past Alice and Wares without even noticing they were there, his eyes fixed on the flap tied open at the back of the performers' area, which gave access to the wagons. Within a few heartbeats he'd vanished into the daylight outside the tent, ducking slightly as he passed beneath the canvas. Something about him had struck Alice as odd – as *dangerous*, even – and she couldn't suppress her curiosity.

She'd counted to five before clicking her tongue to get

Wares's attention and then they'd slipped out after him.

Keeping low, crouching behind crates and stray equipment, they followed the stranger as he hurried, stiff-legged, through the camp. He stopped at the edge of the circle of wagons as though looking for something, his head turning from side to side. Alice and Wares ducked quickly behind a large, empty gas cylinder – but as Alice crouched, she knocked against something that looked like an old unicycle frame, making it *clang* against the tank. Alice's breath dried up as the stranger's eyes landed on their hiding place and then the dog set off at a run, tearing across the campground, yapping as he went.

"Wares!" she hissed, reaching out to grab him, but she wasn't fast enough. The stranger's head whipped round to look as Wares barrelled past him, but then Alice saw him relax. Clearly, he'd decided the noise had been made by the dog. She gave a shaky grin, silently giving thanks for the tricks Wares had learned as part of Mrs Palmer's gang, and then the stranger started walking again. Alice steeled herself and crept after him. *You're up to something*, she thought, frowning at the man. *And I'm going to find out what.* She slipped between two wagons, pressing herself against the side of one of them and peeking around its front wheel until she had a clear view of the stranger.

Then from behind a cart with the words *Bracklebrick Farm* on the side, Alice saw a roustie appear – a man with

a speckled neckerchief and a dusty, patched waistcoat –
who nodded at the stranger. The two men cast wary looks
around the campground before approaching one another.

Alice watched the roustie mutter something in the
stranger's ear, at the same time as the stranger slipped
something – a banknote? – into the roustie's waistcoat
pocket. Her breath hitched as the roustie nodded in the
direction of Crake and Bastjan's wagon before he hurried
away. Alice watched him go, hardly able to believe what
she'd seen. *Did he just tell that man where Crake and Bastjan
live?*

The stranger looked around once more, before walking
towards Bastjan and Crake's wagon, striding up the steps as
though he had every right to. He pulled open the top half
of their door and leaned in to unlatch the bottom panel.
Then he let himself into their home. Alice's hand travelled
to the box she had in her hidden pocket. She squeezed it, as
though checking it was still there, and watched the wagon
for several long moments, unsure of what to do.

"Bauer!" came a voice from behind her. "Dr Bauer!"

Alice froze for a moment before dropping silently to the
ground. She crept beneath the belly box of the wagon and
wriggled out of sight just in time. The ringmaster came
striding across the campground, his expression thunderous.
He passed her hiding place without giving it a glance.

The stranger emerged from Crake and Bastjan's wagon

nonchalantly, his eyebrows raised politely. "Mr Quinn," he said. "What is it, please?"

"Just wondering where you'd gone, Doctor," Quinn said, stopping with one foot on the bottom step of Crake and Bastjan's wagon. Alice couldn't see his face properly, but she saw the tension in his arms and shoulders. "Circus camps are dangerous places for people who aren't used to 'em. I wouldn't want you coming to any harm."

Bauer gave the ringmaster an indulgent smile. "I have handled myself in far more challenging environments than this one, Mr Quinn. I assure you of that. But I thank you for your concern."

Quinn straightened his shoulders and folded his arms. "Is there anything I can show you, sir? Would you like a tour of the animal enclosures? We have a magnificent bull elephant on site, you might—"

"Mr Quinn, let me be honest. I am not at this wagon by accident." Bauer's smile flattened before fading completely. "I am here because I hoped to find some small keepsake, a trinket which once belonged to your late wife, something which I – as a great fan of her work – would enjoy having for my own."

There was a moment's silence and then Quinn spoke again. "I think I'm seeing the truth of it now," he said, leaning against the wagon's railing. He looked up at the smaller man, who was standing on a higher step. "You want something of Ester's, and if you don't get it, you'll be skedaddling off back to London with your money. Is that about the size of it?"

Bauer's mouth tightened. "You've been a man of business for a great many years, Mr Quinn. I see you are nobody's fool."

Quinn snorted. "Fools don't last long in this line of work. Tell me what you're lookin' for, Dr Bauer, and let's get the deal done."

Bauer pulled out a handkerchief from his top pocket and dabbed at his lips. "I seek a box, Mr Quinn. It is made of dark wood, with an enamelled lid. Possibly, this lid will have a fish design, as it comes from a village which makes its living from the sea, and such artistry is common there. It belonged to Miss Manduca and I believe she brought it with her from Melita, many years ago."

"Well, you won't find it in there," Quinn said, and Alice gripped the box again as she listened. Her pulse hopped in her fingers. "The boy doesn't have anything of his mother's. And that's not even the wagon Ester lived in, anyhow. I forget which one was hers."

A flash of irritation crossed Bauer's face. "Ah. That is a shame. Do you know whether the boy – Bastjan, is it? – has maintained contact with his family on Melita? Perhaps the box has remained there."

"Dr Bauer, I don't know what this box is, or where it is,

but I can tell you that boy has nothing to do with anyone on Melita. I don't even know if he has any relatives there. Not living ones, at least. Why's it so important, anyway?"

Bauer descended one step, putting him face to face with the ringmaster. "It is not important, Mr Quinn. Not to anyone else, at least. It is simply something I would have liked and I felt sure it would be here. But it is of no consequence." He tucked his handkerchief back into his pocket. "If it turns up, please keep it for me. I shall hope to collect it in a month, when I am back in Britain."

"And if it doesn't turn up?"

"You shall be generously compensated for your time and effort in looking for it, Mr Quinn," Bauer said. "Perhaps that will help it to turn up."

Bauer descended another step, forcing Quinn to stand back to let him pass. The ringmaster's eyes were unsettled and thoughtful, like a stirred-up riverbed, suddenly full of things long-buried. Alice frowned at him, wondering what he was remembering, but then he blinked and the strange look disappeared. "How about the rest of that tour now, then?" he said, to Bauer's back. The other man turned.

"I'm afraid I must return to London immediately," he said, bowing very slightly as though in apology. "My airship leaves from there at eight this evening, bound for the Americas. I have associates in Antarctica at present, conducting research into one of my other business interests, and I am to meet them in the Argentine Republic in a little under a fortnight's time. But I shall be back, as I say, in one month, and I am already looking forward to a return visit to your circus."

Quinn raised an eyebrow. "The feeling's mutual, I'm sure. Well. The tour can wait until next time, then."

"Exactly so. I hope to find your circus in rude health, and the box waiting for me, when I return." Bauer gave a courteous nod. "And perhaps I will have the honour of meeting young Bastjan in person when I come for the box. Please extend my best wishes to the boy in the meantime."

The pale stranger turned and walked away, and Alice lay trembling in her hiding place. She squeezed her eyes tight, wrapping her fingers round the box. *He'll pay you for it!* said a voice inside her head. *You heard him – he's willing to pay anything. Enough for you to disappear completely and never be found.* She opened her eyes again. The ringmaster was still at Crake and Bastjan's wagon, looking troubled and thoughtful, and as he turned, making for his own wagon, Alice knew this was her chance to follow Bauer, box in hand. If she didn't go now, the chance would be lost.

Your firemark, Crake's gentle voice whispered in her memory. *A mark of power. Given to the best among us...* Alice wiped away a tear, her heart slowing. Crake and Bastjan hadn't cared about her face. They'd been kind –

kinder than anyone had ever been. *They trust me. I can't let them down.* She took a deep breath and slowly released it, waiting to feel steady again. *I have to find Crake and Bastjan and tell them what I've seen,* she told herself. *And Quinn's got something on his mind too – something that could be important.*

Once she was sure the coast was clear, Alice wriggled out and got to her feet, making straight for the big top, the box safely tucked inside her coat.

"Bastjan!" Alice sounded out of breath. He looked up at her, scrubbing away his tears with the heels of his hands. His chin and jaw still ached from where the ringmaster had grabbed him, and his breath sounded like molasses in his lungs.

Alice's thoughts about what she'd just witnessed vanished as she stared at him. "Bastjan, are you all right?" She dropped to her knees, reaching out her arm to help him.

"Fine," he managed. "*Whoop.* Jus' need a minute."

As Alice hauled him up, they were joined by a woman dressed in a performance costume. The woman walked with Bastjan and Alice to the ringside barrier and helped Bastjan on to it, where he sat with his body slumped and his sweaty hair stuck to his forehead. Alice was bursting to tell Bastjan her news, but didn't want to while someone else was listening.

"Nanette van Hemel," the woman said, reaching over to shake Alice's hand. "At least, that's what they call me here." She smiled. Alice recognized her from the Grand Parade as the lady in the ring. She took in Alice's face with interest and the girl shrugged her birthmark into her hair. "Are you new around here?"

"I'm a ... a friend of Bastjan's," Alice said.

"Righto," said Nanette, when it became clear Alice didn't want to say anything more. "I'm glad someone's here to keep an eye on the boy. I'd better go and track down Mr Quinn, see what's going on with tonight's show." Nanette gave Bastjan one last pat on the shoulder and then she was gone.

Alice watched until Nanette was out of earshot and then she turned back to Bastjan. He looked washed-out and weary, his face clammy and his eyes downcast. "Hey!" Alice said. "The stranger – the sponsor. He's been in your wagon!"

Bastjan turned to her. "What?"

"He's looking for your mum's box, as a souvenir. Though he didn't say why it had to be the box and nothing else," Alice said. "I heard him talking to the ringmaster about it."

"*Quinn?*" Bastjan coughed thickly. "So now 'e knows too?"

"That's not all," Alice continued. "When he was talking

137

to the sponsor about it, Quinn started to look strange – like he was remembering something. I'm not sure what. He took off for his own wagon straight afterwards."

Bastjan breathed slowly for a moment as he thought. "Lookin' for Mum's chest, maybe," he said. "Checkin' it for the box. Only he won't find it there."

Voices outside the tent drew their attention and daylight pooled in the entrance. Two silhouettes became visible – a woman's and a man's. Nanette and the ringmaster, on their way back to the ring. Alice's heart began to pound. *So much for staying out of sight, you idiot!* she berated herself, but it was too late to hide now.

"Whatever you want, Mr Quinn," Nanette was saying as they walked into the tent. "The sooner we get practising the better. I'm sure we can have an act in place before Dr Bauer's return."

"Just do your best," Quinn said. He looked away from his aerialist and his eyes fell on Alice. "And here she is, then – the girl you were telling me about?"

"That's her," Nanette said, smiling down at Alice. "Her firemark, sir. Remarkable, isn't it?"

"Just as you described," Quinn agreed. He bent forwards, tilting his head slightly. "Hello, there," he said, falsely bright. "I'm Cyrus Quinn. And you are?"

"A friend of Bastjan's," Alice replied. "Passing through."

Quinn straightened up. "I'm sure." Then he looked

at Bastjan. "You'll get back to work, boy. Dr Bauer was inspecting the circus's assets just now." Quinn paused as he cast his gaze around the big top, before fixing Bastjan with a stare. "The last thing I want is to hear of him selling my property off, bit by bit. So if you want a home to call your own, you'd better start to fly. We have one month, tops."

Bastjan swallowed hard. "Yessir," he muttered.

Quinn gave a sharp nod. "Now. If you'll all excuse me, I'm sure you have work to do." With that, he turned and made his way out of the ring.

Nanette heaved a deep breath. "Right, then," she said, giving Bastjan a fleeting smile. "Will we get started?"

Chapter Sixteen

Flames danced against the night, crackling like laughing tongues, spitting out sparks. Everywhere was noise; voices shouting, words rattling and clattering like stones, like bones, and the sound of breaths tearing through pained lungs somewhere close by. Eyes, wide with terror, reflecting the fire. The terror of being found. We must not be found!

And then an explosion, louder than the end of the world...

Bastjan jolted awake, sitting straight up. His heart was racing painfully fast and his chest felt tighter than a clenched fist. His breaths squeaked, in and out. He placed his hand against the wall, his fingers rasping against the paper glued there, the pictures of his mother. Moonlight shone on the rim of the washstand mirror and on the fittings of the quenched oil lamp. Crake, safe in his bunk, snored lightly. And overhead, slung in a spare bedsheet, hammock-like, slept Alice, with Wares tucked in at her feet. *Everythin's fine*, he told himself. *A dream, that's all it was.*

Slowly, Bastjan's pulse returned to normal and his breaths began to fill his chest.

"Are you all right?" Alice's whisper made Bastjan jump. He blinked into the darkness.

"Did you hear it?" he asked. "The screamin'. An' the bang."

"All I heard was you, whimpering."

"A dream, then, for sure," Bastjan said. "Din't feel like it, though." He reached to pull the box out from beneath his pillow. It was unlocked and he popped it open, drawing out his mother's notebook. It sat on his knee like a rectangle of night, dark against the white of his bedsheets.

"Do you want to read some?" Alice whispered.

Before he could answer, Alice had already slid out of her precarious hammock and landed on the floor. Barefoot, she was clad in one of Crake's old shirts as a nightgown. She clambered on to Bastjan's bed, wrapping herself in a blanket while he lit a candle and set it in a nook on the wall.

The children blinked as they got used to the glow. Bastjan tried to drive the images from his dream out of his head, but they stubbornly refused to move. They seemed planted in his brain, like a memory. *But not one o' mine*, he thought. *One o' Mum's.* His thoughts turned to the creature his mother had drawn. *Or maybe one o' theirs, instead.*

"We should probably start at the beginning," Alice said as Bastjan handed her the notebook. "Or the beginning of the entries written in English, at least." She began to flick through the pages of his mother's sketches, pausing for a moment at the one of the strange half-human creature.

"Wish I knew what that was," Bastjan said, leaning in.

"The bracelet in the box," Alice said. "This is it, isn't it?" She pointed at the creature's arm.

Bastjan nodded. "Think so," he said, frowning. He wanted to tell her how the bracelet made him feel, every time it touched his skin, but he couldn't get the words past his tongue.

"And there's this," Alice continued, taking the torn-off page out of the back of the notebook and unfolding it. "I wonder if these creatures have anything to do with the one your mum drew?"

Bastjan shrugged. "Must 'ave," he said. "Why would she 'ave kept this page otherwise?"

"They're shapeshifters," Alice said thoughtfully. "All different sorts. So I wonder if your mum's creature is too."

Bastjan stiffened. "*Shapeshifters?* 'Ow d'you figure that out?"

"It's in French," she said. "I know a bit. I had a tutor, for a while, when I was younger." She coughed, hurrying

142

on. "And I know this word." She pointed at the writing beneath one of the drawings which, to Bastjan, looked the same as all the other black squiggles. "*Le métamorphe.* The shapeshifter."

"Shapeshifter," Bastjan repeated, feeling a chill run through him.

Alice slid it back into the notebook and continued to flick through the pages. "Ah – here we go." She stopped and folded the notebook flat, running her fingers along its spine. Bastjan drew his knees up to his chest as she began to read.

"*June 6th. The weather was cruel hot today. Baba felt it too. He was quite out of sorts. Q would not excuse us from duty. I am too tired to write more.*" Alice looked at Bastjan, but he kept his eyes firmly on the page.

"*June 15th. I had a tincture from Carmen tonight to help my aches. I have been working hard. She also gave me an oil to add to warm water, for soothing sore feet, and she and Ana watched Baba for me while I bathed. Cornelius returned from town with extra milk (for Baba) and some roses (for me). I think they dislike Q as much as I have grown to. He pushes me too hard and I have no choice but to allow it.*"

Alice scanned the page, turning to the next one. "It goes on like that for a while," she said. "Short entries, mostly about tiredness and working too much."

"What about the last thing she wrote?" Bastjan said.

"Can you find that?"

Alice nodded and turned over one final page. The writing stopped midway down, leaving all the other pages blank.

"*August 7th. I thought a lot about Bastjan today,*" Alice began, "*and Mama's face when they told us about him and Papa, and how they were gone. I remember their boat and its colours. I remember our house and Mama in the door. I remember Bastjan—*"

Alice paused, confused. "She's not talking about you here, is she?"

Bastjan shook his head. "Her brother," he whispered. "He was Bastjan too. She named me after 'im."

Alice took in a deep, sympathetic breath and then began to read again.

"*I remember Bastjan, and his hair which was always too long, and his crooked tooth in front. Going home … it's a dream. Would Mama be there? Would she welcome me? I hope she would understand. I had to leave, because she wouldn't let me fly. I had to fly. Bastjan understood. He knew. He sent me to the wall. He gave me the wings I needed and I flew.*"

Alice paused again. "What wall?" she whispered.

Bastjan sat forwards suddenly. Wide-eyed, he rummaged through the box until he found a smaller piece of paper – a piece of paper which had once been neatly folded around a key. The drawings on it hadn't made sense the first time he'd seen them, but now, like a coin dropping into the right slot inside his mind, they suddenly did.

"How 'bout these?" he whispered, showing the paper to Alice. Between blocks of the same looping handwriting, the letters tiny, were drawings of what looked like walls, towering high above a stick-figure person. They were drawn again and again, from every angle, and on the paper's other side, there was a large 'O' mostly filled in with dark ink scratchings, enclosed within a carefully drawn outer circle. At the centre of the 'O' was an irregular shape, drawn with waves across its surface, like it was a pool. Along one side of the outer circle were more scribbled wavy lines, some curled at the top like sea foam.

"But what is it?" Alice said.

"A map," Bastjan replied. He pulled the loose sheet from inside his mother's notebook once again. The picture of the lizard-lady glowered up at him, but he ignored her. "Look," he whispered, jabbing at the drawing in the corner of the page, the one which, he now saw, looked just like the map his mother had made. "This is on Melita, in't it? The same place Mum was from?"

Alice nodded. "*La Cité du Silence*," she read, running a finger under some tiny words printed beneath the image, above the word 'Melita'. "It means the Silent City." She met his eye. "And your mum drew it too."

"So she must be talkin' about these walls," Bastjan said.

"The walls of this place. The Silent City."

Alice ran her hand over the page with the creatures on it. "And look," she said, pointing at the half human, half fish inside the walled space of the Silent City. "Here's something, inside the city. Something not fully human."

The children looked at one another.

"So behind the wall – inside this Silent City. That's where it is – the creature Mum drew." Bastjan swallowed hard.

"Let's read the rest," Alice suggested, picking up the notebook once again. She took a breath and began. "*I dream that Mama is there, in our house, and that when I put the key into her door – the key I took the night I ran, the key I keep always to remind me where my home is – that she will hear me and open before I turn it, and that she will kiss my cheeks and call me darling, as she always did. And that I can explain, and she will understand, how I needed to be free – but not free of her. Then together we can walk to the walls and I will climb one last time, and I will leave the bracelet there. I hope the Slipskin will find it and then I can be at peace. The bracelet is not mine. It helped me to fly, but it is not mine, and I have kept it for too long.*"

"She wanted to give it back," Bastjan said, blinking hard. "That's why she was goin' home. An' bringin' me with 'er. She was goin' back to her mum, an' goin' to make things right. But she never got the chance."

"What's a Slipskin?" Alice frowned at the page and then her expression cleared. "*Le métamorphe*," she said.

"Eh?" Bastjan muttered.

"The Slipskin," Alice said, turning to Bastjan, "must be the creature your mum drew. Maybe it's a shapeshifter too, like the others on that bit of paper. And somehow she had its bracelet."

"An' now I have it," Bastjan said slowly. "So it's up to me to get it back where it belongs."

"How are you going to do that?" Alice said. "Melita's in the middle of the Midsea, somewhere north of Afrik. It's miles from here!"

"Has to be a way," Bastjan said.

"But this creature – this Slipskin – mightn't even be there. Maybe it's *dead*." Alice peered at Bastjan in the gloom.

"Even so, I got to get the bracelet back," he replied. "No matter how long it takes. Mum din't make it, but I will."

"I believe you," Alice whispered. Then Bauer's oddly pale face floated in her memory and she remembered the cold gleam in his eyes as he'd described the box. She glanced down at it and carefully began to replace its contents. "We've got to keep this stuff out of Quinn's hands, and away from that Bauer person too. I don't believe his story for a minute – he's not just some fan of your mother's. He wants this box, which means he knows something about it

– probably more than we do. Maybe he even knows about the Slipskins."

"Yeah. You're right. Whatever 'e might want Mum's things for, chances are it's nothin' good," Bastjan whispered as Alice closed the lid. His eyes were gritty with tiredness and his limbs ached. It had been a busy day of rehearsals and performance, and he knew tomorrow, and the day after, and every day as far as he could see, would be just the same. He needed to sleep, but he was afraid to in case the dream-memories, the ones not his own, wrapped themselves around him again.

"D'you reckon you can give your memories to other people?" he said, the words stretching around a yawn. "Y'know. When you die or whatever. Do your memories, or your dreams maybe, sort of go up into the air an' wait there for someone else's head to settle into?"

Alice gave him a quizzical look. "I've never thought about it," she said. "Why do you ask?"

Bastjan licked his lips, searching for the right way to say what was on his mind. "Mum's box," he finally said. "I think it's makin' me see things. The bracelet 'specially. It's like it puts memories in my 'ead or somethin'. I can't explain it."

Alice frowned thoughtfully. "I had a doll of my mum's which I had to put in a drawer eventually, because I couldn't bear to look at it. It made me sad, you know, because I had so few memories of my mother. Or my dad. All I had was this blank-eyed thing, staring at me across the room, and I was supposed to love it because it had been hers." She stopped suddenly, as though afraid she'd shared too much. "Anyway," she finished. "Thinking about people you've lost can do funny things to your brain."

Bastjan sighed. "Yeah. Maybe," he said. "I'll try gettin' some kip, an' we'll see. Things always look different in the mornin', eh? An' listen. I'm sorry about your folks."

Alice gave him a smile. "Sleep well."

"You too," Bastjan whispered as she climbed back into her hammock. "An' you too an' all, Mum," he added, tapping the lid of the box with one finger before sliding it back into its hiding place beneath his pillow.

"G'night, you pair," murmured Crake, making Bastjan jump. Alice's head popped up out of her hammock, her tousled hair barely hiding her surprised grin, and Crake chuckled.

"Can't keep nothin' to yerself in this place," Bastjan grouched, before blowing out the light.

CHAPTER
SEVENTEEN

"What's this slop, then?" Bastjan muttered, slipping into his seat beside Crake. In his hand he had a bowl of too-thick gruel. It looked like a grey worm curled in the bottom of the bowl and seemed about as appetizing. The atmosphere in the mess tent was subdued. There was no sound of bacon frying, no smells of kippers or toasted crumpets in the air, and the other performers sat in sullen clumps, with barely anyone attempting to make conversation.

"The boss wasn't jokin' about savin' money, I s'pose," Crake said, poking at his own breakfast. "Here," he whispered, leaning close. "Save some of yer bread for Alice. I don't think she'd be too fond of this stuff."

Bastjan grimaced. The bread was probably the only edible part of the meal, but he slipped it into his pocket and hefted his spoon, ready to tackle the gruel. He was barely halfway through it when the flap to the mess tent was knocked aside and the ringmaster himself strode through, flanked by three of his burliest rousties. Bastjan swallowed his sticky mouthful and sat to attention.

"Morning, folks," Quinn greeted them. Instantly, the low buzz in the tent fell silent. "I'm here to give you all a warning. I'm about to conduct a thorough search of the campground, my friends. I'm not looking for contraband or anything of the sort—" Quinn raised his hands against the sudden flood of muttering coming from every corner of the tent and slowly it died away. "I don't care what you've got hidden in your cubbyholes and stuffed inside your socks. I'm looking for something in particular and when I find it I'll leave you in peace. All right? I simply wanted to let you know, so that nobody's left wondering why things might be in a bit of disarray when you get back to your wagons." Quinn nodded at his rousties, who turned and marched out of the tent.

Someone near the door piped up with a question, and while Quinn was distracted Crake took the opportunity to lean back on his bench, pulling up the side of the mess tent with one huge hand. "Now," he whispered to Bastjan, all the while keeping his eyes on the ringmaster. The boy was gone in a blink.

Got to get to Alice, an' get 'er out of sight, Bastjan told himself. *An' the box!*

Skirting the back of the mess tent, he took advantage of the rubbish heap to hide his progress, gritting his teeth against the smell, and kept his ears tuned to the sound of approaching rousties. His blood froze at the first whistle; they were talking to one another in their code, the secret language that only they understood. He muttered under his breath and kept going, breaking cover as he reached the first wagon. He crouched behind it, watching for movement – and finally he spotted the rousties. The men paused at the top of the campground before splitting up, each one going in a different direction.

A tall roustie with close-cropped black hair looked at the wagon Bastjan was hiding behind and made a move towards it. Bastjan waited, letting the man reach the wagon's front steps, and then he grabbed hold of the downpipe. Quickly, silently, hand over hand, he hauled himself up on to the wagon's roof. He kept low, flattening himself against the canvas, his heart thumping against his ribs.

Soundlessly, Bastjan inched forwards until he could look down into the wagon through its skylight. The roustie was searching the interior, shaking out pillows and cushions, feeling beneath the mattress, going through drawers. A quick glance out into the campground told him the other rousties were going over their wagons just as thoroughly.

Bastjan took a couple of deep breaths and rolled to the edge of the wagon's roof. He swung his body out, holding on to the gutter with his strong hands. Then he pushed away with one foot, landing lightly on the ground. He sprinted to the cover of the next wagon, stopping at its back wheel to take stock of the camp. Nothing stirred besides a skinny dog poking about near the fire.

Before he could lose his nerve, Bastjan took off again, crouching in the mud behind the back wheel of the next wagon.

This really is a proper goin' over, he thought, his eyes skipping from wagon to wagon. *He's determined to find this box, an' I can't let 'im have it. I can't let* anyone *'ave it.*

The next wagon was Magnus Ólafsson's, the one after that was Ana and Carmen's. And the one after that was his and Crake's, across a slightly wider gap. He sucked his teeth in frustration; he'd be out in the open for a dangerously long time.

Just as he prepared to move, a roustie emerged from a wagon halfway across the camp. The man whistled and the signal was repeated as the other rousties appeared in the doorways of the wagons they'd just searched. Each man moved to the next wagon over and Bastjan waited for a few moments before bolting from his hiding place.

He skidded and fell at the back of Magnus's wagon, landing with a *splash* in a pool of muddy water. He glanced up and noticed an open window, through which he could hear a gentle snore. Magnus didn't usually take breakfast with the others, preferring instead to sleep late. *Please*, he begged. *Don't wake up an' give me away.* Bastjan held his breath as Magnus's snoring stopped. He didn't exhale until it started again, ten long heartbeats later.

He crept around the back of Magnus's wagon, before sprinting across the gap to Ana and Carmen's. He was halfway there when the rousties reappeared and Bastjan slid forwards, landing in the thick mud beside the back wheels. He scuttled beneath the sisters' wagon, peering out from behind the front wheel, to get a proper look at the camp.

The rousties had gathered at the fire, too far away for him to hear what they were saying to one another. They seemed to be passing something between them, a bottle, and one of the men threw back his head and laughed, loudly enough to carry to Bastjan's ears. The boy held his breath as he thought about what to do next. He had no choice but to run, but he knew he had to time it just right. If he was seen, everything would be wasted.

"What's the problem?" bellowed a voice to his left. Bastjan slowly turned to look – though he'd recognized the voice straightaway. The ringmaster was coming, striding up the path that led from the mess tent. "I told you to check the boy's wagon first and here I find you lollygagging." The rousties stood to attention and the one holding the bottle – *prob'ly stolen jus' now from someone's wagon*, Bastjan thought

154

– put it behind his back in the vain hope that he wouldn't be caught with it.

Bastjan slowly got to his haunches. He had to move or Alice was a goner. He checked behind him, but the way was clear. Then, with one final glance at the ringmaster, who was subjecting his rousties to a tirade, Bastjan ran, keeping as low as he could. Finally, he reached the back of his own wagon.

He leaped on to the footboard and rapped, one-two-three, on the windowpane, their code to let Alice know it was safe to open up. A second later, she pulled the curtain back, her face bright, and unlocked the window. She had his mother's notebook in her hand and she was sprawled on Crake's bunk. Bastjan looked in; the contents of the box were spread on Crake's coverlet, the empty box beside them.

"Bastjan, your mum's book is so interesting!" Alice began eagerly, pushing open the window. "She's talking all about—"

"It'll 'ave to wait till later," Bastjan said. "C'mon. Pack up the stuff. We gotta go."

Alice's smile vanished. "Go? Where?"

"Out of 'ere. Come on! Quinn's lookin' for the box."

Alice did as she was asked without any further questions. Faintly, Bastjan heard the rousties' whistles and his eyes widened in fear. Alice heard it too and her fingers trembled as she struggled to push the box's contents back inside it. She slapped the lid shut and Bastjan reached in to take her hand.

He hauled her through the window and helped her, one leg at a time, out on to the footboard, then they jumped together into the muck. Hand in hand, they made straight for the long grass behind the wagon. They trudged in as far as they could, hoping their tracks wouldn't be noticed, and then they crouched low.

Seconds later, the children saw the ringmaster enter the wagon. They'd closed the window behind them, but left the curtain open, and they had a clear view right through the tiny space.

"You got everythin'?" Bastjan whispered, watching as Quinn looked around his home.

Alice nodded. Then her eyes widened. "Wares," she breathed. "Oh no!"

"What? Where is 'e?"

"Somewhere in the camp," Alice said. "But if he smells us, he might give us away."

Bastjan looked back at the wagon. It shook a little as the ringmaster strode around inside. He thought of his wall of pictures and imagined the look on the ringmaster's face when he saw it.

"Forget about the dog," he said. "Let's just hope Quinn gives up quick an' leaves my things in peace."

"Thanks for coming to get me," Alice whispered, squeezing Bastjan's hand.

"Ain't nothin' to thank me for," he said. "If you was caught, we'd all be for it. Quinn would 'ave the box, an' I'd never see it again."

"I was reading about the Slipskins when you knocked on the window," Alice said. "I was right – they are shapeshifters. Your mum said everyone on the island knew the stories. And they lived in the Silent City, but it was because they'd been forced there. Hunted and persecuted by humans." Alice paused, taking a long breath. "Anyway. The bracelet has something to do with their shapeshifting power. Your mum didn't know what, exactly."

"Fascinatin'," Bastjan muttered. "I jus' wonder what everyone wants with this box. The more I'm learnin' about what's in it, the less good it all sounds."

"I was thinking about that too," Alice said. "D'you remember how your mum said that the bracelet had helped her to fly, but that she'd kept it for too long?"

Bastjan shrugged. "Not really. But if you say so."

"Well, mightn't that mean that a person who wore the bracelet got some of the Slipskin's powers? Maybe? It's a theory I'm working on," she finished, her cheeks turning pink.

Bastjan considered this. "Sounds like a reason for stealin' it, don't it?"

Alice frowned. "Perhaps. Though why anyone would want—"

"Shh!" Bastjan put a finger to his lips. Quinn strode out of the front door of the wagon and spat on the ground. He scrubbed at his forehead with one hand, his mouth tight with anger. A roustie jogged over to him, holding a wooden box in his hands.

"Found this in Lady Z's, sir," he said, handing it to the ringmaster. Quinn snatched it and flipped open its flimsy catch, before stirring through its contents with a finger. Then he upended the box, scattering its contents on the ground.

"Tat," he said, grinding Lady Zenobia's jewellery beneath the heel of his boot. He flung the box away. "Rubbish! This isn't what I'm looking for. The box I want has got a fish on the lid, man. It can't be that hard to spot."

"Yes, sir," said the roustie.

"Any luck with those books I sent you to find?" Quinn said.

The roustie seemed visibly relieved. "Yes, sir. Left 'em in your wagon. I could get all of 'em besides one, sir." The man fumbled in his pocket for a piece of paper, which he unfolded. "*The Physio-ol-ology and Anatomy of Rare Species, Midsea and North Afrik Region*, by Martin J. Widget. Bookshop fella said it would have to be ordered in."

"Good work." Quinn slapped the roustie on the back.

"That's something, at least. Got to play these toffs at their own game, don't we?"

"Yes, sir," said the roustie.

Alice and Bastjan looked at one another as the men walked into the centre of camp.

"Rare species," Alice whispered.

"From the Midsea. An' North Afrik," Bastjan continued. "In't that where Melita is?"

Alice nodded. "You don't think…"

"I dunno *what* to think," Bastjan said. "Din't even think Quinn could *read*, never mind a book like that. I wonder what else I've bin wrong about."

"Well, it looks like he's doing his homework on this box," Alice said, giving it a squeeze. "So we'll have to try to keep one step ahead of him for as long as we can."

"Yeah," Bastjan said. "An' stay out of his way, an' all."

"And what about Bauer?" Alice asked. "He'll be back in a few weeks."

Bastjan glanced back at his wagon. He wondered what it might feel like to roll it out of this camp, away from everyone he had ever known. *Might 'ave to roll it all the way to Melita.* "I'm workin' on that one," he told her. "I'll let you know when I got a plan."

CHAPTER
EIGHTEEN

"Look at that," Bastjan whispered to Alice. They were sitting in Bastjan's favourite place behind the scenes, a spot high in the rigging with a perfect view of the ring. There were sturdy planks to sit on, a handy metal bar to lean against and acres of empty space perfect for leg-swinging. They'd even smuggled up some snacks – half a bottle of warm lemonade, some squashed chocolate which still tasted fine, and a bag of roasted peanuts.

"Look at what?" Alice replied, the words muffled through her mouthful of food. She had one hand free to feed herself peanuts; the other held Wares carefully by the collar, keeping his inquisitive nose away from the chocolate.

"The crowd," he said, as if it was obvious. "The place is really fillin' up tonight."

"I heard there was a new headline act," Alice said,

popping in another handful of peanuts. "Some kid in a ring?" She threw Bastjan a grin. Tonight was the night he was to make his debut.

The circus had left St Wycombe several days before, moving a few miles down the road as they gradually made their way to London. Bastjan and Nanette had been practising every moment they got and she had finally pronounced him ready to fly. Earlier that morning, someone had been dispatched to the nearest printers' to run off some handbills and posters. Alice had one tucked into the pocket of her coat. It showed a child in a silver hoop, with eye-catching words over his head – *the Skyborn Boy*. As soon as she could, she was going to stick it on the wall of his wagon, right beside the pictures of the Flying Girl.

Bastjan returned the grin. "Maybe if we start gettin' our audience back, it'll solve a few problems at once," he said. "Might be no need for Bauer, that ol' mushroom head, to bail us out."

"I hope his airship runs out of steam in the middle of the ocean," Alice said, with feeling. "And that he *never* comes anywhere near us again."

"Knowin' our luck, he's prob'ly in the audience somewhere," Bastjan said darkly. "Keep yer eyes peeled."

Alice, alarmed, looked back out at the crowd and Bastjan took his opportunity to raid her peanut bag.

He managed to grab a handful before she pulled the bag away and he crammed them into his mouth, chuckling, as he got to his feet. It was time for him to head to the performers' area – the Runner Beans were up soon. Down below, the circus band was beginning to play and the clowns were gambolling into the ring. Ana and Carmen would be ready to go on after them, aboard their polished-pearl ponies, and then Bastjan would join the rest of his troupe for his first performance of the evening.

"Make sure to stay out of sight, yeah?" he said. He was already on the ladder leading to the ground. "We don't want anythin' like yesterday to happen again."

Alice gave him an apologetic look. She'd taken to lying on the roof of Bastjan and Crake's wagon during the day, just in case the ringmaster decided to spring any more no-warning searches. She'd found a good hiding place behind some of the ornate scrolling woodwork that decorated the roof's edges, but the day before, lost in reading the notebook, she'd glanced up and noticed a roustie on the far side of the campsite look in her direction for a too-long moment. She'd quickly flopped down, throwing the blanket over her head, and when she'd looked up again the roustie was gone. But she hadn't been able to shake the fear that she'd been seen.

"Nobody knows I'm even up here, right? Wares and I'll take good care of your mum's things. Won't we, boy?" She patted the dog and threw him a peanut, which he crunched happily.

"See you afterwards, then," he said, and was gone.

Bastjan bounded into the ring alongside his fellow Runner Beans when their act was announced, almost losing his footing when one of the other boys jabbed him with an elbow as they took their places for the first tumble. As the son of a performer who'd died in the ring, he was considered bad luck by most of the other Beans. But they didn't normally go so far as to try to interfere with his performance. He pushed the thought away as he listened for the cue, poised for his first trick.

Sandrine, one of the smallest Beans, came sailing through the air as the music surged. Bastjan reached up to catch her and her foot landed perfectly in his palm. As she bent forwards to grab his other hand in hers, ready for her next move, Bastjan glanced up at her.

"Think yer too good fer the likes of us now, do yer?" Sandrine whispered, her sneer made worse by the fact that she was upside down. "Mister fancy pants on yer flyin' hoop."

Bastjan's mouth dropped open, but his grip didn't slip as Sandrine did a handstand over his head. As the audience applauded she flipped to the ground and jogged away.

The rest of the act passed without incident, but Bastjan couldn't shake his sense of foreboding as he and the other Runner Beans made their way backstage. He looked around the performers' area. There was no sign of Crake, and even though he knew Alice had to be safe in their hiding place, he wished she was here where he could see her.

And he would have given anything for a reassuring look at the box, and a stroke of its enamelled lid.

"Bastjan," came a familiar voice, and he turned to see Nanette. She wore a brown robe with its hood up over her hair, but her tights and shoes were white. Unexpectedly, the woman dropped to her knees in front of him and gathered him into a hug. After a moment, Bastjan hugged her back.

"What's up? Everythin' all right, Nanette?" he said.

"Come on," she replied. Her voice sounded strange, muffled somehow. "Let's get you ready." She got to her feet still holding his hand. Her grip was tight. Bastjan tried to wriggle his fingers free, but Nanette didn't let go.

"No need to drag me," he said as they approached the dressing room, which was blocked off from the main backstage area with thin plywood boards. "What's goin' on?"

"Mr Quinn wants a word before we go up," Nanette replied. She closed the dressing-room door behind them and turned to check herself in a mirror. "So we've got to hurry."

Bastjan muttered under his breath as he lathered a

flannel for his face. He had to clean all traces of the Runner Beans' green paint off before he could get ready for the headline act. Nanette had left out his sticks of face paint – they were silver and white. He frowned at them as he scrubbed at his ears.

"Nanette, is this the right stuff?" he said, turning to her. Nanette stood in front of the door, watching him warily, her mouth a thin, quivering line. "Ain't it red we're usin' tonight?"

"There was a change of plan earlier. Mr Quinn'll tell you about it."

Bastjan shrugged and turned back to the mirror, but he kept watch on Nanette all the time. She stood with her arms folded, her shoulders stooped and tense. *Somethin's wrong*, Bastjan thought. He towelled his face dry, trying to stay calm. Then he pulled out his costume from the rack. He froze. It was white and covered with silver sequins. *Like a snowflake*, he thought.

Bastjan turned to Nanette with the leotard in his hands. "What's this, then? Some kind of a joke, is it?"

Nanette didn't answer. Instead, she loosened her robe and pulled down her hood. Her curled hair was piled on her head, dotted through with silver stars. She pulled the robe fully open, dropping it to the floor. Bastjan stared at her properly and finally understood. The white-and-silver leotard, the sparkling face paint on her cheekbones, the glittering headpiece.

The Dance of the Snowflakes. She's dressed in Mum's old costume!

"No way," he said, every inch of his chest feeling hot. The heat erupted up through his nose and mouth and eyes, making them water. "I ain't doin' this!"

"He wants a triple tuck, you flying and me catching, just like we practised," Nanette said. She closed her eyes and two fat tears ran down her cheeks, smudging her make-up. "Only we've got to do it dressed like this. He's got me over a barrel, Bastjan, and there's nothing I can do. I'm sorry."

"What? Nanette, tell me what's goin' on." Bastjan crushed the satin of the silver costume between his hands as he gripped it.

"I've got a daughter," Nanette said, blinking her tears away. "She has two babies and her husband's dead. She's sick and she relies on what I send her to keep those babies fed. Quinn's goin' to sack me, without the pay he owes, if I don't do as he tells me tonight." Nanette's eyes filled again. "They're only *babies*, Bastjan. And I'm all they've got. I can't lose this job."

Bastjan stared, incredulous. "Nanette, jus' *tell* me. What's any of this got to do wi' me?"

The woman looked him in the eye. "It's your friend. The girl with the firemark. He knows she's got the box."

Bastjan blinked, his brain a whir. "*What?*"

"Ester's box, Bastjan. He wants it." Her voice dropped to a whisper. "And it's all my fault. I told him about her. I told him about Alice."

"How … how d'you know her name?"

"Her grandfather's been looking for her since the day she ran away from his house. Her face is in all the papers, Bastjan. *Everyone* knows her name."

Bastjan's heart skipped. *Alice ain't safe*, he thought. *I gotta warn 'er!* But Nanette was still blocking the dressing-room door, his only way out. "Alice ain't got nothin' to do with any o' this."

Nanette shook her head. "Someone saw her, Bastjan. One of the rousties. And now Quinn's convinced she has the box. He's goin' to do whatever it takes to get it."

"Whatever it takes?" Bastjan felt dizzy.

"We're going up," Nanette said. "And if that girl won't hand over the box, I'm to make sure you don't come down."

High overhead, Wares began to growl.

"What is it, boy?" Alice said, reaching out to scratch his head. Her eyes didn't leave the ring. Bastjan's act was coming up soon and she didn't want to miss a moment of it.

"He can probably smell an intruder," came a voice from behind her, and Alice turned sharply, knocking over the open bottle of lemonade. It tinkled away over the boards, leaving a sticky trail. Cyrus Quinn stood on the ladder. In his hand he held a knife with a long, wide blade.

Wares bared his teeth and barked. In the swelling noise of the ring, nobody heard. Alice picked him up, feeling his small body quivering in her arms.

"What—" Alice began, but her throat closed over with shock. "What do you want?" she finally said, as Cyrus Quinn stepped up on to the platform. Alice knew there was nowhere to run, but she took a step backwards anyway, almost tumbling over a coil of rope.

"I'd forgotten about you, you know," Quinn began, taking a step towards her. "After that day we met beneath my big top. Remarkable as you are, young lady, I've had a lot on my mind and somehow you managed to slip out of it." He paused, his smile thin-lipped. "And then one of my men reported seeing a girl, and a dog, on top of a wagon, and certain things began to fall into place."

"I'm not staying, I promise," Alice said. "I just needed somewhere—"

"There's a box," Quinn interrupted, "made of fine dark wood, with a fish on its lid." He twirled the knife in his hand. "I think you have it. You must have, as I've scoured the camp and found no trace of it."

Alice gripped the bar beside her, afraid she might faint. "Don't be ridiculous," she said, her voice shaking.

"I am many things, Miss Patten – or should I say, *Lady* Patten – but ridiculous is not one of them." Quinn stared at her. "In my pocket I have a telegram, ready for sending, which is addressed to your dear old grandad. In it, I tell him I've found you safe and well, and I'm claiming the fat reward he has out for your safe return."

"Grandfather?" Alice said, blinking fast against her tears. "He has a *reward* out for me?"

"Terribly worried, he is." Quinn pursed his lips in a mockery of concern. "Been searching for you up and down the country." He leaned casually against the railing, tapping the flat of the knife against his open palm. "So it's like this. You hand over the box, I claim the reward, you go home and live in luxury for the rest of your life. Or," he continued, raising the blade and pointing it at her, wagging it with every word he spoke, "you *don't* hand over the box and I send a different telegram to poor old Lord Patten. One in which I tell him that, before I could secure her safe return –" Quinn took a step closer, tightening his grip on the knife – "his darling granddaughter met with an unfortunate accident."

CHAPTER NINETEEN

Wares leaped from Alice's arms, scrambling on the boards and launching himself at the ringmaster. Quinn bared his own teeth at the charging dog and Alice screamed as he grabbed Wares by the scruff of the neck, lifting his tiny body high.

"No!" she shouted. "Don't hurt him!"

"After you," Quinn growled, indicating towards the ladder with a wave of the blade. Wares wriggled his legs for all he was worth, but the ringmaster held him at arm's length. Sobbing, Alice made her way to the ladder and began to descend. Quinn's stare followed her all the way. As soon as she reached the ground, he placed the blade of his knife between his teeth and climbed down one-handed. Once at the bottom he removed the knife, wiping its blade on his sleeve.

"Please," Alice said, reaching out for the dog. "Give him back."

Quinn stuck the knife into a scabbard strapped to his chest before gripping Alice around the arm. Wordlessly, he led her through the forest of struts and scaffolding until they reached the performers' area – just in time to see Bastjan burst through the dressing-room door with Nanette at his heels. He was still wearing his Runner Beans trousers, but with nothing on top besides a stained old vest. In his hands he carried a sparkling white costume.

"Bastjan!" Alice shouted, and he turned to her. His eyes widened.

"Let 'er go!" he shouted, but Quinn only tightened his grip. Alice winced, trying to wriggle free.

"We all need to have a little talk, I think," Quinn said. Bastjan threw the costume to the ground and Nanette ran to pick it up, shaking the dirt from it as best she could.

"I *ain't* goin' up," Bastjan said. "Ain't no way."

"Well, then, I'm afraid we've got a problem," the ringmaster said. "Because, you see, there's an audience out there expecting a high-flying showstopper of a finale." As he spoke, there was a gush of applause from beyond the curtain as an act came to an end. "Not to mention the fact that there's something I need. Something you've got." The ringmaster tossed Wares to the floor, aiming a kick at him. The dog dodged it and ran, vanishing into the campground through the open tent flap.

"Mr Quinn, I tried to explain," Nanette began. "Bastjan knows what you need. He—"

"Then why isn't he dressed?" Quinn asked mildly.

"Let Alice go," Bastjan said, his fists clenching.

Quinn pulled his knife free, spinning it carelessly in his palm. "Get into your costume," he said. "Time is running out, boy. And the longer you delay…" He stopped the blade's spin with the point close to Alice's cheek. She closed her eyes against it.

"Please, Bastjan," Nanette said, holding out the white leotard. "He'll hurt her. Don't try his patience, lad."

Bastjan turned to Quinn. "If I go up, you'll let 'er go?"

"I get the box, nobody gets hurt. You get to survive your great debut, little Lady Patten here gets to go home safely and I get paid a great deal of money." Quinn cocked a small grin. "And that's just the start of it," he added, half to himself.

Alice opened her eyes and the children looked at one another. "Give it to 'im as soon as I'm back on the ground," Bastjan murmured to Alice, his voice low. "Nothin's worth gettin' hurt for."

"But—" Alice whispered.

"Jus' do it," Bastjan said. He grabbed the leotard out of Nanette's hands and began to pull it on.

Nanette vanished into the dressing room for a moment

172

and re-emerged with the sticks of make-up in her hand. She did her best to paint Bastjan's face despite his glowering expression, until finally he stood ready, his cheeks sparkling in the light.

"Passable," Quinn muttered, shoving Alice away from him. Nanette took hold of her instead, digging in her strong fingers. Then she stood to one side, pulling the children with her, as performers spilled out of the ring and into the backstage area – Lily and Gustav, Lady Zenobia, and Christabel with her dogs.

"Please," Nanette murmured. "Please, don't say anythin'. If this doesn't work, my grandkids are as good as dead. I'm beggin' you."

"Where's Crake?" Bastjan asked, watching the last of the performers disappear into the dressing room.

"There's been an emergency in Mammoth's enclosure," Nanette said, and as Bastjan turned to her, eyes wide, she quickly continued. "Not a real one – don't worry. Just somethin' to keep Crake an' some of the other men out of the way, until… Until this is done."

The ringmaster buttoned his jacket over the knife at his chest, smoothing down the fabric to ensure the weapon couldn't be seen. "I'm off to give you the best introduction I can muster," he said, throwing Bastjan a wink. "Break a leg." Then, with a laugh, he was gone beyond the curtain.

Bastjan quivered as he closed his eyes and listened for

the ringmaster's voice. "Ladies and gentlemen! Boys, girls, *friends*! We're nearing the end of our evening and I wanted to thank you all, most sincerely, for being part of our family here tonight." The audience responded with a gentle ripple of applause.

"You've seen tumblers and jugglers, flying knives and spurts of flame. You've witnessed the finest dancers and singers this side of a circus ring. You've marvelled at creatures from distant lands. You've seen things that – I hope! – you'll be talking about for years to come." Bastjan grimaced as he listened. "But now, my friends. Now the time has come for our highlight of the evening." Quinn paused and Bastjan held his breath.

"It's rare, my friends, to come across a talent so incandescent as the one you're about to see," Quinn began. Bastjan imagined him walking around the ring, his hands behind his back, the audience hanging on his every word. "You think you've seen performers in the air? You think you've seen artists on the trapeze? They pale beside my next act, ladies and gents. Not since the days of the Dance of the Snowflakes have we seen a performer of this level of artistry. No, my friends! Prepare yourselves for skill beyond compare." The drums rattled, growing louder and louder. "Ready yourselves for acrobatics that go beyond the bounds of what is possible. Without further ado, I present to you my most trusted aerialist, Miss Nanette van Hemel, and the young man known only as…" The drums rolled for a moment that seemed far too long.

"*The Skyborn Boy!*" the ringmaster shouted, and the crowd erupted.

In the next moment, Quinn ducked beneath the curtain again. He grabbed Alice, but Bastjan didn't have a chance to say anything before Nanette was pulling him forwards. Just before they passed through the curtain and into the ring he looked back, but all he could see were Alice's angry, tearful eyes and the ringmaster's jaw, set tightly.

Then they were through the curtain and into the spotlights' glare. Nanette released his wrist and raised her arms in the air before bending into a graceful bow. Knowing he had no choice, Bastjan copied her movements exactly. He jogged lightly to one side of the trapeze apparatus while Nanette jogged to the other, and as they rose into the air, he could feel the piercing weight of her gaze with every foot they climbed. He closed his eyes as the platforms settled into place and tried to breathe.

Behind the curtain, Alice edged away from the point of the knife which the ringmaster insisted on holding against her side.

"Can't you put that away?" she asked.

"Afraid not," he said, as they peered out through the

gap. The spotlights were trained on the sparkling figures high above. The music soared as Nanette and Bastjan readied themselves to swing. "It's multipurpose, you see. Keeps you from getting too feisty and it also acts as my failsafe. If you try anything –" the ringmaster angled the blade, just enough to catch the light – "it has other uses."

Quinn angled the blade further, reflecting the light straight into Alice's eyes. She squeezed them shut against the glare and turned her head away, her pulse booming in her ears. "This is how we pass messages in the circus, you know, when shouting and whistling won't do. A simple flashing signal. Although normally we use mirrors," Quinn continued, a note of amusement in his voice. "Nanette is ready and waiting for a sign from me. If you give me any trouble, all I need to do is let her know."

Alice blinked as the band struck up a loud, rolling tune. The audience began to clap along, all eyes on the performers – Bastjan on one silver swing and Nanette on another. Then they were off, swooping effortlessly across the dizzying space. Alice glanced down at the poles holding the tent aloft; there was no safety net.

If he falls, he's done for, she thought, and with a lurch, she made a guess at what the ringmaster had been hinting at.

"You mean – he's going to fall," Alice said, turning to Quinn. "If you signal to Nanette, she's going to drop him."

"Ain't you the clever one," Quinn said. He kept his eyes on his performers. "Sharper'n this blade, young Lady Patten. It'd be tragic, eh? Going the same way as his dear old mum. But headlines are headlines, and there's no paying for coverage like that. Can you imagine? I'd have to beat them away from the door."

If I fight, he'll signal, Alice realized, glancing up at Bastjan's swinging form. *If I scream, the same. And if he thinks there's any chance I won't hand over the box...* Her thoughts cascaded, one after the other. *But he doesn't know whether I've got it on me or not. I can still delay things. Maybe just long enough to get Bastjan down from there.* She frowned. *But I won't give up the box, even then, no matter what Bastjan said.*

"You're not getting anything until Bastjan's safe," she said.

"He'll be perfectly safe so long as I don't give the signal," Quinn replied. There was a hard edge to his words.

"Even so..." Alice forced the wobble out of her voice. "I'm not handing anything over until he's back on the ground."

Quinn turned to her. "In that case, I think we'll have to come to a compromise, *milady*."

Alice curled her lip. "Stop calling me that," she snapped.

Quinn leaned forwards, raising the knife so that the blade was between his nose and Alice's. "You see, I have this," he told her. "And with this, you'll find things get done a little more easily. Things like searching a person for something they shouldn't have."

Alice swallowed hard and looked away from the blade, back into Quinn's face. "I'm still not giving you anything until Bastjan's safe."

"Once he's back in Nanette's arms, he's as safe as a baby in a cradle," Quinn said. "So I propose this." He lowered the knife, looking back out into the circus ring. "As soon as Nanette has caught Bastjan – and she *will* catch him – you'll give the box to me. And if you don't –" Alice yelped as the point of the knife was again pressed against her side – "I'll make sure to take it from you anyway. Maybe Lord Patten will pay out for your return, even if you're missing a piece or two." He gave a low chuckle. "I'm willing to take my chances, at any rate."

The tempo of the music shifted and Alice focused on Bastjan, glittering high above. He was hanging from his swing, getting ready to fly.

Alice closed her eyes, trembling, and prepared herself for what had to come next.

CHAPTER
TWENTY

Bastjan sat on the bar of his swing, running through the act in his head as he performed every movement. He and Nanette mirrored one another; his swing matched hers exactly, their timings precise. They swung towards one another, leaning back with their toes pointed, stretching their legs until the tips of their slippers almost touched, before gravity pulled them apart again. Below them the audience applauded.

He swallowed back a mouthful of sickness that had nothing to do with the height, or the movement. *Got to get this right*, he told himself. He crunched his eyes shut, knowing without having to look exactly where he was in the roof space. *He'll hurt Alice if I muck this up.*

The swings moved forwards once more, and Nanette and Bastjan leaned backwards to propel them along.

On the count of three they each released one hand, letting the spotlight dance along their sparkling costumes; far below, the audience gasped and clapped as the swings began their return journey. With the next swing, they released their other hands and flew holding on with only their legs, bending backwards to reach out for one another at the swing's highest point. They came close enough for Bastjan to see the fear in Nanette's eyes and then the swings began their downward journey.

Bastjan sat back up on to his swing as Nanette landed lightly on her platform. She paused, bowing to the crowd and allowing their applause to wash over her, as Bastjan built up his speed. He tried not to think about the drop that yawned beneath him. The only thing he had to rely on to keep him from falling to the sawdust below was Nanette. His mouth filled with sour-tasting saliva and he had to swallow it back.

As he started his descent, Bastjan quickly swapped his grip from the ropes to the swing, holding on tightly with both hands while his legs swung clear. Now his whole body hung beneath the swing like a sparkling teardrop, and he knew he had two more swings left before it would be time to let go. The band began to roll their drums once more but he pushed the sound out of his mind.

She smelled like roses, heavy and sweet. Her smile shone as she swung, gripping the rope with one hand and holding him in the crook of her other arm. Holding him close beneath her chin, kissing his forehead with her red lips, swinging her legs as though she hadn't a single care in the world. Then she hooked her infant son to her leotard and began to swing with all her strength, pushing forwards through the empty roof space, going so high the spotlights could hardly find her.

And then, just as she started her descent, his mother unhooked him from her chest, gave him a single kiss and flung him into the air…

Bastjan's eyes snapped back into focus. His lungs were burning – but not with exertion. It felt like he was drowning, his chest struggling to open. "*Whoop*," came the sound, unasked for, out of his mouth. "*Whoop*." He looked towards Nanette's platform – she was hanging beneath her swing with her legs bent around its bar, and she was beginning to move.

He finished his swing, knowing that the next time he flew forwards, he would hear Nanette's signal, just like they'd practised, and he would have to let go.

He would have to fling himself into the air and hope she would catch him.

"Ayup!" came Nanette's voice. Bastjan heard it, clear as clear – the signal to release and fly.

He let go of his swing and tucked his legs to his ailing chest, counting his spins. *One. Two. Three.*

Quick as a thought, he uncoiled, his hands seeking

Nanette's, his head swimming from a lack of air. And then Nanette's face was right beside his own. Her hands were stretched out and Bastjan reached for them.

"Got you," she said, trying to smile, as her fingers closed around his wrists. They began the return swing, ready for their final trick – but just as they began to move, Bastjan saw Nanette flinch, dazzled by a flash of light. She closed her eyes against it but Bastjan saw it again, so bright that it made him sick with dizziness. He stared up into Nanette's face. She opened her eyes. They were dark with grief and Bastjan knew what she was about to do.

"I'm sorry," she whispered, her face twisted with pain – and then she let him go.

At the same second as Nanette loosened her grip, Bastjan reached up as high as he could, grabbing at whatever he could find. He got a handful of Nanette's hair, and the woman screeched in pain and surprise. The swing began to wobble dangerously as Nanette tried to fight off Bastjan's hold and the boy knew he was seconds away from losing his grip completely.

One. Two. Three. Alice counted Bastjan's spins as he sailed through the air, and then, with a crashing of cymbals from the band, he was caught and held. Bastjan and Nanette began to swing and the audience's applause swelled like a wave.

"Now!" Quinn bellowed into her ear. "The box. Give it to me!"

"I don't have it," Alice said, fear making her words tight. "Not with me. But I know where it is. Just let him get back on the ground, and then we can all go together and fetch it. Please!" *Stall him, just long enough, and maybe we can take the box and run...*

"What?" Quinn turned to her, snarling with rage. "You little—"

Alice tried to pull away, but Quinn held her tight. Then he hefted the blade of the knife — but instead of using it to hurt her, he angled it towards the light. Once, twice, he flicked it.

"No!" Alice cried. "*Please!*" She fumbled through her inside pocket. Her sweaty fingers met the edge of the box and she pulled it out. "It's here! You can have it – just get him down!"

"It's too late," Quinn panted, his eyes fixed on the box. "The signal's sent. It's over."

A shriek of horror made Alice look out into the ring, where she saw Bastjan and Nanette grappling on the swing. Before she could break away, Quinn threw Alice to the floor. The box flew from her fingers. Alice had no time to reach for it before Quinn grabbed it up, and in the next moment, he was gone.

Suddenly, amid the clamour from the audience, there

was another noise. A noise Alice recognized – a sharp, angry yap.

"Wares," she whispered, hauling herself up on her hands and knees.

A group of people were running across the circus ring, led by a tiny patchwork-coloured dog. Crake was right behind Wares, Jericho and Ana and Carmen right behind him – and just as Bastjan began to lose his grip, three clowns came running from the far side of the ring. Between them they carried a trampoline, their eyes focused on the boy. They'd barely got into position before Bastjan finally dropped from the trapeze. Alice lost sight of him then, amid the forest of arms and hands which rushed in to help.

From high overhead there was a scream and Alice looked up. She saw Nanette suspended upside down from a harness – but something had gone wrong. She was hanging awkwardly, one leg pulled horribly out of shape. The woman kept screaming, her cries becoming bellows of agony as a pair of rousties began to lower her to the ground. Alice grimaced and looked away. She hauled herself up using the ringside curtain, stumbling her way towards the spot where Bastjan had landed.

Crake was lifting the pale-faced boy into his arms just as Alice reached them. She dropped to her knees and Wares launched himself at her.

"Good dog," she said, kissing the top of his silky head. "Good, good dog."

Crake got to his feet, carrying Bastjan as though he were a baby, and strode out of the ring. Alice, Jericho, Ana and Carmen followed him, ignoring the restless audience all around as they made for the performers' area.

"Not this way," Alice said, pulling at Crake's arm. "What if Quinn sees us?"

"He'll keep out of my way if he knows what's good for him," the strongman rumbled, ducking beneath the curtain. There was no sign of Quinn in the backstage area. All they saw were abandoned props, sandbags, piles of rope and haybales – and the open flap in the tent leading to the outside.

Ana ran ahead of the group. "Bring him to our wagon. We have medicine." Crake followed without a word.

The strongman creaked his way up the steps and through the door of the sisters' wagon, Alice close at his heels. A moment later he laid Bastjan gently on a bunk, going down on one knee on the floor. He kept one hand on Bastjan's chest, as though to check he was still breathing. Every inhalation and exhalation was marked by a gentle *whoop*, and the boy's breath sounded sticky and thick.

"This will help," Carmen said as she held a bottle to Bastjan's lips. Crake helped him to take a mouthful, and the boy sat up and coughed, wiping his mouth. He coughed again, his lungs clearing, and slowly his colour began to come back. He looked around and found Alice as Crake eased him back on to the pillow.

"You're all right," she breathed. Wares licked away the tears that suddenly began to flood out of her eyes and she turned away, embarrassed.

From outside, the sound of raised voices was heard. Crake got to his feet. Ducking his head around the lamp hanging from the wagon ceiling, he hurried to the door. He looked out and then he turned to the others, his eyes wide with rage.

"He's burnin' our wagon!" Crake shouted, and then he was gone.

Ana and Carmen bounded to the door, Jericho only barely beating them to it.

"Gimme a hand," Bastjan muttered, and Alice helped him out of bed. Then the children and Wares followed the adults out of the wagon and down the steps.

Across the campground the only home Bastjan had ever known was aflame, gouts of fire bursting from its roof and licking along its wooden fittings, smoke billowing in a black cloud out of the half-door. Alice watched as Crake ran towards the burning wagon, helping with a bucket chain that some of the other performers had set up. But it didn't seem to matter how quickly they poured water on the blaze. The wagon was lost, along with everything in it.

Alice didn't know how long she stood and stared. Eventually she turned to find Bastjan, her heart filled with sorrow for his loss, and regret for how badly she'd guarded his most precious thing, but her words died on her tongue.

For where Bastjan had been standing was now an empty patch of muddy grass.

CHAPTER
TWENTY-ONE

All Bastjan knew was the rocking of the world and the animal stench and the bursting, burning pain in his head.

Things came and went, like he was slowly opening and closing his eyes.

Nothing he saw or heard made any sense.

Voices. Voices he knew.

"How much longer?"

"*Ahyuk*, not too far now, sir, just down this lane, an' then…"

"… has to work, Hubert. I won't let the circus fail. Not while I'm in charge."

"I know, Mr Quinn, sir. I know."

"As soon as the boy is out of the picture, we'll leave for London. The airship will be ready, with any luck. We've got to reach the island before…"

Then all was darkness, for longer than Bastjan could name.

Suddenly, his head whacked painfully off a strange, hard surface. He moved one hand over it. Boards? Rough wood? Everything smelled different. He could hear birdsong. He opened his eyes, but all was blackness.

"*Ahyuk. Ahyuk.*" The sound was so familiar.

"Hubert," Bastjan tried to say. His voice sounded like he had cloth in his ears.

There was a scrambling nearby and then the warmth of a face near to his, the feeling of breath on his cheek. The smell of whiskey and sweat and animal dung. The smell of home. "Lie still, lad. *Ahyuk.* You'll be all right. You'll be minded here and you'll be fed, an' everythin' will work out fine. *Ahyuk.*"

"Home," Bastjan said, the throbbing in his head becoming unbearable.

"Best forget about it, boy. *Ahyuk.* Best for you, just to put it all away."

Then the feeling of a warm, calloused hand on his forehead, stroking back his hair, and Hubert was gone.

Bastjan felt himself burst through a barrier, like waking up suddenly from a bad dream. His head was lolling painfully to one side. Wheels rumbled beneath him, over a rough and rutted road. He knew he wasn't in a wagon, where the going would have been smooth; whatever he was riding in, it was jolting and jerking him as it rolled. He opened his eyes, but he still couldn't see. Then he realized he was wearing a rough, itchy blindfold and he tried to lift his arm to pull it loose – but his arms were tied behind his back, the rope cutting painfully into his wrists. A pole ran up his back, pressing uncomfortably hard against his spine as it kept him sitting upright, and his wrists were tied around it. Quickly, he drew up his legs. They were bound at the ankles, but that didn't stop him from catching the blindfold between his knees and pulling it down.

He squinted. It wasn't quite dark, but almost. Everywhere he looked, all he saw was sky and trees. And somewhere close by, someone was whistling.

"Hey!" he shouted, struggling against his ropes. "What's goin' on?"

"Awake, are yer?" came a voice. Bastjan turned his head as far as it would go. Finally, he could see enough to make sense of where he was.

He was tied up in the back of a plain, tall-sided cart, empty of anything besides him and a few stray bits of straw. Up ahead, his back turned to him, sat a stranger. By the clicking of his tongue, Bastjan knew he was driving a horse. Just as he worked all this out, the cart rolled over a bump in the road, jostling him painfully against the pole.

"Who're you?" Bastjan shouted.

"Yer new boss," came the reply.

Bastjan blinked. His head was clearing, but it still thumped with pain. There was a horrible taste in his mouth too. He spat, dislodging a thread of fabric that had been lying on his tongue.

Quinn knocked me out, Bastjan realized. *Shoved a rag over my face, an' knocked me out.* "An' then he sold me," Bastjan said out loud, remembering the ringmaster's words. *I should sell you, I should!* The boy squeezed his eyes tight, imagining the circus wagon leaving him behind, rolling and bumping down a narrow laneway, getting smaller and smaller as it vanished into the distance. *But why?*

"You were a bargain too!" chortled the stranger.

Bastjan roared, bracing his feet against the boards beneath him. He pushed against the pole keeping him tied in place, gritting his teeth with the strain.

"Don't get any big ideas there, sonny," came the driver's voice. "If you want my advice I'd tell you to rest as much as you can while you've got the chance. I don't abide slackers, me. No dead weight on my land, I can tell you."

Bastjan ignored the man and tried to think. Where was Crake? What had happened to Alice? He swallowed back his fear that the ringmaster had hurt her. *Crake'll take care o' her, won't he?*

He pressed his face against his knees, feeling hot tears soak through his tights. The last thing he remembered from the circus was the sight of his wagon going up in smoke, and his heart tore in half at the thought of all the pictures of his mum turning into ash, floating through the evening sky. *An' does Quinn have the box?* He hoped against hope that Alice hadn't handed it over.

He looked around, peering out through the gaps between the cart's slats. There were no buildings anywhere he could see – no tents, no wagons, nothing familiar at all. He had no idea where he was, nor any clue how to get back to the circus. He let his face fall forwards against his legs again, trying to keep warm. He shivered as the night drew in; all he had on was his performance costume, and eventually it became all he could do to simply keep himself going, one heartbeat at a time.

Finally, the cart came to a stop in a small, cobbled courtyard, surrounded on three sides by low, neatly kept buildings. Bastjan jerked awake, his senses jangling. At one of the windows a candle burned and overhead all he could see were stars. Somewhere close by a dog growled, low in its chest, before letting free a volley of loud barks.

"Put a sock in it, you!" the man shouted, and the dog fell silent. A door opened and a figure stood in the gap, holding a lantern high. The person – a woman, Bastjan saw, wrapped in a warm-looking shawl, her face a wary scowl – came down the garden path and handed the lantern to the driver. He took it with a muttered grunt. The cart rocked as the man climbed down and a heartbeat later Bastjan heard him undoing the backboard.

"Here we are, then," the man said, hanging the lantern from a hook at the cart's far end. "Let's get you settled. It's milkin' first thing. I need you hale and hearty, an'—"

Bastjan drew his bound legs up and tried to kick at the man's face, but he simply took an angry step to one side, batting away the boy's flailing feet with one huge hand. He climbed aboard the cart, grabbing hold of the front of Bastjan's leotard.

"There's two reasons I'm not bringin' you to the barn for a thrashin', an' the first is that tomorrow's your first day," the man growled. "The second is I admire a lad with a bit of backbone. But not too much backbone, sonny. Too much backbone gets you the back of my hand." The farmer peered at him, his eyes narrowed. "I'll 'ave to keep my eye on you, an' no mistake."

A wave of exhaustion washed over Bastjan, and his mother's face bloomed in his memory. He closed his eyes, desperate to keep hold of it, and to dig even deeper, to remember the fragmentary descriptions his mother had given him of his father, but they slipped out of his grip. Bastjan tried as hard as he could, but his father's face gradually became Crake's face, the only real father he'd ever known, and his pain grew overwhelming. Here, miles from home, all he had left of his family were these memories and the smeared remnants of face paint on his filthy, ripped costume – the ringmaster had taken everything else away. "Mum," he whispered. "Dad." Hot tears broke through and his thoughts shattered into pieces.

"You ain't got no dad now," the farmer muttered, smacking Bastjan on the side of the head as he leaned around behind the boy to cut his wrists free. "Sooner the better you remember that."

Alice sat in Ana and Carmen's wagon, wrapped head to toe in a blanket. Wares was huddled on her lap too, but even with his extra warmth she was frozen to the bone. It wasn't because she was cold – Ana and Carmen had their stove lit and kept handing her things to drink, hot chocolate, honey in warm milk, a spicy-smelling tea – but because she'd never felt so deeply hopeless before.

I gave him the box, she kept telling herself. *I gave Quinn the box and I broke my promise to Bastjan.*

Ana sat cross-legged on the end of her bunk, a guitar in her hands. Her hair fell over the instrument in a shining dark wave as she plucked a mournful melody from it. Carmen, at the washstand, hummed along. Finally, Ana stopped playing, throwing the guitar on the bed, and

Carmen rose from her stool to comfort her.

"Someone has to know where Bastjan is," Alice said, and the sisters looked at her.

"Crake and the others, they have sent search parties out into the park, into the city, everywhere. We have to wait, to see if they find any trace," Ana said.

Alice threw off the blanket and a drowsy, half asleep Wares sat up. "No," she said. "We can't just *sit* here, like … like … *mannequins*, waiting for something to happen. Someone in this camp must know where Bastjan is."

Alice pushed herself up off the floor. Wares dropped from her lap, landing with a skitter on all four paws. He bounded towards the wagon door as Alice reached out to unlatch it.

"Wait!" Ana said. "*Pequeña*, you cannot go alone." She and Carmen slipped on shoes and shawls.

Alice opened the door and thumped her way down the steps. The remnants of Crake and Bastjan's wagon sat, blackened and skeletal, a few feet away; the smoke from the fire still rose into the air and Alice choked on it.

She turned to the sisters. "We need to search the camp. See who's missing. Besides Bastjan, I mean, and the ringmaster. And I'm going to pay a visit to Nanette."

Ana and Carmen conferred in Iberian and then they looked at Alice. "In that case, wait one more moment," Ana said, before vanishing into her wagon again. When she re-emerged, Alice caught a glimpse of a tiny glass bottle with a stopper in its neck before Ana slid it into her pocket.

"Now," said Ana, "we are ready."

Chapter
Twenty-two

"I will go and ask among the roustabouts, see if any of them have been missed since the end of the performance," Carmen said. "Ana will go with you, Alice."

They split up without another word. Soon Ana, Alice and Wares drew near to Nanette's wagon, where she'd been brought to recover after the show. Lily sat on the steps. She was feverishly knitting, a thick shawl tight around her shoulders and a lamp by her side, burning low.

"She's sleepin'," Lily said.

"We would like to see her anyway," Ana said. "We will not stay long."

Lily's knitting needles went *clickety-clack, clickety-clack*, and she made no reply. After a moment Alice realized the woman was weeping. "Known her since we were girls," Lily was saying, her eyes never leaving her knitting. "Known her since she were plain old Nancy Harrington – none of this Nanette van Hemel stuff. Never knew she could do anythin' like this." She looked up at Ana, her eyes shining with tears. "She could've *killed* that boy."

Ana nodded. "Yes," she said.

Lily wiped her eyes and shuffled to one side. "Go on, then. But don't upset 'er. She was in a lot of pain. I gave her somethin' for it, so she mightn't be all there yet."

"Thank you, Lily," Ana said, dropping one hand to the older woman's shoulder as she passed her by.

Alice followed Ana into the wagon, Wares lolloping up the steps at her heels. The aerialist lay on her bunk. Her eyes seemed sunken and her face pale; her hair was undone where Bastjan had pulled at it and there were scratches along one cheek. Ana and Alice got to their knees and watched her sleep for a moment, while Wares stood on his back legs and placed his front paws on the bedspread, gazing at Nanette with his head cocked to one side.

"Bastjan told me the ringmaster threatened to sell him," Alice said, still watching Nanette's sleeping face. "Do you think he actually would?"

Ana took a deep breath. "If it got him what he wanted, I think Cyrus Quinn would do anything," she said. "So yes."

Alice turned to her. "But who would buy a *child*?"

Ana shrugged, one-shouldered. "Anyone who needs someone who can work. Someone they do not need to pay." Her dark eyes settled on the girl. "Plenty of people would give money for a young, strong boy to pick their crops or feed their animals or fix their machinery, in return for a place to sleep and some food. Quinn, like all ringmasters, knows many farmers and factory men who send him workers when he needs them, and often he returns the favour."

Something popped in Alice's memory. "A farm," she whispered. "I saw a cart with the name of a farm on it, only a few days ago. It was in St Wycombe, but we're not far away from there. Perhaps they're still supplying the circus?"

"Try to remember it, *amor*. And let us talk to Nanette while you think." Ana reached into her pocket and pulled out the small bottle. "Hold your breath," she said, and pulled out its stopper. Ana waved it beneath Nanette's nose once, twice and then a third time – and finally, with a spluttering cough, the injured woman woke up. Instantly, her face was pulled into a grimace of pain.

"We will not keep you long, Nanette," Ana said as she re-stoppered the bottle of smelling salts and slipped them back into her pocket.

"Get out," Nanette said, closing her eyes tight. "Lily!" she called, before her words were lost in a fit of coughing. She grabbed at her side and her hip, groaning.

"I don't want to make things worse for you," Alice said. "But we need to know where Bastjan is."

Lily appeared at the door. "Tell 'em, Nance. Do that one kindness for the lad."

Nanette's eyes stayed closed and she shook her head slightly. Alice watched her hands tense and clench on top of her blanket, and on instinct she slid her own fingers through Nanette's. The woman gripped them hard. "Please," Alice said. "We know Quinn sold him. Was it to a farmer? Is it close by?"

"Has Cyrus gone?" Nanette asked, opening her eyes and looking for Lily.

"He has, love," Lily said, from the doorway.

"Did he leave my money?" Nanette asked. Lily looked at the floor and didn't answer, and Nanette closed her eyes again. "I've been such a fool," she whispered.

"Tell us what's going on," Alice begged. "Why did you do it?"

Nanette's eyes opened again and tears ran down her cheeks. "I had no choice," she whispered. "It was do what Cyrus wanted or my grandkids were goin' to starve." Her lips trembled. "But he don't care about my grandkids, I know that now. An' I've gone an' hurt that boy, for nothin'."

"The farm," Alice prompted. "They were supplying the circus with hay for the animals, weren't they? Is that where he sent Bastjan?"

"He said he was goin' to sell the boy, get what he could for him. Far as I know, the whole thing was arranged days ago. But it was the box he really wanted. He said we'd know all about it when he got back – he'd show us what a *real* ringmaster looked like."

"Back? From where?" Ana asked.

"I don't know," Nanette said miserably. "He's leaving from the airship station in London. That's all I know. He were boasting about something or other, the size of the ship he's bought or something like that. And said he had to have the box before he left."

"Bracklebrick Farm," Alice said, the memory coming back to her in a rush. Her eyes opened wide. "That's it. That's the name I saw on the cart!"

Nanette looked up at her, her eyes clouded with pain. "That's it, love," she said. "The boy'll be there."

Alice turned to Ana. "It can't be far, can it?"

"I hope not," she said, getting to her feet. Alice followed suit, clicking her tongue for Wares's attention. They turned to leave and from behind them came Nanette's voice.

"I'm sorry," she said, her eyes drifting closed into sleep once more. "Please. Tell Bastjan I'm sorry."

Alice turned to her and gave one short nod, and then they were gone.

Alice and Ana, with Wares in tow, hurried across the campground in search of Carmen. They found her by the animal enclosures, talking to a young handler.

"Left me 'ere, they 'ave," the young man was complaining. "I've never taken care of all the animals before, not on me own!"

"And you don't know where they've gone?" Carmen asked, with barely controlled impatience.

"Naw, but Hubert said they'd be back within the week, an' I was to be ready for somethin' none of us has ever handled before. He din't tell me anythin' more than that."

"We need horses," Ana told the man. "One each for my sister and me."

"And directions to Bracklebrick Farm," Alice put in.

"Where?" he said.

"The farm where the feed comes from," Alice said. "For the animals."

The handler frowned, reaching into his top pocket for a sheet of paper. "Bracklebrick Farm it says, right enough," he muttered, showing it to Ana and Carmen. Alice stretched on tiptoe to see. The paper was a receipt for straw and fodder, but there was no address.

Alice folded her arms tightly around herself and Ana slid her arm across her shoulders. "Never mind," the woman whispered. "It's a good start."

The man put the receipt back into his pocket. "The horses," Carmen reminded him, and he nodded before vanishing between the wagons.

"What about one for me?" Alice asked.

"Can you ride?" Carmen asked, her eyes questioning. She didn't wait for Alice's answer before continuing. "I did not think so. You can share a horse with me. All right?"

Alice nodded, feeling a bit foolish, and Ana gave her a warm grin.

"Now. We must get ready," Carmen said, striding towards their wagon.

Alice, who had nothing to pack but Wares, helped Ana and Carmen with their saddlebags. Blankets and sparc clothes, hairbrushes, medicine and water skins were all deftly rolled up and stored, taking up barely any room at all.

The young handler was as good as his word. When they returned to the animal enclosures, they found two horses tethered to a stake, their breaths misting around their heads. Ana and Carmen settled the saddlebags and checked the horses' tack; everything seemed to their satisfaction.

Just as Ana was about to heave herself into her saddle, the sound of approaching hoofbeats was heard – *lots* of hoofbeats. Ana slid back to the ground and the trio turned to see what was happening.

Into the camp rode a cluster of people, with Crake at their head and Jericho riding right behind. As they made for the sisters, Alice peeked out from behind a horse. Wares, at her feet, was a bundle of jangling nerves, yipping furiously. She picked him up, in case one of the horses trampled him.

"Get fresh horses," Carmen called to Crake. "We know where he is."

Crake threw himself out of his saddle before his horse had come to a stop, landing with ease. He caught the animal's reins and drew it to a halt, shushing and calming it with a gentle voice.

"Alice should tell you," Carmen said, standing back to shove her towards Crake. "If it had not been for her, we would never have worked it out."

Crake crouched in front of Alice and held out his hand. Alice ran to hug him and the man held her tightly. "Bracklebrick Farm," Alice said. "That's where the ringmaster's sent him."

"We'll find it," the strongman rumbled. "Good work, girleen."

"But that's not all," Alice said, standing back to look Crake in the face. "The ringmaster – he's got the box, Crake. And Nanette said he was going somewhere. He's got an airship, ready to fly."

Crake frowned at her. "An airship?"

"Think about it!" Alice said. "He's got the box. He's not keeping it to hand over to Bauer. He's *going* somewhere with it." She realized something else. "And the animal handler – just now, he said he was told to get ready for something big. Something big is coming back with the ringmaster – an animal the likes of which they've never handled before. Quinn is taking the box with him and I think I know where."

Crake frowned in genuine confusion. "Why would he? When the box is worth money to him here?"

"It must be worth more than money to him somewhere else," Alice said quietly. "Somewhere like Melita."

Crake's eyes widened. "Glory," he muttered.

"We have to stop him, Crake," said Alice.

"I can't make halves of meself, girl. I can only go to one place and that's to Bastjan."

Ana stepped forwards. "Carmen and I, we're ready to ride," she said. "We will go to London. The airship station is on the Isle of Dogs. We shall stop Quinn's ship, Mr Crake. Or delay it as long as we can." As she spoke, Carmen put her foot into a stirrup and hauled herself on to her horse. She gazed at the strongman, eye to eye.

Crake nodded at each sister in turn. "I'm goin' to get my boy," he said. He turned to look at Alice. "An' I hope I won't be goin' on my own."

Alice took Crake's hand and the strongman gave her a quick, sad smile.

"We will be waiting for you in London," Carmen said. "*Adios – y buena suerte.*"

She nodded at Ana, who mounted her own horse and urged it into motion all in one swift movement. Then the sisters vanished into the night.

CHAPTER
TWENTY-THREE

The *clunk* of the lock on Bastjan's prison being pulled open woke him. He jerked upright, blinking hard in the dusty air as he pushed himself into the corner of the tiny space. He looked up, but it wasn't the farmer who stood there; it was his wife. She carried a plate in one hand, covered with a cloth, and in the other a tankard of water. Beneath one arm was a bundle of cloth.

"So," she greeted him. "You're the latest one."

"What's goin' on?" Bastjan said. "When am I goin' home?"

The woman sighed. "This is Bracklebrick Farm, lad, and I'm Mrs Mythen. My husband is the farmer. You're here to work for us now, bought an' paid for, an' there'll be no goin' home. This is home, from now on."

Bastjan stared at her. "No, it ain't," he said.

The woman sighed, resigned. "Here's the only breakfast you're goin' to get, an' somethin' to wear. Goodness knows it's got to be warmer than that affair you've got on." She placed the plate on the floor and tossed the bundle towards him. It landed at Bastjan's feet, coming half undone. It was a shirt, Bastjan saw, wrapped around thick work trousers and a pair of old boots.

"Whose are these?" he asked.

"Yours, now," Mrs Mythen replied. "But I can't say whose they were, in the beginnin'. Those clothes have done several of you lads, over the years."

Bastjan looked up at her. "How many lads?" he asked, but Mrs Mythen didn't reply. Instead, she put the tankard of water beside the plate of food and stood with her arms folded.

"If you're eatin', then eat. An' if you want to milk cows and dig the land dressed like a sugarplum fairy, by all means have at it. But I'll bet you'll be beggin' me for those clothes by the end of the day."

Bastjan pulled the trousers free. They were patched, worn thin in places, and much too big. The boots were the same, but there was a pair of thick socks tucked into them, which made them as comfortable as they could be.

Mrs Mythen turned her back long enough to let him dress, and as he uncovered the plate of food, she bent to scoop up the scraps of leotard. "Might be able to make somethin' with these," she said, tucking them into a pocket. "They'll fancy up my workbox, an' no mistake." She tried to smile at the boy, but all Bastjan could do was chew the hard crust of bread she'd given him. Mrs Mythen's smile faltered and she leaned against the wall while Bastjan ate.

He took the chance to look around. The wall was stone, up to the height of Mrs Mythen. Above that, iron bars stuck out and up, fixed to a ceiling above, and the door was wooden and thick, heavy-looking, with a panel cut into it. The panel was blocked with more iron bars. There wasn't enough space at the top or the bottom of the door to wriggle out – not even Wares would have made it. And the bars were too close together to let Bastjan stick much more than his arm through.

Mrs Mythen saw him looking. "You'll not get out, lad," she said. "Not from in here, at least," she added quietly. "All of you manage it, in the end. But don't be in a rush."

Bastjan chewed and swallowed. "Why not?"

The woman sighed. "Because he takes it out on the next lad," she told him. "The sooner a boy runs away, the worse it is for the chap that comes after him. Anyway, maybe you'll end up happy. It's not so bad, this life."

Bastjan took a swig of water. "I got things to do, far away from 'ere," he said. He wiped the water from his mouth on his new-old sleeve.

"You look so like him," Mrs Mythen said unexpectedly. She reached out, as if she wanted to touch Bastjan's hair, before realizing what she was doing and snatching her fingers back. Her face crumpled and she turned away. "Maybe you all do. I'm seein' him in all the faces that pass through here. It'll be my age, I expect." She sighed. "Fifteen years he's been gone, our Joseph. Fifteen years, an' now here I am, lookin' at you. You could be his double, I do swear it."

Bastjan frowned, wondering what she was talking about, but before he had a chance to ask, a deep voice startled them both.

"What are you doin', woman? Is he fed? Dressed? There's cows here needin' milkin'!"

"Coming, Ivor," the woman called, fumbling at her belt for the key. The floor was covered with straw and the stone walls were whitewashed; Bastjan thought it could have been a stable, once. *But now it's a cell,* he thought.

Mrs Mythen let them both out, keeping one hand on Bastjan's shoulder. Her grip was loose and he could have thrown it off, but there was nowhere to run. The cell was at the back of the milking parlour, he now saw, and the farmer stood in the parlour's wide door. The early light was weak outside and gentle lowing from the cows in their byre along the wall filled the air.

Mr Mythen pointed to a stool and bucket on the floor

beside the first byre. "Get to it," he said, before ushering his wife outside.

Bastjan stared at the bucket and the stool. After a moment, he crept to the open door and peeked through it. On the far side of the yard he saw the pigsties, low brick walls separating the animals from one another. Attached to the milking parlour and running around the side of the yard, facing the farmhouse, was a large hay barn, its door standing open. He took a step outside, trying to see more.

Instantly, he heard a low, warning growl and he looked down.

The farmer's dog was there, its lip pulled back to reveal its teeth. The animal's hackles were raised and Bastjan stumbled back through the door. This dog was three times Wares's size and only a fraction as friendly.

"Good boy," he muttered. "Good fella, ain't ya?" But the dog's growl deepened and it began to creep forwards, as though it were used to herding lesser animals – and Bastjan got the distinct impression that included him. "All right," he snapped, going back into the milking parlour. "I'm not goin' anywhere. Leave off!"

Bastjan took his seat on the milking stool and the dog draped itself over the threshold of the door. As the boy tried to work out the mechanics of milking, it never took its eyes off him for a moment.

"You'd swear they'd nothin' better to look at," muttered Crake. Alice grinned at him. They'd come back to St Wycombe looking for any clues that might lead them to Bracklebrick Farm, but so far all they'd found were curious stares. Crake was so tall that Alice's head, as she sat on the horse's back, was barely higher than his own. He wore an ill-fitting suit he'd borrowed from Magnus Ólafsson and his hair threatened to spring loose at any moment. Two gigantic plaits of beard trailed across his expanse of stomach and he was leading a horse topped with a firemarked, mongrel-holding girl. They may as well have been followed by a pack of gambolling clowns.

Alice raised an eyebrow. "Goodness knows what they find so interesting," she said, straining against the stirrups and standing as tall as she could. She was sure she could see a square coming up, a water pump in the middle of it.

"I have an idea," she said, tucking Wares into the crook of one arm while she slid down from the horse's back. She pushed her hair behind her ears in a determined fashion. "You go and find somewhere out of the way," she said. "I'll be back in a minute."

Crake turned away, gently urging the horse forwards with a click of his tongue. Alice set off in the other direction, heading straight for the busy square. All around the water pump were women, chatting and laughing, holding pots and pans and buckets, and between their legs scampered children, mostly barefoot, but all of them rosy-cheeked and clean. Sitting in a circle not far from the pump was a group of older children, closer to Alice's own age. They were playing a spirited game of knucklestones, and she settled close to them without saying a word. She put Wares on the ground beside her, a piece of twine around his collar. She held its other end tightly in her fist.

After a few minutes, one of the girls glanced her way.

"Want to play?" she asked, shuffling aside to make room. Wares lolloped forwards a step or two, and the girl gave him a friendly pat on the head.

Alice grinned and settled in, quickly picking up the words of the rhyme they sang every time someone threw a playing piece in the air. Wares sat beside her, watching proceedings with interest, his pink tongue hanging out.

"Who're you, then?" asked the girl who'd invited her to sit.

"Just passing through," Alice said, keeping her eyes on the game. "Here with my dad. We're on our way to Bracklebrick Farm."

The girl's nose wrinkled as she turned away, picking up the words of the rhyme without missing a beat. Both she and Alice scrambled to pick up the playing pieces, and then the game began again.

"Where's that?" the girl asked, and Alice's heart sank.

"Somewhere around here," she answered. "Not sure where, exactly."

"Out towards Mop End," a boy beside Alice piped up. He was deftly tossing some of the bones in the air and catching them on the back of his hand as he spoke. "Go past the train station an' up the hill, an' then follow the road. 'S out there somewhere, a few miles along." He flipped his hand over and caught the bones in his palm.

Alice gave a relieved grin. "Thanks," she said.

The boy threw the bones on the ground and looked at her. "What's wrong wi' your face, eh?" he said rudely.

Alice felt herself reddening. "Nothing," she muttered. She pushed herself to her feet and began to walk away, pulling gently on Wares's lead.

"Hey!" called the girl. "Where you going?" Alice put her head down and kept walking, leaving a slight commotion in her wake. The curious eyes of the women at the pump followed her. A beat of panic began to sound inside her head – *get away from here!* She pulled her hair out from behind her ear, covering her cheek with it.

As she walked, Alice thought again about the things she'd stolen from Mrs Palmer. Coins, jewellery – and the ring. *Now's my chance. Get on the train, get to London, sell the ring. Disappear.* She shut her eyes for a moment, desperate to quieten her thoughts. *I wouldn't last a week,* she told herself, knowing it was true. Before she'd joined Mrs Palmer's gang, she'd had a life that most people could only dream of. She'd wanted for nothing, besides a friend.

She opened her eyes again and saw Crake, standing awkwardly in an alleyway. He looked around nervously, rubbing the horse's neck, still drawing disapproving stares. As soon as he saw her, Crake's face broke into a relieved smile. Alice returned it and he led the horse out of the alley to meet her.

"Past the train station," Alice told him as he fell into step beside her. "We'll find it from there."

"Good work, girleen," Crake said.

Alice shrugged. "It was nothing," she said, but as she spoke she caught the eye of a passing woman, a full water pail in one hand and a struggling child in the other. She gave Alice a look that was bright with curiosity, her gaze searching Alice's face. "Now let's get out of here, Crake, as quick as we can."

CHAPTER
TWENTY-FOUR

Bastjan ate his midday meal sitting on the kitchen step. The back of the farmhouse gave way to a small paved courtyard with a water pump at its centre. The sunlight pooled there, warming the flagstones and Bastjan's bones. The meal was simple; a hunk of dry-crusted bread, some pickle and a hard-boiled egg, but Bastjan was grateful for it.

A tiny kitten rubbed and purred its way around his ankles, and Bastjan bent forwards to scratch it gently between the ears. "I ain't got anythin' you'd like," he whispered to it. "I'd share it, otherwise."

From inside the kitchen, he heard a *whish-whish-whish* sound as Mrs Mythen called the kitten inside. She slid a platter piled high with fish scraps on to the floor and the kitten bounded away from Bastjan's fingers. The boy watched it eat for a moment, looking at the lumps of wasted fish falling out of the dish, then turned back to his own meal. He took a fierce bite out of his egg, clenched his eyes shut and leaned back against the doorframe, letting the sunlight sink into his eyelids as he chewed.

When he opened his eyes again, there was a small bowl of bread-and-butter pudding at his elbow, a fork stuck into it like a flag. Mrs Mythen was at the sink, busily scrubbing something out and making a point of ignoring him, so Bastjan quietly took up the dish and polished off the rich pudding.

Once he was finished, he slid the fork into his sleeve.

"Bring over your dirty crockery, an' get a drink from the pump," Mrs Mythen told him, over her shoulder. "Then back to work."

Bastjan pushed himself up off the step and did as she asked. Mrs Mythen glanced down at the dish and her scrubbing hand paused for a moment. Then she continued, making no mention of the missing fork.

Just as he was about to walk away, Mrs Mythen turned. "Mr Quinn told us your name was Thing, lad. Just Thing?"

Bastjan shrugged. "Thing'll do. Quinn ain't never used no other name fer me."

The woman's eyes glistened as she blinked at him. "I'd love to call you Joseph, like my boy. Maybe I will, in time."

Bastjan looked away. "I'll get on."

Mrs Mythen nodded, turning back to her work, and

Bastjan went back outside. He took a long drink at the pump, jumping at the sound of Mr Mythen's voice as he came striding into the courtyard.

"Into the barn, boy, an' finish the job that's there," he boomed. "A cart with a broken axle. It's to be done by the time I've had my dinner or there'll be trouble."

Bastjan dried his face on his sleeve, taking care not to dislodge his hidden weapon, and met the farmer's eye as he walked away. He hadn't gone three steps before he felt a stinging slap on the back of his head, which sent him sprawling.

"That was for yer insolence," Mythen growled. "You don't need to speak it for me to hear it. I know what's in your head, you louse."

Bastjan rubbed his head and set his teeth as he clambered to his feet. He hurried down the laneway that led from the courtyard into the main farmyard and stared across at the open barn door. The cart was just visible inside it, propped up on a wooden block.

He looked to his right. The farmyard gate was there, closed and locked, and Mr Mythen's dog sat in front of it with its paws crossed, gazing steadily at Bastjan as the boy made his slow way across the cobbles.

Bastjan stepped into the barn. The hammer leaning against the cart was heavy enough that he needed two hands to pick it up and all his strength to swing it. He got a feel for its weight and then he readied himself.

'Ow's this fer insolence, then? he thought, bringing the hammer down on the axle with a grunt, again and again, imagining he was smashing down the farmyard gate with every blow – and then he blinked out of his thoughts. The wooden axle had split, the crack stretching right across its diameter.

Bastjan dropped the hammer and then, next thing he knew, a wave of freezing water drenched him from head to toe, sticking his clothes to his body and making him cough. He turned in shock to see the farmer standing behind him. Mythen threw an empty bucket into the straw and grabbed Bastjan by the arm.

"You can take a little break," the farmer said, dragging Bastjan towards the milking parlour and the cell that lay at the back of it. "Sit in yer wet clothes an' have a think about the money an' time you've just cost me, an' when yer ready to apologize, you can come out." He threw the boy into the cell and stood over him. "Oh, an' here's hopin' you don't get hungry, or thirsty, or need to use the *lavatory*," he sneered, "because there won't be none o' that until I hear those words from you. *I'm terrible sorry, Mr Mythen, sir.*"

Bastjan stared at the man, shivering, and said nothing for a long moment. Then, as Mythen turned to walk away, Bastjan fumbled in his sleeve for the hidden fork. It fell into his quaking hand and, with a yell, he launched himself at the farmer's back.

Mythen spun on his heel and caught Bastjan's wrist, squeezing it tightly enough to make the boy wail in pain and release the fork. It tumbled to the straw-covered floor and Mythen kicked it away with one boot. "I'll break that backbone o' yours. Just you wait an' see." The farmer stared into Bastjan's eyes until the boy was forced to look away and then he flung him to the ground.

Mythen slammed the cell door shut and locked it. Then he took one last look at the cold, despairing child in the straw and walked away.

Alice and Crake led the horse over a bridge that spanned a river wider than any Alice had ever seen.

"This must run all the way to London," Crake said.

"D'you think Ana and Carmen have made it?" Alice asked.

The strongman's face clouded over. "Let's hope so, girleen," he said. "If that airship leaves before we get there, I don't want to be the one that has to tell Bastjan."

"It means a lot to him, doesn't it?" Alice said. "Doing what his mother couldn't. Trying to put her bracelet back where it belongs."

Crake looked down at her and his large hand rested on her shoulder. "Fixin' the mistakes of the past shouldn't drown out your present, lass," he said gently. "But sometimes it feels like there's no way forward unless you step back a bit first."

Just as they reached a marker stone with the words 'Mop End' carved into it, the sky darkened. Alice made a cloak out of her coat, trying to stay out of the worst of the rain that began to fall, while Crake's greased hair ran with droplets. The horse trudged on, its hooves sticking in the mud of the path, and Wares took refuge in a saddlebag.

They passed through a tiny village, its streets empty, and on its far side, a signpost greeted them, each marker carved to look like a pointing finger. "Missenden-by-Water," Alice read. "Five miles. And there's another – Holmer's Isle, four miles."

"Here we are," Crake said, from the far side of the post. "Bracklebrick. Seven miles." They turned to look at the road the sign was pointing towards. It was small and winding, soon vanishing around a bend. They set off, following the track as it grew narrower.

Shortly after the rain stopped, Wares poked his head out of the saddlebag and started to growl. Alice glanced at the road ahead. "There's somebody coming," she said.

They pulled the horse on to the grass verge, leaving the road as clear as they could, and within moments the newcomer was near enough to see properly. As he drew up alongside them, Alice could see his curious expression as he tipped his hat. He was driving a cart and Alice fought not to grimace at the stench – it seemed to be filled, mostly, with a mixture of dung and straw.

"Hallo there," the farmer said.

"We're lookin' for Bracklebrick Farm," Crake said. "Be obliged if you could direct us."

The farmer blinked, as though surprised, and sat back. "Right y'are," he said. "Keep on about a mile this way. When yer get to the bit of the road with the tree in the middle take the track to the left. It's bumpy, but it'll see you to Bracklebrick in about another mile. You should be there afore suppertime, all goin' in yer favour."

Crake nodded his thanks, clicking the horse forwards, and a moment later there was nothing left of the meeting but a set of trackmarks and hoofprints oozing gently in the mud.

A little way down the road, beside a tumbledown gate, the farmer pulled his cart to a halt once more. He got to his feet, turning backwards to peer over his dung heap in the direction Alice and Crake had gone. Satisfied that there was no sign of them, he settled himself back on to his seat and spoke, seemingly to the contents of his cart.

"Get yerself over that gate and down to Mythen's," the farmer muttered. "Tell 'im Josiah said there's circus folk on his tail. Right? Circus folk. Remember that."

"Yes, Da," came a tiny-voiced reply. A flap of canvas

tucked in beside the dung heap, small enough not to be noticed, was nudged to one side and a small child clambered out – a little girl of perhaps five, her hair in plaits, her dress holed and dirty and her cardigan mostly made up of patches. She wore boots that looked like they'd served at least three owners before her and she carried a ragdoll older than she was.

"Good girl," he told her, blowing her a kiss as she climbed over the gate. "There'll be posset for you tonight for this, pet."

The girl nodded, sent back the blown kiss and then disappeared into the corn.

CHAPTER
TWENTY-FIVE

"This must be the place," Alice observed as the horse clip-clopped to a halt. A large gate stood open between two stone gateposts, the track beyond it leading to a farmyard. On one side of the wide yard lay a low-roofed farmhouse, smoke trickling from its chimney.

"I reckon so," Crake said. "Let's see what sort of a welcome we get, eh? I wouldn't put money on it bein' good."

"Crake, listen," Alice said, speaking quickly. "Maybe you should go alone and distract the farmer. I'll sneak in to look for Bastjan and get him out if I can."

Crake blinked, a concerned crease appearing in his forehead. "But—"

"I'll take care, all right? Don't worry about me." Wares sat on her foot and Alice gazed down at him fondly. "Plus,

I'm not alone." As she spoke, from inside the gates, a bark was heard. Then another, louder. Wares sat up, his body tensed, and began to growl. "See? He's ready for anything."

"Stay downwind of that beast inside the gate," Crake muttered. "A farmyard dog won't think twice about takin' lumps out of either of you."

"We'll be *fine*," Alice said. "Go and keep the farmer busy as long as you can and I'll search for Bastjan." She pointed down the road at a huge, spreading oak tree. "We'll wait for one another there, beneath that giant. Agreed?"

"Are you sure?" Crake said.

"It was my idea, wasn't it?" Alice gave him a grin. "Trust me."

"I do, girleen." Crake patted her gently on the cheek and straightened himself up. Then he led the horse on, right through the farmyard gate. Alice hid in the hedgerow, peering out as much as she could. Wares was clutched to her chest. The little dog began to whine and she stroked his head.

"Shh, boy," Alice whispered, trying not to feel her courage ebbing away with every step Crake took into the unknown. She heard the loud barking of the farmer's dog. Then a woman emerged from the farmhouse, wiping her hands on a towel. She scolded the dog and sent it slinking into the house while Crake was led somewhere out of view. Alice was too far away to hear what they were saying, but the sound of their voices travelled just enough for her to know when they'd all gone inside.

"Come on, Wares," she said, putting the small dog on the ground. He trotted at her heels as Alice crept along, bent almost double. She kept tight to the garden wall, hoping it would offer her some cover, and when she got to the gate she risked a peek at the house. Through a window she could see a red-faced man talking animatedly and she looked away, her gut tightening.

She dashed past the gate, hoping nobody had spotted her, pressing her back to the garden wall. To her left was an empty laneway leading to a field; facing Alice were the pigsties. She hurried past them, whispering Bastjan's name as loudly as she dared, but there was no answer. Wares was stopping to sniff or lift his leg against everything he saw and she clicked her fingers at him impatiently. He gave up an investigation of an interesting clump of dandelions and trotted towards her.

Crouched behind the low wall of the last pigsty, Alice assessed the rest of the farm buildings. Directly across from her was what looked like a milking parlour. From it, she could smell the distinct odour of cows. To her left, facing the house, stood a barn. In its doorway was a broken cart.

A wandering chicken popped its bobbing head out of the milking parlour, making Alice start. The chicken picked its way across the farmyard, and with one final look left and right, Alice scuttled straight for the door the chicken had come through, holding her breath until she was safely inside.

She inhaled, relieved, and immediately coughed as the smell settled in the back of her throat. She blinked as her eyes got used to the dim light. The byres were ranged along the right-hand wall, each of them empty but for the tossed-up, dirty straw on the floor. Facing them were some sorry-looking sheep pens, also empty.

At the back, along the wall, were several small, box-like enclosures. Each had a whitewashed wall topped with metal bars and heavy wooden doors with an opening, barred and rectangular, set into them at an adult's head height. Something about them made Alice's skin creep.

She hurried towards the back of the huge shed, Wares bounding ahead of her through the straw. "Bastjan!" she whispered. Then, "*Bastjan!*" she called, flinching at the loudness of her voice. "It's Alice. Bastjan, are you here?"

Alice heard a shuffling sound from the last enclosure and saw thin, grubby fingers grasping the bars of the rectangular gap in the door. "Alice?" came a voice, followed by a deep, chest-rattling cough.

Blinking away tears of relief, Alice ran to the tiny cell. She stretched on tiptoe, trying to see in through the opening. She wasn't quite tall enough, but she was able to put her hand through the bars. Her fingers met Bastjan's, who held them as tightly as he could.

"You're cold," she whispered, wiping her cheek with her free hand. "Are you all right?"

"It *stinks* 'ere," came the reply. His breaths sounded thick. "I hate it. I hate the lot of it. Can you get me out?"

Alice looked at the padlock. "I'll be back in a minute," she whispered.

She released Bastjan's fingers and looked around, her gaze flicking from object to object. She ran her fingers up a nearby wooden beam, hoping to find a handy nail protruding from it, something she could use to pick the lock, but there was nothing.

Wares gave a low growl. The tiny dog was tensed, his teeth bared, and Alice dropped silently to the straw-strewn floor.

The dog trotted to her side just as someone appeared at the open shed door. A girl, younger than her, wearing a patched cardigan and too-big boots, her hair in two untidy plaits. She was chewing on the end of one of them and as Alice watched she pulled it from her mouth to shout.

"*Bil*-berry!" the girl called. "Bilberry, where are you? Silly cat!"

"Martha!" came another voice, this one more distant. "Martha McCloskey! Where are you, girl?"

"I'm lookin' for the kitten, Mrs Mythen!" the girl called back, turning to face the house.

A few breaths later, a woman joined the girl at the open parlour door. Alice stayed frozen to the spot, hoping with all she had that neither of them would look in and notice her.

"Martha, child, Mr Mythen wants to know if there was anyone else with that man when you met him on the road."

Martha paused, chewing thoughtfully on her plait. Finally, she spat it free. "Don't think so, Mrs M. I din't see him, 'cos I was underneath the tarp. But I din't hear anyone else talkin', just my da and that man."

The farmer on the road! Alice held her breath. *This little girl must've been hidden in his cart.* She dug her fingers into the mucky ground, wishing she could melt into it, and tried to listen.

"It's just, he's askin' for work," the farmer's wife continued. "Casual labour, like. But your dad was sure he was from the circus. Mr Mythen's wonderin' if he brought anyone else with him."

"That's what my da said, Mrs M," the girl replied, nodding. "I was to tell Mr Mythen my da said there were circus folk on 'is tail. An' he promised me posset." The child looked up at Mrs Mythen hopefully. "Do you have any posset, Mrs M?"

"Posset?" The woman looked wearily at the child. "No, pet. There's some bread-and-butter pud in the usual spot in the larder, though. Off you pop."

The girl darted off, whooping with joy, and the woman stood forlornly in the door for a moment or two, twisting her apron in her hands. For a second Alice was sure she was going to come walking into the milking parlour.

But then a man's voice rang out across the farmyard and the woman took a step back, turning her head towards the house. "Ivor?" she called. The woman vanished from the doorway and, quick as a blink, Alice scrambled up from the ground and threw herself into the shadows beside Bastjan's cell. Wares followed, snuffling contentedly through the murk.

"Thank you kindly, sir, for yer time," said a voice Alice knew well. *Crake*. Beside her, she heard the scuffle of Bastjan getting to his feet and the groan of effort as he struggled to pull himself up to the window in the door. He coughed wetly.

"Bastjan!" she whispered. "Don't say anything!" From the cell, she heard a sniff, like one someone would make if they were crying but didn't want anyone to know.

"I can see why ol' Josiah mistook you fer a circus worker," the farmer said, chuckling. "Yer a beast of a man, an' no mistake. But I'm not lookin' for any help. I've just taken on a new young lad, y'see." He paused and Alice's jaw clenched. "He's more'n enough for now."

"Well, I'm grateful fer the bit of grub, anyway," Crake said. "I s'pose I'd be pushin' my luck if I asked for a corner of yer barn to put me head down in tonight?"

"You would," the farmer replied, his tone turning stony.

Crake cleared his throat. "Right. I'll be off now, so," he said loudly.

"See to it," the farmer replied. "There's a guard dog on duty, I'll remind you. An' thieves aren't met well around 'ere."

Then all Alice could hear was the sound of hooves on the farmyard cobbles, which gradually disappeared. She grabbed Wares around the belly. Footsteps were approaching the milking-parlour door. As quickly as she could, she pulled the dog deeper into the shadows beside Bastjan's cell and hoped the darkness would hide them.

CHAPTER
TWENTY-SIX

"Are you in there, runt?" the farmer said as he stood before Bastjan's door, a mocking leer in his voice. "Dried out yet, have yer?" Alice cuddled Wares close, hoping the trembling in her body would let him know: *don't make a sound.*

"When am I gettin' out of 'ere?" Bastjan replied.

"I think a night in yer wet clothes, without supper, is just what the doctor ordered. Eh?" Bastjan sneezed and the farmer laughed.

He walked away, jangling keys in his hand as he went, and pulled the milking-parlour door closed behind him. There was the sound of a bar being drawn across the door, locking it shut. In the sudden darkness, Wares began to whine.

"Hush, boy," Alice said, blinking in the gloom. "It's all right."

"Alice?" Bastjan whispered.

"I'm here," she told him. "Bastjan, is there anything in your cell that's sharp or made of metal? Like a nail?"

She heard rustling and muttering, and after a minute, Bastjan spoke again. "Come to the door," he said.

Alice did as he asked and this time, when she reached her hand up, she felt something smoother and colder than Bastjan's fingers being pushed into it. In what light there was, she could see the gleaming shape of a dinner fork. She grinned widely enough to make her cheeks ache.

"'Ow's that?" said Bastjan.

"It's perfect," Alice said, and set to work. She put Wares on the floor and stuck the fork beneath her boot, slowly bending one of the tines until it was angled enough for her to slip it into the padlock. Then she forced the tine in and out of the lock, until finally it came undone in her hands.

As Alice pulled open the door, Bastjan fell into her arms and they shared a tight, quick hug. His clothes were still damp enough to soak into Alice's and she grimaced at the touch of them. He shivered and Alice could hear a whistle in his breathing.

"We've got to get you warm," Alice said, relaxing her grip on the boy. "Any idea how to get out of this place?"

Bastjan coughed. "Can't try to force the door, as that'd jus' leave us back in the farmyard," he said. "But we could go up." He looked at the ceiling and Alice followed his gaze. The exposed beams seemed perilously high, but she could see they gave access to the tiny windows set into the roof. They were covered in such a thick layer of grime and moss that they barely let in any light. Bastjan met her eye.

"I don't think I can do that," she said, in a quiet voice.

"Course you can," Bastjan said, wiping his nose. "I'll show ya. Gimme a leg-up?"

Alice cupped her hands. Bastjan stepped into them and she hauled him up with all her strength. "*Whoop*-ah," he said, under his breath, as he leaped to the bars at the top of the wall. From there, he jumped easily to the nearest roof beam and in a blink he was astride it. Lightly as a cat, he got to his feet and walked along the beam with his arms held out, balancing on the tips of his toes. Alice watched him, her mouth agape.

From overhead, there was a cracking noise and the fluttering of a disturbed bird; a clump of moss fell from on high. She turned her head, shielding her eyes from tumbling dust and grit, and when she looked back up, the windowpane nearest Bastjan was creaking as it pivoted on a central hinge. Cautiously, he stuck his head out through it.

"We can get up on the roof, easy," Bastjan said, ducking his head back into the milking parlour. "An' then make it to the road that way."

Alice swallowed back her fear as she watched Bastjan prop open the window with an old piece of slate. Through the gap came the faint sound of lowing cattle and when he made his way back to the ground he gave Alice a worried look. "Mythen's bringin' the cows in. We got to hurry."

She nodded, tucking Wares into the neck of her buttoned-up coat. Bastjan got down on one knee to give her a boost and the next thing she knew, she was clinging for dear life to the bars of Bastjan's former cell, trying not to squash Wares flat. Bastjan climbed up the wall beside her, finding handholds and footholds in the crumbling whitewash. "Right," he said. "Ready to jump?"

Without waiting for an answer, he turned and braced himself against the top of the wall, leaping for the beam with effortless grace. A moment later he was sitting astride it once again, his arm outstretched to Alice and Wares, but Alice was rigid, her grip on the bars white-knuckled. She looked at the distance between the beam and the wall, the drop to the floor if she missed, the climb that lay ahead... Her vision swam and a realization sank inside her like a stone.

"I ... I can't, Bastjan," Alice said. She looked down; the straw-covered floor seemed to undulate beneath her.

"It's easy as pie, Alice," Bastjan said. "I'll catch yer. I promise."

Alice freed one hand and pulled Wares gently out of her coat. She gave him a kiss between the ears as Bastjan reached for him. Then, her heart thudding, she tossed him into

Bastjan's waiting hands.

"Good boy, eh?" Bastjan said, scratching the small dog's head as he placed him carefully on the beam. He reached back for Alice, but she didn't come.

"You need to go," Alice said. "Go and find Crake, Bastjan! He'll be waiting beneath the oak tree down the road. Then come back and get me."

"What?" Bastjan stared at her. "Alice, I ain't leavin' you 'ere! It's ... it's a *pit*!"

Alice's eyes filled with tears and she angrily rubbed them away. "I can't make that jump! Every second you wait for me is a second closer to the farmer finding us," she said. "*Please!* Just go. I'll be waiting."

"Alice, I—"

"Bastjan, you need to go. Listen!" The cows' mooing was close now, and it was even possible to hear the farmer's voice calling to them as they drew near the shed. "You won't make it if you wait any longer. *Go!*"

Bastjan stared at Alice for a long moment, but he didn't say anything else. A heartbeat later he and Wares were gone, through the window and away. Alice closed her eyes, hoping Bastjan would make it and wondering how long she'd be waiting for them to come back for her.

And as the minutes ticked past, she tried to still the tiny voice inside that asked whether they'd come back for her at all.

"Come on, fella," Bastjan muttered, propping Wares on one shoulder as he assessed the journey to the top of the roof. The tiles were old and mossy, and several were loose. He turned to look at the wall which ran around the farm; the parlour had been built snugly against it, the apex of its roof almost level with the top of the wall. And beyond that, he knew Crake was waiting. He leaned his forehead against the window frame for a moment, fighting against the closing-over feeling in his chest. *Get on with it!*

Bastjan gripped the frame and pulled himself the rest of the way out. Then he reached for his first handhold and began to climb. At first the going was good, but when he put his hand on a tile that moved beneath his weight, only the strong grip of his feet kept him from sliding all the way to the mucky cobbles far below. He felt his heart start to gallop and his breaths grow sticky. "*Whoop*," he croaked. "*Whoop*." He coughed, trying to clear his lungs, his head beginning to swim.

Somewhere below him, a dog began to bark – loud and gruff, the sound of a larger animal than Wares. The smaller dog was instantly on the alert, growling as he scrambled across Bastjan's shoulders. He barked in response, his own voice sounding like a *yip* in comparison to the farmyard dog.

"Stop, Wares!" Bastjan pleaded, freeing one hand to

grab the small dog by the collar. "You'll 'ave us both off!" The boy tried to look, desperate to know where the farmer's dog was but he had to close his eyes again and cling to the roof, dizziness threatening to toss him to the ground.

Wares scampered off Bastjan's shoulders and scrambled for the top of the roof, his paws clattering over the tiles. Within minutes he was safely perched on the apex, barking furiously at the larger animal below, and Bastjan decided to save his breath for the climb. He hauled himself up the slope and threw one leg over the point of the roof, getting his balance. Far below him he could see the farmer's dog, in a lather of rage, but there was no sign of Mythen himself – not yet.

Bastjan got to his feet. The tiles beneath his shoes were curved and slick, but he stood tall, his back straight and his arms out to either side. *It's thicker'n the wire*, he told himself. He swallowed hard and began to walk, one foot in front of the other, feeling for balance with his toes before he placed his heel down. His chest felt squeezed, every breath like a pinch in his neck, but he forced himself to keep going.

With every step, the boundary wall grew closer and closer, until finally he'd reached it. Beyond – or so Bastjan hoped – lay the road and Crake. He placed Wares back on his shoulder and prepared himself for the final climb.

"You!" came a roar from down below. Bastjan kept one

hand on the wall, steadying himself, as he stared down. The farmer stood beneath him, rage twisting his face. Wares scrambled off Bastjan's shoulder, leaping for the top of the wall, and Bastjan felt his fingers curling into the gaps between the bricks. He tried to force his legs to push him upwards, over and away, but there was no power left in them. All he could hear was Wares, barking just above his head, as his vision blackened at the edges. He closed his eyes, waiting to fall.

CHAPTER
TWENTY-SEVEN

"Not so fast, lad," came a voice, and Bastjan looked up. Crake's shaggy head appeared over the boundary wall. Bastjan didn't have enough breath to speak, but he reached for Crake's arms as the man stretched to catch him. "I've got ya." Crake hauled the quivering boy over the wall and on to a patch of grass beside the road. Bastjan felt Wares's warm tongue licking his grubby cheeks, and tried to give the dog a pat.

"Alice," Bastjan gasped, forcing air into his chest. "*Whoop*. We gotta go back an' get 'er."

"Don't you worry," Crake muttered, picking Bastjan up and slinging him over the horse, Wares beside him. The horse was snorting and rolling her eyes, disturbed by the barking and shouting from the farmyard. Crake leaped into the saddle behind Bastjan and urged the horse into a canter, and then a gallop.

"No!" Bastjan said as they set off down the road – away from the farm. "Crake, we can't leave 'er!"

"I amn't leavin' that child anywhere," Crake said, bringing the horse into a tight turn as they reached the oak tree. "Now," he whispered, once they were facing the farm once more. "Come on, girl. Let's fly."

They galloped up the road and between the gateposts. Bastjan flattened himself against the horse's neck, keeping one arm round Wares's trembling body. At a wordless command from Crake, the horse sailed over the locked gate and landed heavily, skidding a little on the farmyard cobbles. She reared slightly at a new obstacle – a herd of cows, their udders heavy and ready for milking.

"Hyah!" Crake said, urging the horse forwards. She picked her way between the cattle, turning her head nervously from side to side. The cows moved away, surging to the far side of the farmyard, their desperate mooing intensifying.

"Come on, lad," Crake said, sliding off the horse's back. He reached up to help Bastjan and Wares down, and then all three were running towards the milking parlour. Bastjan's breaths began to twist again as he saw the door standing open, the heavy wooden bar which kept it locked thrown carelessly on the ground. He stared into the gloom, his heart thudding.

"Alice!" he shouted. "*Alice!*"

"So that's 'er name, is it," came a voice. A lantern flared into life and Mythen stepped forward, holding it high. "She wouldn't tell me what she were called, despite my askin' nicely."

Mythen's other hand came into view. He was holding Alice by the arm, and her face was pinched and pale. She looked at Bastjan and Crake with tear-filled eyes.

"Let these children go," Crake rumbled, his huge hands open as he took a step towards the farmer. "An' we'll hear no more about this."

"No more about it?" Mythen spat. He dragged Alice through the milking parlour door and out into the yard. "You're all a bunch of thievin' *louts*! I'll 'ave the lot of you strung up for this, you mark my words. Elspeth!" he shouted. "Bring my rifle!"

Crake's open hands turned into fists. Alice looked at Bastjan, both of them fearful.

From the farmhouse, a voice was heard. "Ivor!" it called. "Ivor Mythen, that is *enough*!" The door of the farmhouse opened, spilling light across the cobbles of the farmyard.

Farmer Mythen faltered. Mrs Mythen, holding a long-barrelled gun and with some sort of bundle beneath her other arm, strode down the garden path and through the gate, not stopping until she stood in front of her husband. She waved the gun menacingly at the air in front of his chest and he took a step back.

"Let that girl go," the woman said. "Let 'er *go*, Ivor."

Mythen threw Alice away from him and she almost landed in the gutter. Bastjan hurried to help her up.

"Elspeth, what on earth—" the farmer sputtered, as Alice and Bastjan carefully made their way towards Crake.

"Get into that house, you," Mrs Mythen growled at her husband, jabbing at the air with the gun. "An' leave these people to their business."

"But they're stealin'!" the farmer said, almost petulantly.

"An' what do you think you did, buyin' that child?" his wife retorted. "You've been takin' children from their rightful places long enough. Every child you've brought here has had people who loved 'em, just like I loved our lad!" Mrs Mythen's words stumbled and she let out a sob. "This is just the first time that someone has come lookin' for one of 'em. And let me tell you one more thing, Ivor."

She took a step closer, the gun steady, and Farmer Mythen took a step back. "Just because our Joe ran away – ran away from *you* – doesn't mean you can take other people's sons away from them. You stole that boy from his family, an' now they're takin' him back."

The farmer stood, stunned, as his wife turned to Crake and the children. She lowered the weapon and took the bundle from beneath her arm, pressing it against Bastjan's chest. He looked down as he took the bundle into his arms;

it was a cloth bag, its top flap open to reveal dry clothes. They smelled clean.

"Be off with the lot of you," Mrs Mythen said. Her eyes glittered with tears. "Quickly, so the cows don't get out. Don't forget that sorry-lookin' horse, an' I hope I never see hide nor hair of any of you again."

"Thank you," Bastjan said, nodding at Mrs Mythen, and she nodded back.

"Goodbye, our Joe," she whispered. "An' good luck."

Under cover of darkness, Crake, Alice, Wares and Bastjan made their way back to the circus camp. They needed a fresh horse and somewhere to get Bastjan warm and dry. It was near midnight by the time they rode into the campground; Jericho, Lady Z, and Gustav and Lily were dotted around the campfire, passing a bottle around along with their stories of the circus in its heyday. They were all glad to see Bastjan's safe return, but when they learned the boy wasn't staying, a despondent mood settled over the site once more. Even Lady Z's tattoos seemed subdued. One by one they peeled off to their wagons, leaving Crake and the children alone.

A pot was found, filled with water and heated over the campfire, and Alice, Crake and Bastjan washed until the stink of the farmyard was almost gone. Bastjan pulled the clean, dry clothes from the bag Mrs Mythen had given him and found, tucked at the bottom, a paper-wrapped parcel of food and a small amount of money in a purse.

"Soon as we can get a fresh horse, we should get movin'," he said, as they shared out the food. "We got to get to London, quick as we can. I ain't lettin' Quinn leave with my mum's box, no matter what." The fire licked the night air silently for a moment or two as a thoughtful hush fell over the group.

Then Alice spoke, her voice quiet. "I know the quickest way to get to London," she said. "The train."

Crake brightened. "There's an idea! St Wycombe station ain't too far. An' I'm sure we'll find a line that goes to the city."

"We will," said Alice, who already knew exactly which train, and from what platform. *Chances are, the place will be bristling with Tunnellers. And when we get to London, there'll be no chance of avoiding them – or Mrs P.* She shuddered. Mrs Palmer, Alice knew, would be in the city. *Everythin' washes up in London eventually,* she'd often said, and Alice was sure that's where the search for her would be focused. *But London's a big place,* Alice told herself, pushing away her fears.

Crake gave her a thoughtful look. "How d'you know so much about the trains, girleen?"

Alice sighed, staring at the fire. "I told you already

about Mrs Palmer," she said, and the others sat in silence, waiting for her to be ready to continue. "Well, she runs a gang. I was part of it, for a while, after I—" Alice paused, swallowing hard. "After I left my grandfather's house. I fell in with Mrs P and the kids she collects. They call themselves the Tunnellers."

"The Tunnellers?" Bastjan repeated.

"They live in the train tunnels. On the platforms, they beg and pickpocket and the like, and they ride the trains, hoping to pick up whatever they can."

"Why'd you leave your grandfather's house?" Bastjan asked, and Crake gave a rumble from his spot beside the fire.

"Sounds a bit like none of our business, lad," the man said. "All I'm concerned with is whether you'll be safe, girleen, if we go by train." He sat forwards, his face lit up by the flames. "You said before that this Mrs P was after you. Will they be lookin' for you too, these Tunnellers?"

Alice shrugged. "Probably," she said. "But we've got no choice really." She paused, thinking. "We don't know how long we've got – Quinn might leave any minute. So the first train's our best bet." She drew her knees up and looked at the others, barely suppressing a yawn. "We'll just have to hope Ana and Carmen can delay him long enough for us to make it." Her yawn finally broke through. As frightening as it was to think of going near the trains again, Alice was glad they'd have time for a few hours' rest.

Crake got to his feet. "Right. I'm goin' to talk to ol' Jericho, try to beat him at one last game o' cards. You pair huddle up an' get some sleep. Leave me the best bunk, won't ye?" He nodded towards Ana and Carmen's wagon as he spoke. They were going to borrow it, knowing the sisters wouldn't mind, for the rest of this short night.

"We'll be goin' before sunup," Bastjan warned as Crake lumbered away. "Not too much whiskey, right?"

Crake saluted with a smile and disappeared into the shadows as the children left the fireside for the cool darkness of the sisters' wagon. They curled up on the creaky bunk, Wares tucked at their feet, and Bastjan was asleep as soon as his eyes closed.

CHAPTER TWENTY-EIGHT

By dawn, they were almost ready to leave. Only Jericho woke to see them off. Crake prepared a quick breakfast by the campfire and they ate hungrily, Wares happily whuffling down whatever scraps he was thrown.

"Man, oh man," Jericho muttered, holding his hands to the flames. "I'm feelin' like I ain't fit for nothin' but Ducrow's Acre this mornin'."

Crake chuckled, and Alice asked, "What's that?"

Bastjan swallowed before answering. "Circus graveyard," he told her. "Where ringmasters an' star performers go." He spooned in another mouthful of beans. "My mum's there," he continued indistinctly. "I ain't never seen it, but I will, one day."

"You will, son," Jericho said. "Bet on it. Now." The acrobat got to his feet, stretching his muscles. "I got my wagon ready. Y'all comin'?"

Bastjan and Alice made ready to leave. Alice clucked her tongue at Wares and he came to her heel. As she straightened up, she tucked her hair behind her ear and Bastjan frowned. Something about her face wasn't right.

"Yer firemark," he said, his eyes wide.

Alice blushed. "I borrowed some make-up from Carmen and Ana to cover it," she said. "The less notice we draw, the better, I thought."

"Come on, you pair!" Crake called. They turned to see him already aboard Jericho's wagon, leaning out the half-door, and they hurried to catch up. Wares raced ahead, scrambling gleefully up the wooden steps.

As they pulled out of camp, Alice's ears pricked up. A voice was singing – and soon that voice was joined by others. Jericho pulled to a halt, and Bastjan, Crake and Alice climbed down to look back at the campground. In the pink morning light, all the wagon doors were open, with people standing in each one.

Alice looked up at Crake. Thick tears spilled down the man's cheeks as he raised a hand to his family, and every hand waved back.

"What are they singing?" Alice asked Bastjan as they climbed back into the wagon.

Bastjan wiped his own cheeks. "*The Lowerin'*," he replied. "We sing it when the tent is put down for the last time, or when one of us ... when one of us dies. It's a farewell."

"You'll see them again," Alice said, slipping an arm round his narrow shoulders. "It's not goodbye. Not forever." Bastjan nodded, but he turned to look through the wagon's back window. His gaze stayed on the camp, and the blackened remnants of his own wagon, until it vanished behind a turn in the road.

They sat in silence for the rest of the journey. Before too long, they reached the outskirts of St Wycombe and Jericho pulled his wagon to a stop by the side of the road. At the end stood an impressive red-brick building – the station.

"Got to leave you here," the acrobat said. "I wish you luck. An' a quick journey home again." He reached out for Crake's hand and the two men hugged briefly. Bastjan and Alice climbed down, waving to Jericho as he turned his wagon back towards the camp.

They set off, watching the red-brick building grow larger with every step. It had arches all along its front façade, topped with a statue of a figure in a helmet, bearing a shield. People streamed in and out despite the early hour.

"If you see me running," Alice said suddenly, "don't follow me."

"What?" Bastjan turned to her. "Why not?"

"Because I don't want anyone to know you're with me.

None of the Tunnellers, I mean."

Crake put a hand on each child's shoulder as they walked beneath an archway into the station. "We're not splittin' up now, girleen. Wherever you go, we're with you."

Inside, the station was a whirl of activity. It reminded Bastjan of opening night in a new place, with the same sense of busy urgency. People bustled to and fro, some with rolled-up newspapers or furled umbrellas beneath their arms; ladies sat on long benches surrounded by bags and children. Whistles and clouds of steam from the chuffing, patient engines, resting at their platforms like sleeping beasts, filled the air. Gaudy advertisements, their words meaningless to Bastjan, assaulted the eye and the scent of food was everywhere.

Alice and Bastjan hid beside a newspaper stand as Crake bought their tickets, using the money Mrs Mythen had put in Bastjan's bag. That same bag was now over Alice's shoulder, and beneath the flap, barely visible, were Wares's bright eyes and curious nose.

"Hey. Look," Bastjan whispered. He nudged Alice in the ribs and she pulled her gaze away from Crake. "Don't he look familiar?" Bastjan pointed at a newspaper, displayed on the stand. On its front page was a face, strangely pale, with sideways-slicked hair.

"*Bauer*," Alice breathed, scanning the newspaper article. "Eccentric millionaire ... business interests in Antarctica...

Someone from a rival firm had an accident, it says. They worked with something called the Order of the White Flower... Frédéric Blancheflour? He died, it seems. Bauer's researching the ice cap, but—"

The paper was whipped up so suddenly that Alice took a step back.

"This ain't a library," the newspaper vendor growled at them, before handing the paper over to a customer.

As the customer walked away, he flipped his paper fully open – and something else caught Bastjan and Alice's eyes. Another familiar face, this one with a birthmark on her cheek.

"Was that *you*?" Bastjan whispered. He turned to Alice. Her mouth was hanging open in shock.

She glanced at him and snapped her mouth shut. "Forget about it," she muttered.

"Nanette said somethin' about your grandad," Bastjan said, trying to recall. "He's lookin' for you, or somethin'."

"He's got a reward out for me," Alice said, more sharply than she intended. "I suppose you'll be handing me in, then."

Bastjan blinked at her. "Is that what you think?" he said. "You think we'd jus'... *give you up*?"

Alice went to answer, but stopped as Crake reappeared, clutching their tickets. Wares poked his head out of the bag, licking the strongman's fingers. "I forgot to pay passage for

251

you, young fella," Crake said. "So keep yer head down."

"Might be good advice fer all of us," Bastjan said darkly.

"Let's go," Alice said, in a clipped tone. "We need to get to the far-side platform for the London-bound train."

The children walked out into the concourse. "Did I miss somethin'?" Crake said, hurrying after them. "What's goin' on with youse pair?"

"Nothing," Alice said, scanning the crowd.

"Right, so," Crake huffed.

Bastjan and Crake followed Alice to an archway set into the wall, and they joined the stream of people making their way down a flight of stairs into a tunnel. The darkness was lifted by gaslights and somewhere, someone was playing a penny whistle.

Just as they saw the tunnel's end, and the steps leading upwards into daylight, the melody changed. Bastjan looked around – the whistler had to be nearby, but he could see no sign of them.

"Come on," Alice muttered, rushing up the steps two at a time. Beneath her make-up, her face was bone-white.

"Hey – hold on!" Bastjan said, hurrying after her. Crake lumbered up behind him.

At the top lay another platform with a train sitting at it, sleek and black and polished to perfection, its brass fittings gleaming in the light pouring through the skylights overhead. Bastjan could just make out Alice's back as she hurried away through the crowd. Then he saw two other children – one a pale girl with short brown hair, the other a tall dark-skinned boy in a top hat – follow her, suspiciously quickly.

"This way, Crake," Bastjan said, pulling at the strongman's sleeve.

The train whistle sounded, and as a cloud of steam cleared, he saw Alice's urgent face. She stood beside an open carriage door, pointing, before slipping up into the train. Crake and Bastjan scurried down the platform towards it.

As Crake hauled himself up the step into the carriage, Bastjan looked at the door to the next carriage down. He stared as the girl with short hair, her wary eyes watching the crowd, vanished inside, followed by the boy in the top hat.

CHAPTER
TWENTY-NINE

"Alice's bein' followed," Bastjan said as soon as he and Crake were aboard the train. "Some kids from the platform. They're in the next carriage."

Crake whuffed. "I'm sure it's grand, lad," he said. "There's no reason to be thinkin' the worst all the time."

"I'm *not*—" Bastjan began, but his words were cut off by the shriek of a whistle nearby, and the next thing he knew, the train had started to move.

Alice stuck her head out of a compartment door. "In here," she whispered, and Bastjan hurried after her. Crake, looking like a sardine in a tin, followed as quickly as he could, his huge shoulders almost level with the carriage roof.

They slipped into the empty compartment. Crake's bulk kept the children from being seen from the corridor and the drape of his oversized coat hid Wares, who was still in his bag tucked beneath Alice's legs.

"Yer bein' followed," Bastjan told Alice, as soon as he'd taken his seat. Alice fixed her gaze on the view outside the train. "Didja hear me? I *said*—"

"They're Tunnellers," Alice said, without looking around. "Monty's the kid with the hat. The girl's called Pork-pie, as that's all she ever wants to eat. They spotted me in the underground passage."

"The whistle," Bastjan said, remembering. "It was a signal."

Alice turned to him, her eyes heavy. "They know I'm on board. There'll be no getting away from them at the other end."

"What're they goin' to do?"

"They'll just follow me, probably. Word will be with Mrs P as soon as the train pulls in that I'm in London."

"You still haven't said why she's lookin' for you," Bastjan said.

Alice grimaced. "I stole from her," she said. "I showed you, when we met. Some coins and a ring. Nothing much, but Mrs P doesn't like thieves unless they're working for her." She sighed. "I only meant to take enough to get away," she continued, in a quiet voice. "Just enough to vanish."

Bastjan nodded. "An' instead, you ended up with us," he said. "Worse luck, eh."

"The worst," Alice agreed, but her eyes shone.

"I'm glad you're 'ere, anyway," Bastjan said. "Ain't nobody I'd rather 'ave on this quest than you an' Wares." Crake cleared his throat, and Bastjan threw him a grin. The big man returned the smile. "An' you too, o' course," Bastjan said.

"I think I'd like someone who knew where they were going," Alice said, with a laugh. "But I'm sure the airship station won't be hard to find. I just hope we get there in time." Her smile faded. "And that we're quick enough to stay clear of Monty and Pork-pie."

"An', jus' so you know, I ain't never goin' to give you up," Bastjan said, and Alice's smile reappeared.

They continued in silence for a few miles, the *clack-clack* of the train's progress broken only by Wares's contented snoring from the floor. Then the train began to slow. Alice nudged Bastjan.

"The Barrier's coming up," she said. "It's a big circular dam around the city, built to keep the water out. London would be swimming without it."

Soon the massive iron-and-steel construction loomed into view, its foundations lost in sparkling water and the lower half of its thick metal wall tinged green by old floods. The train made for a gap in the Barrier's upper half and Bastjan held his breath as they thundered through. The wall rose unimaginably high above their heads and then it was gone.

Before long, they were pulling into a vast train station, the roof arching overhead like a forest of glass and iron.

"Come on," Alice said, pulling herself down from her seat. "Let's try to get out of here before the others spot us." She carefully slung the bag, with its drowsy dog, over her shoulder. Crake left the compartment first, checking the corridor before the children emerged.

The train rocked slowly on its wheels as it drew to a halt, and they disembarked through clouds of steam and noise into the bustle of a station many times larger, and busier, than the one they'd left behind. Bastjan hurried after Alice as she wove her way towards the turnstiles. Joining her in the queue, he glanced back one last time at the train.

A cloud of steam blew aside to reveal Monty. He was scanning the crowd warily, his mouth drawn tight. In the same second as Bastjan spotted him, the boy's gaze landed on Bastjan's face and his dark eyes widened in recognition. Bastjan turned to Alice, but she'd seen him too.

"This way," Alice gasped, once they were through the turnstile, pulling them towards a side door. They followed the flow of people out on to the pavement, keeping their eyes peeled for Tunnellers, and then from the bag on Alice's shoulder Wares gave an angry bark.

"Lady!" came a voice, and Alice turned to face the rail-thin boy in his battered top hat. He was tall enough for his trousers to flap around his skinny ankles and his coat was threadbare.

"Get away from me, Monty," Alice said, through a snarl. The boy put his hands up in a gesture of peace.

"Pork-pie's already on 'er way to Mrs P," Monty said. "I couldn't stop 'er. She was listenin' outside yer compartment door. Said she 'eard you talkin' about the airship station. That where you're goin'?"

Alice tightened her lips. The boy looked up at Crake and down at Bastjan, his face impassive.

"Look," Monty continued. "It's none o' my business. But if that's where you're headin', the sooner you get there, the better."

Alice took in a slow breath. "Thanks, Monty," she said, after a moment.

"Get the tram," he said. "Nearest stop's round the corner. Goes as far as Limehouse, an' from there you'll be on foot. But it's the quickest way from 'ere."

Without another word, Monty disappeared into the crowd. Turning the corner, Bastjan, Crake and Alice saw a tram approaching the stop and they ran for it. Alice hugged the bag containing Wares close as they hopped aboard, and she and Crake pooled the last of their coins, including those she'd stolen from Mrs P, to pay for three tickets. The children stood, mostly hidden beneath Crake's coat, as the tram ground its way through the streets, clanging its bell every few yards to clear the tracks. Eventually it turned slowly round a corner and Bastjan saw the glint of sunlight on water, somewhere beyond the rows of tall, narrow buildings.

"Lime'*ouse*!" called the conductor and the tram came to a juddering stop. "All for Lime'ouse, Isle o' Dogs, Docklands, an' City Airship Station. Take yer baggage, mind 'ow you go."

Crake stepped down from the tram and reached up to lift Alice and Wares down in one arm, and Bastjan in the other. As the tram clanged away, they paused to look around. The river snaked off to their right, between stacks of tall buildings and ribbons of unknown streets. A few hundred yards away, hazy with distance, a ship was making its way into port.

"Look," Alice said, pointing. Near the water's edge, a tall glass-and-metal structure rose into the sky, like a tower made of windows. An airship with a long oval balloon was approaching it, coming into dock. Its anchor rope trailed beneath it, ready to be tied off. "That's got to be the airship station."

Crake nodded to the children, and they began to weave their way through the warren of warehouses and mills, trying to keep the airship tower in view. Finally they turned a corner into a street filled with horse-drawn carriages and carts piled high with all manner of things, the air bursting with noise and movement. Behind a wall on the street's far side rose a prickle-pointed forest of ships' masts, their rigging festooned with flags, and at the end of the street was a wide gateway.

"City Dock," Alice read, looking at the sign above the gate. In smaller letters beneath, it said 'To airship terminal'.

Dodging crowds, carts and horses, they passed through the gate. Ships bobbed in the water, like giants looking down on the world below, their prows sticking out like swords. All along the quayside were men clad in strange weatherproof clothes and hordes of haggling people wanting to buy their fresh fish. And at the end of the dock were three massive cranes, clanking and creaking as they lifted crates to and fro. From all around there was noise – voices and shouting, the grind and crack of machinery, the shriek of seagulls, the slap and ebb of the river.

Suddenly, Bastjan felt Alice go stiff as a statue.

"What's wrong?" he asked. Alice's eyes were fixed, her face pale as milk. The red of her birthmark stood out even through the make-up. He followed her gaze, searching through the crowd, and then, like oil pushing aside the water in its path, a woman came into view.

She was dangerously colourful, her face like old bone and her fuchsia-and-blackberry-hued hair piled on her head in a messy tangle held together with a filthy blue ribbon. Her lips and cheeks were painted red and her eyebrows were swirled on to her forehead with thin black lines, like strange handwriting. She wore a long silk robe, its ends ragged and stained. It had surely been bright once, but was now mostly thin and grey. Her lower arms were bare; they were strong-looking, her hands accustomed to hard work.

As Bastjan watched, a boy ran up to her and handed her something too small to see, which disappeared into her voluminous robe without trace. The woman spoke to the child, her teeth looking yellow in her unnaturally white face. The boy hesitated for a moment and the woman bared her discoloured teeth. The child ran.

Bastjan turned to Alice, knowing what she was about to say. "There she is," the girl whispered, never taking her eyes off Mrs Palmer for a moment.

CHAPTER THIRTY

Ada Palmer's gaze flicked to Alice's face and she smiled. It was a deeply unpleasant thing to witness, like watching a crack forming on the surface of a frozen lake.

Crake moved in front of Alice, blocking her from Mrs P's view, but the girl gave an irritated *tsk*. Tucking her hair behind her ears, Alice stepped around him.

"What're you *doin'*?" Bastjan hissed. "We got to get away!"

"There's no point," Alice said. "She's seen me. And this place is packed with Tunnellers. We wouldn't get ten yards, if we tried to run." She licked her lips. "I've got an idea."

"But—" Bastjan began. Alice only quickened her pace.

"Well, now, if it isn't *Lady* Patten," Ada Palmer said, grinning at Alice with her yellow teeth. "Been looking for you, I have. Got something of mine, en'tcha?" She chuckled mirthlessly. "Not that it really matters what you stole. What you're *worth* is far more important now. Your old grandad has the bloodhounds out for ya, don'tcha know?"

"I am not going back to that man," Alice said between clenched teeth.

"Thing is," Ada Palmer said, "when you're a *child*, you don't really have a *choice*. Do ya?" She stood in front of Alice and reached out one long pale arm, extending her calloused, nail-bitten hand to prod Alice under the chin. "Look at me, little chick," she instructed. "Don't be rude to dear ol' Mrs P."

"Let's make a deal," Alice said. There was the barest quiver in her voice. "Let my friends go. Then you may turn me in for the reward money."

Behind Alice, Bastjan exchanged glances with Crake, his eyes wide with shock.

Mrs Palmer smiled. "I en't got the faintest interest in yer friends, Lady Patten. They can go to Hades an' back, fer all I care."

"*This* is yer plan?" Bastjan said, but Alice ignored him. He assessed his surroundings. The Tunnellers lurked in a semicircle, keeping them hemmed in. The quay's edge was close; the sucking darkness of the water rose and fell like the beating of a heart a few feet from his boots. He looked up at the bulk of the ship that was moored there, close enough to touch. A thick rope tied the ship to a bollard on the shore and its bowsprit stuck out over the heads of Mrs P and her gang, bobbing gently with the tide.

Then Crake took a step forwards and Ada Palmer shouted something – a short, sharp word of command. Her Tunnellers leaped to obey. Crake cried out a warning, but his words were lost beneath a wave of noise as he was besieged by at least a dozen screaming members of Ada Palmer's gang. They swung from his beard, pulling fistfuls of his hair, and as soon as Crake managed to loosen the grip of one child, as gently as he could, three more had limpeted themselves to him.

Bastjan ducked as hands made to grab him. He ran for the bollard, jumping on to it before leaping for the rope, climbing up it from underneath with his hands and knees. Reaching the top, he swung on to the bowsprit. He sized up its movement, getting the feel for the up-and-down rhythm of the ship, and then he began to walk along it, his arms held wide for balance.

On the quayside, Mrs Palmer reached out to grab Alice by the arm. *Move!* Bastjan told himself. Taking the last few steps at a run, he launched himself off the end of the bowsprit, tucking neatly into a human cannonball in mid-air. At the last second he stretched out his body, his arms and legs as wide as they could go.

He landed on Ada Palmer's back with the force of an elephant's kick. The woman let out a muffled shout as she sprawled, skidding along the rough, muddy dock and landing with her face in a puddle. Bastjan hoped it contained something nastier than just rainwater.

Ada Palmer lifted her head. Her white make-up had run, revealing her rather redder skin beneath, and her bloodshot eyes locked on to Bastjan's.

He tried to find Alice in the crowd. "Run!" he gasped, doing his best to get to his feet. The next thing he knew, he felt Alice's hands beneath his armpits, helping him up.

Crake was flinging children off, his job made much easier by the fact that most of them were now too busy making good their own escape, or stopping to laugh at Mrs P. Alice and Bastjan hurried towards him. Just before they reached the strongman, Alice flung the bag down from her shoulder and pulled it open.

"You think you're going to get *away* with this?" Ada Palmer shrieked, heaving herself up off the ground. Her robe was dripping with water and mud, and she'd lost a shoe. Her colourful hair had fallen askew and her long teeth were set in a fearful grimace.

At a whistle from Alice, Wares burst free from the bag and launched himself at Mrs P. With a growl, he sank his teeth into the flesh of her arm. In her desperation to loosen the dog's clamping jaws, she began to spin in circles, shouting at the top of her voice. Nobody came to help her. Instead, the children seemed to urge the dog on.

Alice whistled again and Wares dropped away from Mrs Palmer. Bastjan could see that the worst of the damage had been done to her robe, which was now in tatters, but the woman yelled as though she'd been run through with a spear. Turning blindly to run away, she promptly tripped right over the ship's mooring rope. She teetered on the edge of the quay, before tumbling into the water below.

A raucous cheer rose from the surrounding children and Wares leaped into Alice's outstretched arms, licking her face in delight.

"I think that'll be our cue to get out of here," Crake muttered, herding Alice and Bastjan away from the quayside. Bastjan couldn't help one last look back and caught sight of Ada Palmer's bedraggled head, her wig lost to the water, coming up over the wall.

"She never liked you, did she, boy," Alice said, snuggling her nose against Wares's as they hurried away into the crowd.

"C'mon," Bastjan said. "We got to find the entrance to the airship station – an' fast."

"Airship station, you say," came a voice. Bastjan turned to see a familiar face, black hair curling out through a battered top hat.

"Monty," Alice said. "You're like a bad penny."

The boy gave a quick bow. "A penny's a penny, Lady."

He nodded in the direction they were going. "The airships leave from the far end of the quay. You can't get through the gate unless you've got a ticket, but I know a way to sneak round it without bein' caught."

"Why would you help us?" Bastjan said. "Weren't you tryin' to tail us, back at the train?"

Monty shrugged. "Anythin' that ends up with Mrs P gettin' chucked in the river is good, in my book," he said. "Let's hope she'll be too hoppin' mad to miss me for a bit. Anyway –" he turned to look over his shoulder – "we'd better move or she'll be on us. This way."

The others did their best to keep up as the boy flitted through the crowd. Finally, they reached a wall, slick with green algae and worn smooth by the sea.

"What?" Alice said. "Monty, if this is a trick—"

"Just come on!" Keeping low, Monty crept along until he reached a large seawater drain cut into the base of the wall. "What you waiting for?" he said, ducking inside.

Alice and Bastjan followed, their feet splashing in the thin stream of water that ran down the middle of the tunnel. Crake pushed himself in like a cork squeezing into the neck of a bottle, bending almost double as he forced his way through. At the far end of the short tunnel daylight was shining through the gaps in an iron gate.

Then something caught Bastjan's eye. "Hey!" he shouted. A pile of clothes and rubbish at the tunnel's far end had just sprouted a head – one with dark eyes and a cloud of black hair.

"*Querido!*" came a voice.

Bastjan dashed forwards, pushing past Monty to throw himself into Ana's arms. "*Cuidado!* Careful, please. Carmen is hurt." Bastjan stepped back immediately and Carmen smiled wearily up at him from a makeshift bed on the tunnel floor.

"It's yourselves!" Crake said, his voice filling the tunnel. "What're ye doin' here?"

"They found us," Ana told him. "Quinn and his cronies. They saw us as we tried to climb up the balloon, right after we put a hole in one of the steam ducts. They chased Carmen until she fell."

"I will be all right, Mr Crake," Carmen put in, with a one-shouldered shrug. "A sprained ankle. It is nothing."

"I'll break every ankle he owns," Crake growled.

"Sorry," said Monty. "But what's goin' on?"

Alice explained the situation as briefly as she could, though Monty's face told her he hadn't followed the half of it. "And Ana and Carmen came ahead of us, to try to sabotage the airship and delay it long enough to—"

From beyond the gate came a noise like the loudest hum in the world, the sound of a machine kicking into life.

Ana and the children, with Crake at their backs, raced towards the gate and peered out across the expanse of quay that stretched beyond the tunnel. There was only one airship moored there, but straightaway Bastjan knew it had to be the right one.

And its propellers were spinning, their blades flashing in the sun.

Chapter
Thirty-one

"No," Bastjan said, his gaze hopping from one propeller to another. "We can't let 'im leave!"

"Looks like we've got no choice," Alice said. "But if we can't stop him before he takes off, then we've got to get on board."

Bastjan stared out at the airship. Its mooring ropes were still tied. As he watched, he saw figures beginning to move around the tethered ship, and even from a distance, he recognized some of them as rousties from the circus.

"You need to get on board this thing?" Monty said. His long fingers flipped open a pouch at his belt. "Let me help."

"Thanks, Mont," Alice said.

"Think of it as my way of makin' things up to you," he told her.

"Here – wait." Alice reached into her secret pocket and

pulled out Mrs Palmer's ring. She gave it one final rub, then handed it to Monty. She met his eye. "Enough to get started somewhere new."

"Well, now. Don't mind if I do," Monty said, the ring vanishing into his own pocket. He smiled down at Alice and then, with a nod of farewell to everyone, he slipped his thin frame between the bars of the gate and was gone. The tall control tower stood at the quay's far end. Bastjan flicked a wary gaze towards it, hoping nobody would notice the boy scurrying along the quay towards the moored ship.

"What's 'e doin'?" Bastjan said.

"Wait and see," Alice replied.

Bastjan turned to Ana and Carmen. Without a word, he dropped to his knees and reached out for them. Carmen placed a kiss on his head.

"Thank you," he whispered, and Ana gave him an extra-hard squeeze.

"For you, anything," she told him, as Bastjan pulled away and got to his feet.

"Stand back, girleen," Crake muttered to Alice, raising his leg to kick at the gate. One powerful blow later and it landed on the quayside, wrenching free of its rusting hinges.

At just the same moment, there came a sudden *boom*. Wares began to bark and Alice quickly shushed him as a pop of light showered the back wall of the quay, sprinkling the dingy stone with colour. There was another boom, and another, both accompanied by explosions of light and pigment. The rousties around the ship shouted, starting to move towards the noise, searching for the source of the disturbance. Clouds of sparkling, colourful smoke filled the quay.

"Now," Alice said, pulling Bastjan forwards. Crake squeezed out of the tunnel after them, keeping close to their heels. "That's Monty. He's giving us our chance."

"How's he doin' it?" Bastjan asked as they ran.

"Some sort of compound he invented," Alice said. "It rolls up into pellets and explodes when it lands."

Bastjan's breath began to thicken as they neared the airship. From a distance, it had been disconcerting enough; with every step towards it, it grew stranger still. If ever a vessel had been designed to carry a circus troupe through the air, this was it.

Through the smoke from Monty's diversion he could see its huge, round balloon, red and blue and gold and green, the colours spilling over it in great swoops. It was chained in place above a large vessel which was almost spherical, besides a flat bottom and an extraordinary protrusion of metal and glass sticking out one end, stretching up towards the balloon overhead. On the airship's side there was a giant painted eye and a swirl of grey and blue made to look like the swish of an elephant's ear, and Bastjan let his gaze skip up the length of the glass and metal 'trunk', reaching up to play with the 'ball' of the balloon. Peeling paintwork on the body sketched out a tail, curling around the rump; above the tail, like a decoration on the 'elephant's' back, were three smallish spheres, brightly painted. Along the bottom someone had taken care to draw out four huge feet, each with their greyish-white toenails. And beneath the 'tail' a hatch was open, with a ramp leading from it to the stone quayside below.

Together they scurried towards the ship, using the smoke from Monty's fireworks as cover. Finally they reached the open hatch, trying to catch their breaths before continuing. Up close, Bastjan could see the airship's cracked paintwork and the rust between the rivets.

An angry, familiar voice filled Bastjan's ears. He felt Crake's hand go round his arm as the strongman pulled him and Alice beneath the ramp, out of sight – and not a moment too soon. Boots tramped heavily down the metal ramp and then the voice spoke again. *Quinn.*

"What is it *now*? I can't afford any more delay!" the ringmaster shouted as he walked over their heads.

A distant voice responded – one of the rousties. "A boy playin' tricks, sir! He slipped out through the station entrance. We couldn't catch him." Bastjan felt Alice slump with relief.

"*Ahyuk.* We won't be able to fly until the smoke clears,

Mr Quinn," came Hubert's voice. "Shouldn't take long, in this wind."

"We need to get this thing off the ground, smoke or no smoke," the ringmaster replied. "The pressure gauges have been stable for more'n twelve hours now, ever since we threw those blasted women overboard. This ship *has* to fly, or we're ruined."

"We've fixed the damage the Iberians did, sir," came another voice. Bastjan thought it might belong to a roustie named Lahiri whose job it was to oversee the raising of the king pole every time the circus moved location. "But we won't know until we start up the turbine again whether we're safe to fly. In any case, Hubert's right. We won't be allowed to leave until visibility improves. I'll signal the control tower and get instructions."

"Just get us airborne, as quickly as you can." The ringmaster paused and Bastjan imagined him scrubbing his hands through his hair. "I don't think you boys realize what's at stake here. We're about to change the face of circus life and write ourselves into the history books. A leaky pipe, or a kid trickin' around with fireworks, ain't goin' to stop me, fellas." Beneath the ramp, Crake and the children – and Wares – stayed silent as heavy footsteps strode away overhead.

"He'll get us all killed. *Ahyuk.*" Hubert's voice, when it came again, was low. "We're circus men, not airship engineers. An' the only one of us with any experience of a vessel like this, *ahyuk*, is used to lettin' 'em drop out of the sky."

Lahiri didn't reply for a moment. "Come on," he finally said, sounding weary. "We've got work to do."

When the men's footsteps had fallen into silence, Bastjan and the others emerged from their hiding place. Crake clambered on to the ramp and pulled the children up after him. Then, together, they crept into the ship.

The walls of the interior were metal. Gleaming brass handrails, level with Bastjan's head, were bolted in place. To the left was a wide corridor with doors on either side, at the far end of which was a set of steps leading to the body of the airship. Straight ahead, a pair of huge double doors stood open. Wordlessly, Bastjan and his friends made for them.

The room beyond the doors was gigantic. Against the walls, they could see shapes – boxes and crates, mostly – lashed down tight. Right in the centre was a cage, held firmly in place with straps and ropes. A cold wave washed over Bastjan as he looked at it. *He's goin' to put it in 'ere*, he told himself. *This cage is fer the creature. We were right – Quinn really is goin' after that creature in the Silent City, an' there's no chance he's givin' Bauer the box.*

"This here's the hold," Crake whispered. "Fer storin' cargo, an' suchlike."

"Or the Slipskin," Bastjan muttered, looking up at him.

Crake was about to reply when they heard the sound of footsteps clanging up into the airship and loud voices in the passageway just behind them. The rousties were back. Silently, the stowaways slipped into the hold, crouching amid the shadows.

Bastjan found himself letting out a held breath as the rousties stomped up the corridor towards the metal staircase.

"Here," whispered Alice. She'd found a corner behind a large packing case, big enough for them all to hide.

"Now what?" Crake said, as he settled himself on the cold floor.

"I din't mean for any of this to happen," Bastjan whispered. "What're we goin' to do? We can't go after 'im *now*. The place is packed with rousties. We'd be kicked off – or worse."

"He's after the creature, that much is for sure," Alice said, looking at the cage.

"Yeah. He wants it for a new showstopper, I s'pose – an act nobody else can match." The children looked at one another. "He must be plannin' to use my mum's bracelet to get at the Slipskin. That's why 'e wanted it for 'imself." Bastjan stopped, swallowing hard. "But it's not what Mum wanted. I got to give it back."

Alice nodded. "But how are we going—"

Her words were cut off as the entire airship lurched to one side. Crake raised one arm to keep the heavy packing case from sliding and trapping them all against the wall. The ship righted itself and they could feel a strange, uncomfortable buzzing in their bones as, somewhere beneath them, a massive turbine kicked into life.

"I guess we ain't got no choice now," Bastjan said. "We're goin' to Melita, whether we like it or not."

CHAPTER
THIRTY-TWO

Bastjan woke suddenly from a doze. He jerked upright, blinking hard. Crake was snoring softly in the corner. The hold was dark, except for the faint glow seeping in from the corridor outside, and the walls still hummed as the airship flew.

"Are you all right?" Alice whispered.

Bastjan looked in the direction of her voice. "Yeah. You?" He swallowed carefully. His mouth was uncomfortably dry.

Bastjan felt her come to sit beside him and Wares scampered on to his lap. He rubbed the dog's head gratefully.

"I wonder how long we've been airborne," Alice said.

Bastjan shrugged. "Or what time it is. Hard to tell, wi' no daylight." He chewed on his lip for a moment before continuing. "Listen, there's somethin' I bin meanin' to ask you." He paused and Alice braced herself for what she knew was coming. "Ada Palmer called you 'Lady Patten', back at the quay. An' Monty? He called you 'Lady', like it were a nickname. But I'm guessin' it wasn't."

"Yes. And?" Alice said at last.

"And? Who are you, really?" Bastjan persisted.

She took in a deep breath and let it out slowly. "My grandfather's Lord Patten. My *mother* was Lady Patten. At least, she was, until…" Alice stopped for a moment. "She and my dad caught fever on board a ship from the Mascarene Islands, when I was three." She sniffed quietly. "So my grandfather became my guardian. And yes, he used to serve in parliament, and he's a professor in Magdalen College, and he's got a big house, and all the rest of it. But I'm only his granddaughter." She turned to Bastjan, who could just make out the shine on her eyes. "I'm nobody special."

"Yes, y'are," Bastjan said. "Lady or not."

"*He* didn't think so," she replied, wiping her nose on her sleeve.

"Who? Yer grandad?" Bastjan shifted position on the uncomfortable floor. "Ain't he got the whole country out lookin' for you?" Wares clambered down from his lap and began to pad across the metal floor, his nails *click-click*ing as he went.

"Looking for me to *fix* me," Alice muttered. "Looking

for me to check whether I'm good enough yet, but I'll never be good enough."

"Dunno why anyone'd think that," Bastjan said.

"He kept finding doctors." Alice sighed. "Doctors with fine needles and then doctors with thick needles. Doctors with foul-tasting drinks or horrible, burning ointments that they wanted me to rub on. Nothing worked, and grandfather just got more and more impatient with the whole thing. With *me*." She paused and Bastjan waited for her to continue.

"I was never enough, never *right*, just as I was. Everything I did fell short of what he expected, all because of this *mark* on my face. I could never get him to see that it didn't matter. And then, one day, a stranger came to our house – a visiting professor from another university – and he didn't even introduce me as his granddaughter. 'This is my ward, Alice,' he said. I shook hands with our guest and curtsied like a lady. Then I went to my room and made a rope out of my bedsheets and I climbed out the window." She sniffed again. "I never *ever* want to go back there."

"I wouldn't, neither," Bastjan said.

"So you see why I ended up with Mrs Palmer," Alice said. "But I couldn't stay with her. And now I'm here."

"Well," Bastjan said. "Look on the bright side. Can't get much worse, can it?"

"Anyway," Alice said, a grin in her voice. "Enough about

me. Let's talk about your mother's box. It's likely to be with the ringmaster, isn't it? We need to find him. Or at least his quarters."

Bastjan was about to answer, but then he sat forwards suddenly, scanning the hold. He squinted through the gloom. "Wares?" he breathed, but the dog didn't leap into his lap.

Alice jerked into motion. "Wares!" she whispered, as loudly as she could. She whistled quietly, but it was no use. The dog was gone.

"Maybe he's gone to look fer some grub," Bastjan suggested as his own stomach growled.

"That'll be it," Alice said. "We've got to find him. If Quinn spots Wares he'll know we're on board."

Bastjan glanced at the sleeping Crake. "Yeah. Can't be too hard, right? An' we'll bring back a snack or two for this fella while we're at it."

Alice settled the bag on her shoulder and tiptoed towards the door, Bastjan close behind. Together, they stepped out of the hold and began to walk up the narrow metal corridor. The ship seemed deserted, but it wasn't quite silent. Somewhere, deeper in its workings, there was the regular *chug-chug-chug* of an engine, slow and steady, like a sluggish heartbeat. The walls vibrated very gently, buzzing lightly under the children's fingertips as they crept along.

They drew near the metal staircase and Bastjan slid his hand into Alice's. She gave it a reassuring squeeze as they climbed the steps. At the top, there was a wide corridor stretching in both directions. The right-hand side was dark, while the left was lit by flickering lanterns suspended from the ceiling.

Alice and Bastjan turned to the left and kept walking. Doors and hatchways opened to either side and they passed a wall-mounted case containing a fire axe, its blade fearsome even behind thick glass. Eventually, the floors changed from bare boards to thin, faded carpet and a brass handrail appeared on the wall, curving alongside them like a finger pointing the way. They passed a set of wide-open doors. The vast room they gave way to, filled with empty tables and chairs, reminded Bastjan of the mess tent back at the circus. Then they came to a door with a round dark window set into its upper half. It swung gently open and closed with the movement of the ship.

"Galley," Alice read, looking at a sign on the door. "That's what kitchens are called on ships."

"C'mon, then," Bastjan said, pushing open the door into an unlit room.

Alice followed him through. "Wares!" she whispered. "Are you in here? Come on, boy!"

On the far side of the room, the *click-click* of paws could be heard. Alice dropped to her knees as Wares came barrelling into her arms. She laughed quietly as the dog licked every inch of skin he could reach.

"Come on, you pair," Bastjan grinned. "Let's grab what we can, an' then…" His words trailed off as something reached his ears – the sound of voices. The children scrambled beneath a nearby table, hastily arranging the cloth to try to cover them. Alice held Wares tight and his small body quivered with a barely suppressed growl.

Lights came on inside the room and heavy footsteps made the floor shake.

"Get that kettle going, an' I'll find a tray for the cups," said one of the men who'd come in. Bastjan recognized his voice. He and another man began to stride about the room, and Bastjan tried to press himself into the wall in his desperation not to be discovered.

"Here," came the second man's voice. "The pantry's in a mess! Like somethin' was rootin' about pullin' things down off shelves." Alice and Bastjan stared at Wares, who gave his muzzle an innocent lick.

"Check the room," the first man said quietly. The children listened, barely daring to breathe, as doors were opened and drawers pulled out. Footsteps came closer and closer until, finally, the cloth concealing them from view was yanked up.

A strong hand reached in to pull Bastjan out by the ear.

"Should've known it'd be you," growled the second

man. Bastjan didn't know his name, only that he was a rigger – one of the rousties who helped put up the tent.

Alice scrambled out after Bastjan, Wares in her arms.

"Let him go!" she said. "We're not doing any harm!" The first man grabbed Alice by the collar. Wares leaped down from her arms and was out through the galley door like a flash.

The second roustie raised an eyebrow. "We'll let Mr Quinn decide what harm you're doing." He reached for Alice and the other man handed her over. "Go and find that mutt," he instructed.

The first man nodded.

"An' now," said the second roustie, looking from Bastjan to Alice. "Let's get going, shall we?"

He pulled them through the galley door and on up the corridor until they reached a pair of double doors, which he kicked open. Beyond them was a lobby paved with marble tiles. Plants in large bronze-coloured urns, their leaves edged with brown, were dotted here and there, and a gigantic chandelier hung high above, suspended from the tip of what looked like a tower of glass. A spiral staircase ran up the inside of the tower and right at the very top Bastjan could make out the curving side of the huge balloon, illuminated by the light shining up from the airship.

"Where are you taking us?" Alice demanded.

"Up those stairs," the man replied. "So save your breath."

Their feet tripped on the steps as the roustie pulled them on, up and up, around the twisting staircase inside the great glass trunk. Finally they reached a small, dome-ceilinged room containing several round tables, each surrounded by chairs.

Beneath the glass ceiling's highest point stood the only table in the room that was lit by a glowing lantern. It was also the only table that was occupied.

"Well, then. What do we have here?" said Cyrus Quinn, his face half in shadow.

Chapter
Thirty-three

Bastjan and Alice edged their way between the tables, towards the ringmaster. This room, at the top of the glass trunk, had windows above and to either side, and the floor too was made of thick, reinforced glass. The view was spectacular – if completely dizzying. Far below lay the glimmer of distant cities, their streets laced with dots of light, and waterways glittered as they threaded their way between the expanses of land. Along the horizon, the reddish-gold sunset was just beginning to bleed into the darkening sky.

"Take a seat," the ringmaster said as the children drew near, gesturing to the empty chairs all around him. "We have much to discuss."

Bastjan fumbled his way into a chair. Beneath the table he felt Alice's warm hand squeezing his own.

Quinn watched them as he reached into an inner pocket of his coat. He drew out the box, which he placed in the middle of the table. Its enamelled lid shone with a bright beauty, like the feathers of an exotic bird. Bastjan burned to grab it but Quinn's fingers never left the box for a moment.

The ringmaster chuckled. "Don't worry. I've kept it safe."

"*Safe*," Bastjan spat. He shook with rage as he forced himself to look at the ringmaster's mocking face. "I'll 'ave it back."

"Yes, soon enough," the ringmaster said. "This old thing is making good time. We've been airborne for perhaps eight hours and already we've crossed most of the Continent. We'll arrive on Melita before midnight, with any luck."

"An' then what?" Bastjan said. "We go an' *steal* an innocent creature to perform in yer circus?"

"Steal," the ringmaster repeated. "I hardly think so. Entice, perhaps. I have something the Slipskin wants, and the Slipskin has something I want, and I'm sure we can make a deal."

"Ain't no deal worth makin' if it means someone ends up a prisoner."

Quinn gave a tight-lipped smile. "I can't say I agree."

"Aren't you going to get in trouble when your *benefactor* finds out what you're doing?" Alice said. "I thought you were supposed to hand the box over once you'd found it."

The ringmaster turned his gaze to her. "Lady Patten. What a pleasure." His smile faded. "I've been doing a bit of research into Dr Bauer, actually, and I've discovered a few unpleasant things. If *he* had his way, the Slipskin would end up pinned to a display board in a scientific institute somewhere, pored over and prodded at. Or perhaps kept barely alive, to be used for goodness knows what. Bauer's line of work has made him a very wealthy and extremely well-respected man, but he doesn't care what he destroys in his search for knowledge. As bad as I am, you can't accuse me of that."

Bastjan shook his head in disbelief. "You're no better'n he is!"

Quinn sighed. "Everything I've done – including sending you to the farm, believe it or not – was for the good of this circus. That's the truth. I will do anything to keep this show going, and if I can't have the best aerialist of all time beneath my roof, and if her son is worse than useless –" Quinn's gaze grew piercing – "then I'll take the next most incredible act I can find. I'll put *anything* in the ring, so long as people will pay to see it."

He looked away from Bastjan. "In my haste, I admit I have made one or two mistakes. Once you were dispensed with, for instance, I remembered something I'd read. The Slipskins' remarkable sense of smell, which is acute enough to detect the blood of a Melitan, even from quite a distance. They developed this skill, apparently, as a means of trying to avoid being hunted to extinction – or near extinction, as the case may be. *Now*, I thought to myself, *where shall I find a Melitan, a person whose blood will rouse the Slipskin and draw it out?* And then, of course, I recalled I had one in my family." Quinn began to drum his fingers on the tabletop. "My final piece of luck was our Iberian friends' attempt to sabotage my ship, which I guessed was designed to slow me down. I hoped it meant you were on my trail. So, once it became clear you were, we waited for you to catch up."

"I ain't your *family*," Bastjan growled.

Alice blinked at the ringmaster. "You knew we were coming?"

Quinn met her confused gaze. "I am not an idiot, girl," he said.

Right at that moment, a voice was heard from somewhere beneath them – a loud voice, one the children both knew, interspersed with sharp barks.

"Crake," said Bastjan, at the same time as Alice whispered, "Wares!"

Crake came barrelling up the steps with Wares clutched in one arm, barging past the roustie. His eyes were bulging with rage and his gaze was fixed on the ringmaster. He dropped the dog gently to the floor and then strode towards Cyrus Quinn.

"Cornelius," Quinn said, amused. "I was wondering when you'd turn up."

The ringmaster whistled, the noise a sharp trill – a roustie signal. The next thing Bastjan knew, four men entered the glass room, obeying the command. Crake stopped in his tracks.

"Get behind me, the pair o' youse," he muttered to the children – but as Bastjan moved, he spotted a baton in the hands of one of the rousties.

"Crake!" Bastjan shouted – but it was too late. The roustie hit Crake sharply over the back of the head and the strongman slumped face-forward on to the table, which crashed to one side as Crake landed at the ringmaster's feet.

Amid the shards of the table and the upturned lantern, Bastjan saw his mother's box lying on the floor. Just as he was about to spring forwards and grab it, he felt strong fingers taking a handful of his collar.

"Not so fast," said a voice near his ear. A roustie had him in a vice-grip.

Alice stood amid the confusion, Wares yapping in her arms.

"Take them," said the ringmaster, still calmly seated on his chair. "The firemarked girl, the dog and that lump of useless meat on the floor. Lock them in a pod. Leave me with my *stepson*."

Another roustie grabbed Alice by the arm. "Bastjan!" she shouted, but the boy couldn't reply. His throat was swelling shut and his lungs were beginning to tighten. Stars wriggled across his vision.

Three more men bent to the task of hauling Crake up off the floor. Blood trickled down around his left ear and the back of his collar was stained red. Bastjan watched, his chest on fire, as his friends were taken away.

"Where – *whoop!* – where're you – *whoop!* – takin' 'em?"

"To a pod," Quinn said, bending forwards to pick up the box. He slipped it back into his coat. "A lifeboat. Small, self-contained, easily detached from the main ship." He paused, getting to his feet. "Handy, in an emergency. But it's even more convenient for ridding yourself of people you don't want on board."

"No," Bastjan said. "You *can't* – *whoop* – do this!"

"I can," Quinn said. "And I will. But you can stop it."

Bastjan's eyes blurred with tears.

"Come down to the Silent City with me. Help me find the Slipskin and bring it on board, and once it's safely stowed you can have your friends, and your mother's box, back." Quinn bored through Bastjan with a look. "But if you put one foot out of line, those three will go to a watery end in the Midsea. They'll sink so far that nothing, not even fish that scrape their food off the ocean bed, will ever find them."

Bastjan blinked, the tears rolling down his cheeks. His chest finally closed over completely, and he barely felt the roustie pulling him up, throwing him over his shoulder, and carrying him away.

"Five degrees to starboard. Hold that elevation!"

The words sounded fuzzy in Bastjan's ears, as though the person were speaking through a fistful of cloth. The voice sounded somehow familiar, but Bastjan couldn't quite place where he'd heard it before.

And then recognition washed over him: *Atwood.* Atwood, the circus fire juggler. What was he doing here?

"Three degrees port," Atwood continued. "Got to correct for these crosswinds. Quick, now!"

Bastjan forced his eyes open. Bright lights speared through his head, making him squint. He was lying on the floor of a control room, with gigantic windows to the front and sides. The walls were covered with dials and switches and gauges with hopping needles and pipes which hissed and clanked and rattled. There were several speaking horns – though Bastjan had no idea where they were connected to, or who would answer if you picked one up and spoke into it.

He started to sit up and the room swam into clearer focus. Atwood was standing before the room's largest window, keeping tight hold on the handles of a wheel, while in front of a long lever set into the floor was his son, Clement.

A third figure stood staring out the window with his hands behind his back, his strong legs spread wide for balance. He wore a brown jacket made of leather, and shining black boots. In his hand he clutched a pair of goggles.

"You're awake, then," Quinn said, turning to look at him.

"Where—" Bastjan began, stopping to draw in a deep breath. "Where are we?"

"Come and see for yourself," Quinn said, stepping to one side.

Bastjan got to his feet. The floor hummed unpleasantly, making his teeth buzz. Outside the window the sky was dark. With every step that Bastjan took, he grew surer and surer of what he was about to see, but despite that, nothing could prepare him for the sight when it eventually came.

Beneath the airship, visible even by moonlight, was a huge hole in the earth, surrounded by a high wall. He closed his eyes and all he could see was his mother's sketch. He knew exactly where he was. *The Silent City*.

And somewhere inside the city was the creature that owned the bracelet his mother had stolen. The bracelet he had to return, before it was too late.

Chapter
Thirty-four

The airship sank slowly into the Silent City, its wall rising around them like a fist closing over. When they were low enough, Clement pulled his lever. As soon as it clunked into position, lights began to pop on all around the outside of the airship, flooding the city with artificial brightness. At the same time, Atwood reached overhead to release a switch. The ship rocked very slightly as several loud but muffled bangs were heard, coming from all around the perimeter of the room.

Bastjan saw sharp metal hooks attached to strong ropes come shooting out of the ship. The hooks buried themselves in the crumbling walls, firmly anchoring the airship over the city, each collision of metal and stone throwing up a cloud of dust. The vibration in the floor of the airship eased until, finally, the huge propellers came to rest. The ship was silent, floating above the city. The barest sway gave away the power of the wind, blowing it from side to side.

Bastjan stared at Atwood as the man tied off the wheel. "Why're you doin' this?" he asked. "You *got* to know why we're here."

"What my ringmaster tells me to do, I do. He says it's for the best." Atwood shrugged and looked away, though guilt tinged his eyes. "I believe that."

"Wind's pickin' up, Dad," Clement said, tapping at a gauge on the wall.

Atwood turned to the ringmaster. "It's balloon only now," he said. "I'm keepin' the engines stoked for lights an' liftaway. But we must be quick. Fuel's tight, an' we want to avoid attention if we can." He nodded at the gauge. "Plus, you saw that cloud bank over the Midsea. There's bad weather comin', an' I want to get ahead of it."

The ringmaster nodded. Then he turned back to Bastjan. "Right. Well, let's get moving. We'd best start now and camp in the city if needs be."

"I ain't goin' nowhere," Bastjan told him.

"Either you come with me and lure this thing in peacefully," Quinn said, "or I go down there and bring it in screaming. It's your choice."

Bastjan stared at his stepfather. "I ain't lettin' you hurt anyone. Or anythin'. Never again."

Quinn's face lit up in a smirk. "Well, then. You know what to do. I don't need to remind you what's at stake – not just the creature in the city, but your *friends* too." He turned away, making for the door.

Bastjan glanced between Atwood and Clement, too angry to speak, and finally followed the ringmaster out of the room. Their footsteps clanged on the metal floor as they walked down a dimly lit corridor, until they passed through a round doorway into a small room, no bigger than a circus wagon. It was full of rousties, all of whom seemed to be pulling on boots or wrestling into unfamiliar-looking clothing. One of them was Hubert.

"*Ahyuk*," said Hubert, nodding at Bastjan. "Evenin', young fella."

Bastjan didn't reply. Behind him, the ringmaster slammed a thick iron door closed, making him jump. Then someone shoved something heavy into his hands. It was a jacket, and as he began to struggle his way into it, he barely saved a pair of goggles, which had been wrapped up inside, from crashing to the floor. He looked around – everyone else was putting them on, so he tried to do the same. The leather straps were worn and Bastjan struggled to adjust them. The lenses kept slipping away from his eyes.

"Let me," said Hubert, taking the goggles from him. His strong hands quickly fixed the straps.

"Where's Crake?" Bastjan asked. "An' Alice, an' Wares?"

"*Ahyuk*," Hubert began. "If you mean the girl and that little terrier, they're locked up with Cornelius in one of the pods." He tapped the goggles' lenses. "How's that feel?"

"Fine," Bastjan replied, distracted. "They all right?"

"Far as I know. *Ahyuk*."

"Gentlemen!" came Quinn's voice. Bastjan, Hubert and the other rousties turned to face him. He'd pulled on his own goggles and fastened his jacket up to the neck. "I'm about to open the hatch. Quick as you can, now."

The men braced themselves and Bastjan followed suit. Then the ringmaster turned to a door in the wall, one with a large metal handle. He held up a gloved hand with three fingers raised.

Three, two, one, Bastjan counted as the ringmaster lowered his fingers.

Quinn pulled down on the handle and the door popped open, folding inwards and tucking neatly against the wall. Wind rushed through the tiny room, catching Bastjan's breath.

The ringmaster kicked through a rolled-up rope ladder, which quickly began to unfurl. "Now!" he shouted. "Go!"

The rousties went first. Hubert held out a hand to Bastjan as he made for the opening. "Come on, lad! *Ahyuk!*"

Bastjan was stuck to the wall. His knees buckled.

Quinn grabbed him by the shoulder and shoved him

towards the ladder. Bastjan tried to swallow back his bile as he got a firm grip on the ladder's wooden rungs.

And then, before he knew it, he'd begun his descent.

It was the noise that alerted her first, the loud *thrum* that sounded like nothing in the Silent City. It was a sound from outside – a human sound. She woke, her large black eyes adjusting instantly to the darkness, and straightaway she sat up, her senses on fire.

She had no idea of time. She slept when she was tired, ate when she was hungry. She knew nothing of clocks or calendars, so she did not know how long it had been since her power had been ripped from her. Since that day, she had not grown; her body had remained the same. She was still the child she had been the day she ceased to be a Slipskin and became something else, something without a name.

She did not know where her power, her Relic, had gone. She had been charged to keep it safe and she had failed. She missed it like a knocked-out tooth, the gap where it should be a burning ache inside her. She also knew that it had been taken from her when someone from outside had disturbed her. Nothing good had ever come from outside.

The last human hadn't come with noise, she remembered, just as the gigantic flying creature overhead lit itself up brighter than day, making her hiss and scuttle for shelter.

She peered up and out again, watching the thing hanging in the sky, *her* sky. Its light was too bright, its noise too great. And then it shot out claws, bursting holes through the walls of her city. The girl opened her mouth in a silent scream, huddling in a tight ball, afraid that the ancient walls were finally going to break all around her, just as her mother always told her they would, if ever she tried to go beyond them...

After a moment or two the girl uncovered her face and peered up at the walls again. The claws were still. The walls stood. Nothing had crumbled. She remained.

She, Dawara. The last inhabitant of the Silent City.

Then the floating beast showed it had one more surprise for her. Dawara watched, her eyes narrowed, as a mouth appeared in the belly of the creature – or not a mouth, but a *door*. Something fell through it, something which unrolled itself as it fell, and then the humans began to come.

She could smell them on the wind. They stank of smoke, of dirt, of things Dawara couldn't name. They reeked of death, and Dawara's eyes closed as her mind filled up with the memory of her mother's face, the urgent look in her eyes as she'd pulled the Relic from her arm and pushed it into Dawara's hand. Dawara hadn't wanted to take it – she wasn't ready to own it yet. Her mother still had years of life;

it wasn't time to pass it down.

And then her mother had run, foolishly, into the path of the hunters. They'd taken her. *But it was not foolishness,* Dawara told herself, squeezing her eyes tight. *My mother was not a fool. She did it for me.*

Dawara set her teeth, opening her eyes again. The humans were back, looking for her, looking for the Relic – but it was not here. She'd already lost the power she'd been entrusted with. Grief and fear overwhelmed her, and she hid herself deeper in the rubble, keeping careful watch.

And then the wind brought a curl of something different to her nose – a scent Dawara had not smelled in more years than she could count. Her mouth dropped open in surprise.

A Melitan.

One of these humans was an islander. Her hearts thundered in her belly, pounding hard and strong, making her feel sick and dizzy. The old instincts roared inside her – the urge to run, to hide, to *fight...* But there was more. She closed her eyes and breathed deeply, trying to filter the smells. Beneath the leather and the sweat and the tang of metal, she could detect the scent of a human she knew. The human who had taken her power.

Or – not quite. She frowned, wrinkling her face as she thought. Not quite, but close enough. Kin, perhaps.

The humans had reached the ground now. They were

walking through her city, lights held high, like glow-worms with legs. She allowed herself a chittering laugh at the idea and immediately regretted it; one of the humans stopped dead, holding out a hand to the others. It spoke, its human language sounding like splintering bones in her ear, and the group came to a halt. One of the humans held up its light in her direction and she flinched as it shone directly into her eyes. Dawara knew enough about hunting to know that she had given herself away.

She bolted, moving faster than she'd ever done in her life.

CHAPTER
THIRTY-FIVE

"There!" said the rigger, pointing into the darkness. He turned to the ringmaster, his lantern held high. "Eyes, Mr Quinn. It must be this creature o' yours."

"Let's not be too hasty, Marlowe," Quinn said, though Bastjan could read the delight on his face. "We don't want to rush into things, after all. We want the beast to think of us as friends." Bastjan snorted and Quinn looked at him. "Now, now," the ringmaster murmured. "Let's remember we're a team."

With that, Quinn strode past him. The others followed, laden down with tents and lanterns and cooking equipment, ready to make camp for the night. Bastjan glanced back at the ship and noticed, again, the three round protuberances on the metal elephant's back, painted to look like the balls a circus elephant might use in their act. He squinted more closely and saw the small window set into each one. *The pods*, he thought. He gulped, feeling the chill of the night air trickling down around his collar.

"You! Thing! Get over here," the ringmaster ordered. "Come and help, boy, or you can sleep in the rubble."

Bastjan scowled, making his way to the others. There seemed to be a discussion taking place about where to make camp. Eventually it was decided that half the team would stay behind and maintain a lookout, while the others would continue, as long as their lamps held out, into the Silent City itself.

"You're with me," the ringmaster said to Bastjan, thrusting a lamp into his hands. "Let's get moving."

Four of them set out, Bastjan, Quinn, Lahiri and Hubert, their footsteps quiet on the mossy ground.

"Remarkable," Quinn said, holding his lantern high as they walked. The ruins all around them loomed in the lamplight, huge stones covered with impenetrable markings – rows of incised dots, precisely carved. Some bore swirling patterns which made Bastjan's eyes ache as he tried to follow them. All were covered with weeds and roots and ivy. Occasionally, the stones were marked with black stains, like soot, or the traces of long-ago fire.

"What is this place? *Ahyuk*," Hubert asked. Bastjan looked at him. His eyes weren't fearful, exactly – Hubert was used to staring down lions. But he was wary, like a threatened animal.

"The Silent City. My late wife first told me about it, though I've supplemented her fairy stories with some actual research more recently," Quinn said. He glanced at Bastjan, who pretended to ignore him. "The race of creatures who lived here, the Slipskins, once inhabited this whole island. But when people arrived, gradually the creatures were pushed towards the coast – hunted, of course. Occasionally, so the stories went, the shapeshifters among them would take revenge – snatching children, drowning sailors, that sort of thing – but they were no match for human weapons."

He paused, swinging his lantern this way and that as he decided which track to take. "Eventually, the last dregs of their race were driven here, into a long-ruined place built some time in antiquity. The locals placed the wall around them in the hope they'd just *die*, quietly and without fuss. It was believed they were extinct, but my late wife saw one in her childhood. From what she said, the creature appeared to be alone, living in the ruins. No mention of it appears in any of the books I've read, so it's likely this creature is the last one. And now it's here, waiting for us."

Lahiri adjusted his backpack. "And it's a shapeshifter?"

"Not at present," the ringmaster answered. "But we plan to give it back that power."

"Is that wise?" Lahiri asked, in a quiet voice.

Quinn chuckled. "Don't worry," he said. "We're well

prepared. It's nothing we can't handle."

They walked for some time in silence until, up ahead, Lahiri's lamp began to sputter out. Without his light, the group began to walk a little closer together – all except for Quinn, who strode ahead with his own lamp held high. Bastjan found himself hurrying after Hubert, suddenly afraid of what might come nipping at his heels. Eventually, they turned a corner into an open space, walled off by a ring of ancient stones. The stones were crowded and falling against one another like crooked teeth, each of them decorated with the dotted, swirling markings. The ground was covered with a net of vines and weeds, and the circle was barely big enough to turn a wagon in. The ringmaster began to stride across it, slinging off his backpack as he went.

"Perfect spot for a bivouac, men," the ringmaster called. "We'll continue at first light."

Muttering, Hubert followed his boss. Lahiri followed too, casting a fearful glance at the sky. And Bastjan, every step feeling like lead, joined them.

One by one, the men had fallen asleep. Bastjan had pretended to, but he wasn't the slightest bit tired. This was the quietest place he'd ever known; sounds seemed to vanish before they had a chance to be heard. There were no animal noises, no insects buzzing, no fluttering birds or rootling creatures. It set his teeth on edge.

Beside him, Quinn began to snore, gently at first and quickly growing louder. The ringmaster was lying on his back, his feet crossed at the ankle and his hat perched over his eyes. His hands were folded behind his head, propped up on his backpack – which meant his jacket pockets were unguarded. Even so, Bastjan hesitated. He'd never tried to pick a pocket before and he was afraid of his clumsy fingers.

If Alice were 'ere, she'd've 'ad the job done three times by now, he told himself, flexing and relaxing his hands.

Sucking hard on his lower lip, the boy crept towards the sleeping ringmaster and, as delicately as he could, he lifted the flap of Quinn's pocket.

With the other hand, he slid his fingers inside until they met the cool hardness of his mother's box. Barely daring to breathe, Bastjan pulled it free, clutching it against his chest as he picked up a lantern. Then, with one last look back at the men, he hurried into the darkness of the Silent City.

His feet stumbled over rocks and roots as he walked, and his lantern did nothing except make the darkness seem even more overwhelming. All he could see, when he looked up, were leaning slabs of stone bigger than two tall men standing on one another's shoulders, each of them decorated with the strangely beautiful markings. Once, the light of his lantern caught a face carved on a slab, its teeth bared, and he barely stifled a yell.

No matter how far he walked, or how many turns he took, there wasn't a single landmark he could use to orient himself. He turned. Far behind him, smaller now, was the tethered ship still bathed in its bright light, but he had no idea how he was going to get back to it. He jumped as a fat raindrop hit him on the cheek and the ship rocked slightly on its moorings in the strengthening wind. *The storm's comin'.*

"C'mon," he whispered. "I *got* to find you before the others do. Come out!" He stopped for a moment, closing his eyes as he thought through his half-formed plan. He would find the Slipskin, give it back its bracelet and hope that, somehow, he could ask it to transform into something that could fly, something that was strong enough to pull the door away from the pod containing his friends... *It's got to work*, he told himself. There was no other way of freeing Crake, Alice and Wares, and getting them away from here.

Bastjan kept walking. *Look fer water*, he thought, remembering his mother's map and the pool she'd sketched in the centre of the city. *It might be near water...* He lifted the lantern, looking through the curtain of rain, but he'd barely gone ten steps when he felt his boot catch on something in the undergrowth. It sent him sprawling and he flung out his hands without thinking. The box flew in one direction and the lantern in another. Bastjan cursed his own clumsiness as he got to his hands and knees.

The ground was dotted with holes and his heart thudded with the thought that the box might have fallen into one.

If so, it's gone fer good, he told himself, squinting into the darkness as he crawled towards his fallen light. He held it up, scanning the ground before him for the box. There it was, sitting right on the lip of one of the chasms. Somewhere close, he could hear the gurgle of trickling water, like an underground stream. The lamplight shone into the chasm, gleaming on the fast-moving water below.

Bastjan inched towards the box, careful not to dislodge any loose stones that might send it tumbling, and eventually he closed his fingers around it. He let his head fall on to his arms as he took several deep breaths. Then he got to his feet.

He'd just finished edging his way around the chasm when he heard it – a sound, in the Silent City. A sound not made by him.

Somewhere close by, something moved – something slick, and sleek, and shining-wet. Then that something hauled itself out of a pool and stood before him, its teeth bared.

Bastjan dropped to his knees and put down his lantern. He fumbled his mother's box open and his fingers, numb and nerveless, found the bracelet and held it high. Immediately, his head filled with splitting pain – shouting, blades shining, the terrible tearing pain of loss. His lungs began to tighten, feeling stiff inside his chest; he fought the sensation, forcing his breath in and out.

"Please," he gasped, barely able to hear his own voice through the roaring inside his head. "Please! You gotta help me!"

A moment passed as they peered at one another through the falling rain. Then, the Slipskin pounced.

The cub had been foolish to leave its pack, especially when it was so loud – and so bright – that she would have been able to track it anywhere. She had followed unseen, slipping through the underground waterways as the cub had stumbled through the city, holding its light high. It had allowed the glow to play over the faces of the Old Ones and had run its fingers across the star maps. Finally, it reached the pool at the city's heart.

Its Melitan blood sang to her, but it was Melitan mixed with something else – something different, not of the island. It made her uneasy.

The grown humans had not hunted her and she did not know why. There were far more of them than there were of her but one cub alone, especially so far from its pack, outnumbered nobody. When the cub drew near, for a few careless moments she stopped thinking about the grown humans, and she stopped wondering where they were, and she stopped listening for their footsteps. She hauled herself out of the pool and stood before the cub, ready to attack – but the cub did not run.

Instead, it fell to its knees, its hands in the air. One of them still held the light and she frowned at it. The cub placed the light slowly and carefully on the ground and then held its hands up again.

On its face she saw fear mixed with something else – something that felt like desperation and a plea for help. Dawara stopped, puzzled. The cub slowly reached into the coverings around its body and drew out something flat and shiny, which it broke open. Then the cub pulled something free. Dawara saw it was the Relic, the wind making it twist and spin, and her hearts beat faster.

The cub said something Dawara could not understand – the words were like stones in its mouth. But as it spoke she heard something deeper – she heard the whistle of its breath, the sticky sound of the air trapped in its lungs. She heard its fear and sorrow and anger, and she knew its rage was not for her.

Her gaze hopped between the Relic and the cub's pale face, its eyes too round and too big. Dawara forgot to remain watchful, forgot about everything except the Relic and how much she wanted it.

She looked at the cub. Its arm trembled with fear as it held out the Relic, but still it did not run.

And then she leaped, reaching for her power, her Relic, woven from her mother's hair and the hair of all her foremothers, as far back as anyone could remember – but the *crack* of a weapon sounded nearby, sending her sprawling, and there was a crushing pain in her leg. She looked down to see a ferocious-looking barb protruding from her calf. Her pale pink blood gushed out of the wound, running into the soil of her city, trickling between its fallen rocks and dripping into the caverns far below.

Hands grasped her, pulling her across the stony ground, away from the pool. Dawara tried to fight, to crawl and claw her way back towards the Relic, but it was no use. The hands were too many and too strong and the pain in her leg was much too great.

Her hearts raced sickeningly fast as a bag was placed over her head. She tried to bite at the hands that placed it there, but the human fingers were covered with thick gloves and the voice in her ear, though still speaking the cracking, terrible language she could not understand, was warm and soothing. She breathed heavily through the throbbing agony in her leg, blinking in the darkness, trying to understand. Then she felt herself lifted off the ground, and something hard and cold going around her wrists and ankles, something that bound her. Something she couldn't fight.

Dawara howled and somewhere close by she heard the sound of the cub, its wails long and loud.

CHAPTER
THIRTY-SIX

"I gotta say, nice try," said Marlowe, the rigger, as he dragged Bastjan along the airship corridor. Bastjan's stomach lurched with the movement of the airship as it flew and also with anger and guilt; the sight of Quinn's triumphant face as he'd pulled the bracelet from Bastjan's fingers still danced, mockingly, in his mind's eye. "But I mean, you'd no idea you were bein' followed, did you? Not a clue." He paused to chuckle.

Bastjan made no reply. Instead, he focused on looking for anything he could use as a weapon and trying to quell the flood of ice-cold rage in his brain.

"And it wouldn't surprise me if someone had a little accident over the Midsea, dropped you lot right in it," came Marlowe's sneering voice again, this time accompanied by the jingle of keys. "Very easy thing to do you, y'know, pressin' the wrong button up in the cockpit and releasin' an escape pod by mistake. No, wouldn't surprise me one tiny bit. There are controls to fly it, o' course, an' enough power to get yourselves to land, maybe, but that's no good to youse lot. You need to 'ave a clue what you're doin' first."

Bastjan's eyes slid to the man's free hand, where a ring of keys – one of which had to unlock his friends' prison – were dangling. They clattered their way up a short flight of metal stairs and turned a corner. As soon as they did so, Bastjan knew his time had run out. At the corridor's end were three doors, each with a thick round window set into the top – the pods. *Now or never*, Bastjan told himself.

Marlowe held Bastjan tightly by the collar, but the boy's arms were free. As Marlowe fumbled one-handed with the keys, Bastjan lunged forwards and grabbed hold of Marlowe's nearest leg. Before the man could react, Bastjan buried his teeth in his captor's thigh, biting down hard. Marlowe yelled and swore, and the keys dropped from his hand as he struggled to pull Bastjan's head away. Without missing a beat, Bastjan hooked his foot around Marlowe's other leg, yanking him to the ground. He hit the metal floor with a resounding *clang*.

Bastjan scrambled to his feet, stopping only to grab the ring of keys. "Crake!" he shouted as he began to run. "Crake! You there? Alice!"

Distantly, like it was coming from the bottom of the

sea, Bastjan heard the sound of barking. He strained his ears as he ran, trying to figure out which pod it was coming from.

"You little *brat*!" roared Marlowe, from behind. "You'll pay for that!"

Bastjan ignored him, focusing on the sound of Wares's bark. He dropped to his knees before the keyhole of the left-hand pod. As quickly as he could he checked through the keys, trying to guess which one might fit, all the time painfully aware of the rigger limping down the corridor behind him.

No sooner had he felt the correct key click and turn in the lock than the door was hauled open from the other side. Bastjan looked up to see Alice, her face rigid with terror. In her hands she held something large and red.

"Duck!" she shouted, and Bastjan did as he was told.

Alice threw the thing she had been holding as hard as she could. It was a heavy metal fire bucket, which smacked the pursuing Marlowe full in the face. He hit the floor with a *thump*, out cold. The bucket landed beside him, sand spilling everywhere.

Bastjan was still staring at the unconscious rigger when he felt himself pulled into a fierce hug. "What on earth?" Alice gasped into his ear. "How are you here?"

"He was goin' to put me in there with you," Bastjan said. "Where's Crake?"

Alice released him and stepped back, letting Bastjan look further into the escape pod. Crake was slumped against the wall, still looking dazed from the blow to his head. He saw Bastjan and tried to smile. At his feet stood Wares, his tongue hanging out and his tail flicking back and forth so quickly it could barely be seen.

"Come on," Bastjan said, hurrying into the pod. "We've got to get out of 'ere."

Alice rushed to Crake's other side. The children slotted themselves in beneath the strongman's armpits, doing their best to haul him to his feet. Crake tried to help, but he was worryingly unsteady. Almost as soon as the children got him upright, he stumbled heavily against the wall of the pod.

"Leave me," he panted. "I'll follow ye."

"We can't *leave* you, Crake," Bastjan said, bracing himself against his friend's bulk and trying to push him up.

"Quicker without me," the strongman mumbled. "I'm awful dizzy." He slumped again, seemingly unable to keep his eyes open for long.

"Crake," Bastjan said, pulling at the strongman's arm. "C'mon. Please! We need you!"

Crake looked up at the boy, blinking as he tried to focus. "I'll be behind you, son," he said. "I's promisin' you that."

"Listen, maybe he's right," Alice said, casting a glance out of the pod door. "We *will* be quicker, just the two of us."

"But I can't go without 'im," Bastjan said miserably.

Alice took him by the shoulders. "We'll come back," she said. "I promise. Let's just get him out of this pod and leave him somewhere safe. Once everything's done, we'll come and find him. Right?"

As she spoke, a bellow sounded from somewhere inside the ship – a deep, guttural noise of rage and pain. Alice looked away from Bastjan, her face paling.

"That's 'er," Bastjan said, once the noise had faded. "The Slipskin. They speared 'er in the leg, down in the City."

"Brutes," Alice whispered. "*Monsters!* They can't be allowed to do this."

"She's just a kid," he replied. "She's no bigger'n you, anyways. She don't deserve to be caged up. We've got to get 'er off this ship."

The agonized roaring sounded again, coming from beneath their feet, several floors below. Bastjan crouched in front of Crake. "We'll be back fer you," he told him. "I promise."

"I'll be waitin'," Crake said.

Alice bent to give Crake a kiss on the top of his head and he smiled at her briefly. Then they helped him out of the pod and down the corridor a little way, settling him against the wall as comfortably as they could.

"Now go on," Crake said, waving the children away.

"I'll be grand."

Bastjan threw himself at Crake, giving the strongman one final hug, and then the children got to their feet and ran.

Wares scuttled in front of them, looking back every few feet to check they were following. With every step, the noise of the trapped Slipskin girl grew louder and louder. Bastjan's head began to fill with thoughts about what might be happening to her and how on earth they were going to help… He stumbled, falling hard on one knee.

"*Whoop*," he said, digging his fingernails into the carpet. He shook his head, trying to clear his thoughts and settle his breathing.

Alice stopped and turned. "Are you all right?"

Bastjan scrambled to his feet. "We jus' need to hurry," he said.

They raced on down the corridor, listening at every turn for the Slipskin's cries. Before long they arrived in the airship's lobby, their feet squeaking on the marble tiles as they dashed across its expanse. To their left the staircase wound up into the trunk, and through its glass they could see the sky outside the ship. It boiled purple, the clouds rolling against the panes, and every few seconds the air was lit with the jagged brightness of a lightning bolt.

"The storm," Bastjan said. He swallowed hard, hoping the windows were sturdier than they looked. "Atwood said it was comin'.'"

"At least it'll keep everyone busy," Alice said, looking up. At the top of the trunk she could make out the curve of the balloon, its chains rattling, and the propellers struggling against the wind.

Bastjan glanced around. The lobby was deserted, but somewhere, not far away, they heard the sound of adult voices raised in argument. "C'mon," he said.

They hurried past the base of the glass trunk towards the back of the lobby, where the next set of descending stairs led into shadow. On the wall above them was a brass plaque.

"Crew only," Alice read. "The hold has to be this way."

As they reached the stairs, a sudden tilting of the ship threw them off balance. Alice and Bastjan found themselves being thrown against the wall, clutching at one another as they struggled upright. They carried on as quickly as they could, keeping a tight hold on the banister.

Another staircase down, and then another, and finally Bastjan was sure the corridor they were running down – and the double doors just ahead – looked familiar. Beyond the doors, Bastjan could hear the shriek of the Slipskin. Without a second's delay he burst through them, Alice and Wares at his heels.

In the centre of the huge room was the lashed-down cage, but it was no longer empty. It now contained a tiny, ragged, wild-eyed girl who bared her sharp teeth and screamed one more time, the noise bursting from her throat seeming far too big to fit inside her. Bastjan's steps faltered as the girl roared at him, her dark eyes filled with fury and hatred.

He glanced at Alice, whose terror was plain. Staring at the Slipskin, she took a step closer until she was right at Bastjan's side. He turned back to the child in the cage. This was the first time they'd seen one another properly and yet Bastjan felt as though he *knew* her. He'd seen her face in his mother's memories. The bracelet connected them to one another – Ester, the Slipskin and him.

"'Sall right," Bastjan said, forcing himself forwards. Despite the iron bars that stood between them, the Slipskin was more frightening than anything he'd ever seen. She was no bigger than him, but somehow that didn't seem to matter.

"Maybe I look like 'er, eh? Maybe I do. An' maybe you're thinkin' of 'er right now, lookin' at me. So I don't blame you fer bein' mad." Bastjan licked his lips nervously and took another step. "I don't know fer sure what happened the day my mum met you, but I do know this. She din't mean to steal nothin' from you. It was an accident – it *had* to be. An' she tried to get it back to you, all those years ago. She just din't make it."

The Slipskin was staring at him now with fixed intensity,

her teeth bared and her chest rising and falling, rising and falling with her deep, rattling breaths. "She died, y'see. My mum. It was an accident." Bastjan sucked his lips in, so hard that it stung, and then he continued. "I miss 'er. Even though I don't really remember 'er, not clearly. In't that odd?"

Bastjan could tell she was listening. He met her strange eyes, dark black and too large in her long, narrow face, and he remembered the pain he'd felt the last time he'd held her bracelet, the searing loss. "I know you've lost someone too. You're all alone, ain't ya? You know how it feels. So let's work together, me an' you, to get you out of that cage. Right? And then we'll work on gettin' your bracelet back. It's what my mum would've wanted." He paused to catch a breath. "An' it's what I want too."

The Slipskin was quiet. Her breathing had calmed. She dropped her hands from the bars of the cage and moved back, flopping on the floor of her prison with her long legs tucked beneath her. Even though her wary eyes never left him, Bastjan took this as a sign that he could approach. He walked slowly to the cage and wrapped his fingers round the same bars the Slipskin had just released, rattling the door as hard as he could – but it was securely locked. He looked around, desperately hoping to see something he could use to break open the door.

"Bastjan!" Alice called, and at the fear in her voice the

boy turned. Two silhouetted figures emerged through a doorway at the far end of the hold. If there had been any doubt about the taller of the two figures, it was quickly put to rest by the familiar sound of a throat being cleared.

"*Ahyuk,*" said Hubert, stepping into the light, and behind him came Cyrus Quinn.

CHAPTER
THIRTY-SEVEN

Hubert's arms were laden with a harness, its leather straps hanging loose beneath it like trailing tentacles. His eyes were clouded with concern – or perhaps shame.

"And here you are again, like a stubborn stain," the ringmaster said, striding past the animal handler. He looked down at Bastjan with a curl to his lip that made the boy's blood rise.

"Let 'er out," Bastjan said, his voice low. "Let 'er out *now*."

"You must be joking," the ringmaster replied. He snapped his fingers at Hubert. "You! Get in there and get that harness on her."

Hubert fumbled at his waist for some keys and Bastjan's heart gave a pang – but before he could make his move, Wares flung himself from Alice's arms and shot towards

Hubert, leaping up to knock the keys right out of his uncharacteristically careless fingers. The dog caught them before they had a chance to hit the floor.

"Ouch! *Ahyuk!*" Hubert shouted, nursing his hand.

Wares dropped the keys at Bastjan's feet and the boy crouched to pick them up. The ringmaster surged forwards, his teeth bared in a rictus of fury. But before he could get anywhere close to the boy, a familiar voice rang through the room.

"Come one inch closer to him, Cyrus, and you'll be lookin' for yer teeth," said Crake. Bastjan whipped his head round, his mouth falling open in amazement. Crake, pale but determined, stood in the doorway, and in each huge hand he held a fire-axe, sharp and deadly. Crake flicked his gaze towards Bastjan and the boy could see how hard he was fighting to stay upright.

The ringmaster froze, his fury replaced by a sneer. "You wouldn't dare, Cornelius."

Crake made no reply. He simply hefted one huge axe, tossing it into the air. It spun, slowly, before falling again. He caught it, his eyes never leaving Quinn's.

"Crake, we got to get 'er out," Bastjan said.

Quinn darted forwards, his hand raised to strike Bastjan, but Hubert was right behind him. Taking hold of either end of the harness, Hubert threw it over the ringmaster's head. Using the harness as a restraint, Hubert compressed Quinn's arms tightly against his sides. With one quick move, he passed a thick leather strap across the ringmaster's face, where it made a very effective gag.

"*Ahyuk*," the animal handler said into his former boss's ear. "That's enough now, Mr Quinn. The boy's right. I ain't havin' nothin' more to do with harmin' kids." Bastjan saw him glance at the girl in the cage. "An' that includes the one we stole."

Quinn's eyes filled with fury, but he said nothing.

Hubert looked at Bastjan, his eyes urgent. "The box is in his right breast pocket. *Ahyuk!*" he called, and the boy pushed himself up off the floor. The ringmaster aimed a kick as Bastjan drew near, but Bastjan dodged it.

Just as Bastjan felt his fingers close around his mother's box, Quinn made a desperate grab for him, freeing one hand from the harness and wrapping it around the boy's forearm. Bastjan dug his fingernails into the back of Quinn's hand, scratching hard enough to draw beads of blood. Quinn released him with a hiss.

Bastjan turned away and opened the lid. His fingers brushed against his mother's treasures – the notebook, the key, the feather – and finally they rested on the bracelet. Placing the box on the floor, he held up the bracelet and walked towards the cage. Inside, the Slipskin was breathing fast, her skinny chest going up and down like a pair of bellows as she watched Bastjan.

"I'm sorry," Bastjan said, blinking hard. "An' my mum would 'ave been too." The Slipskin's eyes were wide, her gaze flickering between Bastjan's face and the bracelet in his hand. Slowly, with his other hand, Bastjan held up the key to her cage and the Slipskin reared back, chirping out something that sounded like a warning.

"It's all right!" Alice said, appearing at Bastjan's side. Slowly, his eyes on the Slipskin, Bastjan slid the key into the lock. With a squeal, the cage door opened outwards. Together, the children stepped inside.

The Slipskin stood, trembling, at the far side of the cage. Emotions flicked across her face – fear and want, trust and terror and rage – as she looked between Bastjan and Alice.

Bastjan slid the key back into his pocket and held out the bracelet, taking a couple of slow steps towards the Slipskin. He extended his arm as far as he could, the strap quivering in mid-air as it dangled from his fingers. He closed his mind to the screams of agony and grief – and then he glanced at the Slipskin's face. Her features were contorted and he knew he wasn't the only one who could hear the cries. His eyes slid closed and for a moment it felt like he and the Slipskin were together, hiding in the dark, while somewhere nearby her mother screamed her last…

"Go on," Alice said to the caged girl, her voice calm. Her words pulled Bastjan out of his thoughts and he opened his eyes. "You can take it now. Nobody's going to hurt you."

The Slipskin crept forwards slowly, dropping to all fours. Her wounded leg was bandaged, a pinkish stain marring the bright white cloth, and she dragged it stiffly behind her. As she neared them, Bastjan and Alice inched towards her, crouching down as they got close.

For a few long heartbeats, the Slipskin's eyes searched their faces. Then the girl reached out – but not for Bastjan. She brushed her fingers against Alice's face instead, her touch on the firemark as gentle as a butterfly's wing.

Alice gasped, a jolt of some strange power passing through her body. Her skin hummed where the Slipskin's fingers had been and she gazed into the Slipskin's eyes. They were so large, and so dark, that Alice could see herself reflected in them. Her firemark was there, of course, bright and bold and part of her. Instead of closing her eyes or looking away, she smiled to see it – to see herself – and the Slipskin let out a throaty chuckle in response. Slowly, the humming feeling in her skin drained away.

"I think," Alice whispered, blinking, "if I were you, and had your power, and I could look like anything I wanted…" Her smile grew wider and a tear rolled down over her firemarked cheek. "I think I'd choose to look exactly like myself."

Alice turned to Bastjan. He gave her a companionable nudge and she nodded at him, wiping her cheeks dry. Then they looked back at the Slipskin.

Bastjan held the bracelet out once more, his hand trembling a little less this time. "Here," he said.

The Slipskin reached out and Bastjan laid the strap of woven hair on her palm. The pain in his head lessened a little as the Slipskin held up the bracelet, crowing proudly. Bastjan couldn't help but smile and Alice did too, hiccupping away the last of her tears. The Slipskin wrapped the bracelet around her arm and fastened the clasp, and the noises in Bastjan's head finally hushed.

Then the Slipskin glanced back at Bastjan and his smile faded. As she got to her feet, standing awkwardly on her wounded leg, she looked just like the drawing in his mother's book. Strong and powerful, otherworldly, her eyes began to change from black to glowing gold, alight with knowledge beyond anything humans could imagine. From outside the cage, Bastjan heard Quinn spluttering with rage as he fought to free himself from Hubert's gag, but he ignored him.

"We got to get 'er out of 'ere. Off the ship, I mean," Bastjan muttered.

"Is … is she going to change?" Alice said.

"I ain't one for gamblin'," Bastjan replied, "but if I was, my money'd be on it."

He scrambled for the cage door, pulling Alice with him, and together they ran straight for Crake. The cage door clicked shut behind them.

The strongman wobbled on his feet, his face greyer than it should be. "We've got to get the ship on the ground," he said, staring at the Slipskin. She throbbed with power now, like a snake about to strike, and her eyes, fully golden, were glowing.

"Prob'ly should've done that bit first, really," Bastjan said, and Crake cracked a grin.

Behind them Hubert released the ringmaster's gag and Quinn slumped forwards in his restraints. His face was red and slick with sweat, and his eyes were narrowed but still sharp. Bastjan looked away.

As he did so, his gaze fell on something attached to the wall by a shining metal bracket, something with a brass horn and a long, flexible hose. Something he'd seen before, elsewhere on board the ship.

"The speakin' tubes! Crake, there's a speakin' tube up in the control room – I saw it! We can shout up an' tell Atwood to get this thing down!"

Crake and the children quickly made their way to the wall. Crake leaned one of his axes against it as he pulled the speaking tube free. The apparatus whistled. "Hello?" he shouted into the horn. "Atwood! Are ya there, man?"

For several long moments, nothing happened. Then, finally, there was an answering whistle and a tiny voice, so low they could barely hear, replied. "Who's this?"

"It's Crake! We're in the hold. You've got to get the ship down!"

Frustrating seconds passed before the reply was heard. "Not without Mr Quinn's say-so."

"But the storm!" Bastjan shouted into the mouthpiece. "The storm'll wreck us, even if the Slipskin don't."

"The Slipskin?" Atwood sounded cautious and afraid.

"She's loose!" Crake roared. "Get us down, quick as you can, or none of us will survive what might happen if she changes while she's still on board."

The speaking tube in Crake's hand whistled again and nothing more was said. The strongman hung it back in its wall bracket and they braced themselves. Crake and Bastjan exchanged a worried glance.

Then, without warning, everything began to tilt.

CHAPTER
THIRTY-EIGHT

The Slipskin stumbled, grabbing the bars of her cage for support. From behind, Bastjan heard Hubert shouting. The next thing he knew, Crake's arms were round him, pulling him and Alice back into a corner of the hold. Unsecured cargo began to tumble all around, boxes and crates smashing as they fell, and somewhere there was a *crash* as glass toppled over, shards scattering all over the floor.

Bastjan could see the huge loading doors, held shut by a large metal bolt, rattling on their hinges as the ship came down. He glanced at the Slipskin. The door to her cage wasn't swinging with the movement of the ship; it seemed to have locked itself, and he recalled the *click* it had made as he and Alice had made their escape. The Slipskin glowed from within with a golden light, which looked like it could

330

spill over at any moment. Her gaze was fixed on the doors. Beyond them lay her freedom and she didn't look like she was willing to wait for it much longer.

Bastjan pulled himself out of Crake's embrace and ran, dodging falling objects and fighting for balance. He heard Alice and Crake calling him back, and Wares's fearful yapping, but he knew what he had to do.

His fingers shook as he reached the shuddering doors. The bolt was jammed through two metal loops and attached by a short chain to a panel nailed to one of the doors. Bastjan hauled at the chain with all his strength. The great bolt began to shift, lifting upwards, and Bastjan pushed at it until finally, and with surprising speed, it popped right out of the loops.

And then, with a groan of metal, the doors to the airship's cargo hold began to grind open. Bastjan flailed for something to hold on to as the wind sucked at his hair and clothes and buffeted against his breath. Beneath him, all he could see were mountains, jagged and snow-capped, far too close for comfort. Just as he felt sure he was about to tip forwards into emptiness, he felt someone grab his hand firmly, pulling him to safety.

They both tumbled against the wall in a jumble of limbs and hair and muffled apologies.

"You're welcome," Alice muttered, pushing him off.

"Where are we?" Bastjan said, staring out at the view.

The mountains were rushing by beneath the ship, coming closer and closer with every minute, and it couldn't be long until they'd come in to land.

A noise from the cage drew their attention towards the Slipskin. Her eyes were fixed on the outside world too, reflecting the white of the snow beyond the door. She blinked, slowly and purposefully, and her glow intensified, wrapping around her body like a shroud. Then it disappeared as quickly as if the shroud had been pulled away – and when it did, the Slipskin girl was gone. In her place was a tiny bird, no bigger than a wren, small enough to flit between the bars of the cage with ease.

The bird flew to Bastjan and perched on his knee. She looked up at him with her golden-brown head to one side, her shining eyes regarding him curiously. And then she slipped through the cargo door, disappearing into the sky so quickly that she seemed to vanish completely. Bastjan watched her go, and from somewhere very deep, he felt a bubble of loss and pride and sorrow rising up through him.

"Bye," he whispered, his throat aching. "I 'ope I did all right, Mum."

In the next second, the airship landed, hitting the snowy mountainside with a *crump*. Alice grabbed hold of Bastjan again as he almost hurtled out of the door. They held one another tight as the ship skidded along the rocky ground for several hundred yards. Finally, the airship gave one last lurch and settled, metal groaning all around as it found purchase on the mountain.

Bastjan turned to see Crake coming towards him on unsteady feet. Empty-handed, his axes lost in the collision, he slumped down beside the children.

A noise made them turn to see Quinn scrambling to his feet, pulling loose the harness that Hubert had used to overpower him. The animal handler was lying on the floor, his face slick with blood down one side. It looked like he'd been hit by something, perhaps one of the crates that had been dislodged in the crash-landing. Quinn bent over Hubert's prone form, pulling something free from the unconscious handler's belt, and then staggered forwards. After a step or two Quinn stopped again, bending to pick up an object from the floor.

As the ringmaster slid the object into his pocket, Bastjan recognized it – his mother's box. His lungs were suddenly tight, as though drawn shut with thread, and the words he wanted to shout at his stepfather were stoppered up before they reached his tongue. Without so much as a backwards glance, Quinn staggered out through the doors and into the morning light, his eyes fixed on the sky. In his hand was the harpoon gun he'd pulled from Hubert's belt, its point shining and death-sharp.

Bastjan looked out to see Quinn fighting his way through the knee-deep snow as he skirted around the ship, getting further away every second.

"*Whoop*," Bastjan said, shaking his head in irritation at the sound. He coughed, painfully deep, and got to his feet. "C'mon," he said. "We ain't jus' goin' to let him go, are we?"

"What harm can he do now?" Crake said. The big man winced as he began to drag himself up.

"Harm? He can do plenty! He's got Hubert's gun. He's goin' after 'er again – you *know* 'e is. Please, Crake. *Please.*" He sucked hard on his lip. "And my mum's box, Crake. I got to get it back."

Crake's body throbbed with pain, but the strongman pushed it aside as he got to his feet, shaking with effort. He leaned heavily on Bastjan's shoulders.

"What about Hubert?" Alice asked, as Crake held out a hand to her.

"Help's comin'," Crake said, nodding his head towards the sound of voices. Bastjan turned. Some of the crew members were entering the hold from the other side, smashing their way through the doors that led into the body of the ship.

"We gotta go," Bastjan said. The big man nodded and began to hobble forwards, supported on one side by Alice and on the other by Bastjan. Together, they picked their way over the chaos of the upturned room and when they reached the doors Crake slid to the ground first, stretching up to help the children down.

They hurried through the snow, following the

ringmaster's tracks around the ship. The air was thin and cold as a knife. All around them mountains rose into the sky. The ship had come down in a snowfield, held in a hollow between the peaks like sand in a cupped palm.

"There!" Bastjan said. The ringmaster was a hundred yards ahead of them, kicking up snow with his boots as he strode across the frozen ground. The ramp, beneath which Bastjan and his friends had hidden the day before, had been wrenched open in the collision. As they watched, someone appeared in the opening. He jumped towards the ground, landing softly in the snow.

"Who's that?" Alice asked as the man came towards Quinn.

"Lahiri," Crake answered. "He does the king pole."

"The what?" Alice asked, frowning.

"The first pole to go up when we're raisin' the big top," Bastjan muttered, keeping his eyes on the men. The ringmaster was shouting something at Lahiri, who looked confused. Lahiri's hand strayed to his belt.

"I said *now*!" The ringmaster's shout was loud enough to carry. Lahiri fumbled at his belt and unfastened a ring of keys, which he handed to Quinn. Once he had the keys, Quinn struck Lahiri with the butt of his harpoon gun, hitting him smartly on the side of the head. Lahiri crumpled to the ground.

Bastjan's breath began to come in thick gloopy gusts

once more. He and Alice shared a horrified look.

"What on earth is he playin' at?" Crake murmured, and then something struck Bastjan with almost as much force as the harpoon gun had struck Lahiri. *The pods*. Marlowe, the rigger who'd tried to lock him up, had had a set of keys just like the one Lahiri had just handed to Quinn.

He looked at the airship, lying on its side. Its hull seemed undamaged, but the balloon was slumped against its tethers, gradually deflating. The pods, hanging sideways, were still attached to the back of the ship, rocking slightly on their moorings. Bastjan remembered what Marlowe had said: *There are controls to fly it, o' course, but that's no good to youse lot. You need to 'ave a clue what you're doin' first…*

"The pods," he said to Crake. "The ringmaster's goin' to fly one. He *is* goin' after her!"

Before the strongman had a chance to reply, Bastjan was off, chasing after Quinn as fast as he could, his legs pistoning through the snow.

"Look!" Alice gasped as she and Crake scrambled after him.

The ringmaster had climbed up a bank of snow and churned-up dirt and launched himself from it, landing awkwardly on top of the nearest pod. He reached down to undo the lock on the pod's small round escape hatch using the keys he'd taken from Lahiri. It fell open heavily. As Bastjan and his friends drew near, the ringmaster swung himself through.

Bastjan scrambled up the snowbank and launched himself from the top of it, grabbing hold of the hatch's handle just as Quinn tried to haul it closed. The hatch was made of thick, heavy metal and Quinn didn't look at all pleased to be pulling against Bastjan's weight too. The boy clung to the door, staring up into the pod – and into the ringmaster's enraged face.

"If you know what's good for you, *thing*," Quinn snarled, "you'll let go of this door and leave me in peace."

"Not a chance," Bastjan wheezed. "*Whoop*."

"Come on, Mr Quinn, sir," Crake said, gasping as he reached the pod. "Give it up. It's time."

"What would you know about it being *time*," Quinn snapped at Crake. "You should've been retired years ago."

"Fair enough," Crake said, with a shrug. "And I would have gone with me honour intact. Don't you want to do the same?"

"*Honour?*" Quinn spat. "What has honour to do with anything? I've discovered the most incredible headline act anywhere on earth and you expect me to step away from it?" He stared at Bastjan with hard, sharp eyes. "I thought it was in your blood, boy. The circus. I couldn't have been more wrong."

Bastjan took a deep breath. "I know what's in my blood," he said, trying not to lose his grip on the hatch.

"My *mum*'s in it. An' she wouldn't've let you do this."

Quinn coughed out a humourless laugh. "Your *mum*," he sneered, "performed with you before you could even *walk*, for goodness' sake. There was nothing she wouldn't have done, if an audience would applaud her for it."

"She'd never 'ave hurt me! She'd never 'ave hurt anyone!" Bastjan shouted, tears filling his eyes. "An' I'm sure she wouldn't've gone up if you hadn't *made* her."

The ringmaster snorted. "Me? I didn't make her do the Dance of the Snowflakes. In fact, the act wasn't even my idea." He leaned forwards out of the pod, his eyes narrowed. "It was *hers*."

Bastjan felt like someone had punctured him. "What?"

Quinn's face shone with malice. "If you don't believe me, ask your friend Cornelius. I'm sure he remembers." He turned to Crake. "Don't you? Don't you remember our dear Ester and how she *begged* me to put her and the baby on top billing? How she assured me it would get the crowds in? And it did – for a while." The ringmaster chuckled. "Yes indeed, I'm sure old Crake remembers that all too well."

Bastjan turned to his friend. He felt as though all the blood in his body had begun to drain out through his heels. His hands, on the hatch, were numb. "Crake? What's 'e talkin' about?"

The strongman was grey in the face, staring at the ringmaster with hatred in his eyes.

CHAPTER
THIRTY-NINE

"Your mother loved you, lad," Crake said.

"And old Crake here loved *her*," the ringmaster jeered.
"But she chose me. Didn't she, Cornelius? Not for love, of
course. But for everything that came with being married
to a ringmaster. She wanted the circus. She wanted fame.
She wanted to be known all over the world. The Girl Who
Flew!" Quinn waved his hand in the air. "So marriage to
a moth-eaten circus strongman wasn't part of her plan –
whatever her *heart* might have told her." He turned to
Bastjan. "Your beloved mum endangered you every night
of your life and she did it because she wanted to."

"Because *you* wouldn't let 'er out of a silly, hasty promise
that she made in desperation!" Crake shouted, so suddenly
that Bastjan jumped. "She was newly widowed, in need
of a home an' a job to provide fer a young baby, an' she

was willin' to do whatever she had to, to keep her child safe. She promised you a headline act that nobody could top, an' she delivered you the Dance of the Snowflakes. She only meant to perform it once, but when she showed you what she could do, you wouldn't let 'er stop. Nothin' was good enough – not even the new act she was workin' on, the one that would've let 'er keep the child on the ground, where he belonged."

"I wasn't going to allow her to take my act away," Quinn replied, his voice tight with rage. "The Dance of the Snowflakes *made* me."

Crake blinked, a new understanding dawning on his face. "I heard you, shoutin' at her the day she fell," the strongman said. "You found out about her wantin' to leave. Didn't you?"

Quinn's face twisted. "She wanted to visit her *mama*, she said. But she wouldn't tell me when she was coming back. I knew, then. She was taking her act somewhere else. I couldn't allow that."

"She weren't goin' to any new circus!" Bastjan said. "She jus' wanted to *fix* things."

Quinn turned to the boy. "So she wanted to give up her talent and stop performing?" he said. "How's that any better? She would've ruined me."

Bastjan's mouth was tight as he stared at his stepfather. "Yeah. Well, you managed that all by yerself."

A sudden noise from the sky made them all look up – a terrible shriek. Bastjan saw a gigantic shape against the weak morning sun. A spiralling tail covered with sharp barbs, claws that shone like metal and a pair of wings, their feathers like sharp plates of armour, which were wide enough to block out the light. The creature's head was huge, with a curved, powerful beak, and her golden eyes glittered. *The Slipskin.*

Bastjan had no idea what sort of creature she'd become – perhaps one that only existed in her nightmares. She was circling the downed airship, her massive head turning from side to side as though she were looking for something.

"What's she doing?" Alice said. Wares, at her feet, growled at the wheeling Slipskin and then took off at a run, yapping at its shadow. "No! Wares! Come *back* here!" Alice yelled, racing after the dog.

Cyrus Quinn growled, regaining his grip on the handle of the pod door and hauling it up with massive effort. Bastjan's hand slipped; he landed with a *whumpf* in the snow.

"Wait!" he shouted, desperation making his chest burn. *I can't jus' let him leave!* "Wait jus' one minute! You made me a *promise.*" Bastjan was sure he could see the corner of his mother's box poking out of Quinn's pocket, just out of reach. "You promised me my mum's things."

Quinn let the door fall open a crack. "So I did. I'm afraid, however, that in this case my word is not my bond."

"Then take me with you!" Bastjan shouted.

Crake turned to Bastjan, incredulous. "What? You can't mean that. Son, you're not thinkin' right!"

Bastjan didn't look at Crake. He spoke again, the words thick and tight in his throat, pushing painfully out through his mouth. "Take me."

After a heartbeat's pause, Quinn reached down and grabbed Bastjan by the collar, hauling him aboard the pod. Then he reached for the control panel on the wall and pressed a button. Gas-powered engines kicked into life, blasting Crake off his feet. The clamps attaching the pod to the side of the airship released one by one, each with a hollow *clunk*.

Crake scrambled to his feet as the pod began to lift off. He grabbed hold of the hatch, gripping a pipe on the side of the airship with the other hand, and Bastjan saw the strain on his face as the force of the pod's engines grew stronger and stronger.

"Please! Stop! You're goin' to *kill* 'im!" he shouted.

"What a capital idea," Quinn said, pulling out the harpoon gun. Without missing a beat he braced himself to fire and shot Crake in the chest. The harpoon hit with a strange-sounding *clang*, skittering off into the snow.

The strongman finally released his grip and fell to the

ground, and the pod rocketed into the sky. It righted itself as it flew and Bastjan dropped to the floor. His lungs felt like they were slowly filling with water. All he could think about was the look on Crake's face – the fear, the sorrow and the betrayal. *An' now Quinn's shot 'im*, Bastjan thought, despair swallowing him up. *I ain't never goin' to get a chance to tell 'im how sorry I am…* He wiped his nose on the back of his hand and swallowed hard, pushing the pain away just enough to keep going. Getting his mother's box back wasn't worth this – it wasn't worth any of it. *But I can still save the Slipskin.*

"Come on!" Quinn shouted, steadying himself against the pod's erratic movements. He tucked the harpoon gun under one arm as he reached for the hatch. "Help me get the door shut!"

Bastjan pushed himself to his feet, finding his balance as he would on a swaying rope. He could feel the pod gaining height with every second, but he was not afraid. Not any more. As he came within range of the ringmaster, he bent low and threw himself at the man, almost knocking him flat.

"Take care, you fool! You'll have us both overboard!" Quinn tore Bastjan away from him, his eyes filled with rage.

"You're *not* goin' to hurt anyone else!" Bastjan roared. The noise of wind in the tiny pod was overwhelming.

It was hard to breathe and the pod's movement was dangerously unpredictable. They had to get the hatch shut, or soon they wouldn't be doing much of anything at all.

"I'm not going to *hurt* her, you simpleton! I'm going to give her a new life, one she couldn't dream of in that wreck of a city she called home." Quinn's eyes searched the boy's face. "I thought you were throwing your lot in with me," he said, blinking. Bastjan could have sworn he looked disappointed – almost wounded.

"I never wanted anythin' to do wi' you," Bastjan said. "My mum tried to get away from you an' she died before she could. I ain't goin' to let you destroy her memory too."

A shadow fell over the pod. They both turned to look out of the hatch, which was flapping and groaning in the wind. The Slipskin was outside, flying beside them. Her gigantic golden eye peered in through the door. Taking advantage of the momentary distraction, Bastjan launched himself at Quinn once more, shoving his hand into the ringmaster's pocket.

His fingers found the familiar shape of his mother's treasure box, but the ringmaster jerked away before Bastjan could tear it free. With a savage kick, Quinn threw Bastjan off. He fumbled for his gun, a crazed look in his eyes as he slid a new harpoon into the chamber.

"You're not goin' to use my mum's mistake to hurt

anybody else!" Bastjan cried. Heedless of the gun, he ran straight for the ringmaster. A sudden jerk of the pod threw off Quinn's aim, sending the gun skidding over the floor. But just as Bastjan reached him, Quinn shoved the boy hard, knocking him out through the open hatch.

The heavy metal door hit the side of Bastjan's head as he fell and then everything in the world went dark.

"Wares! What are you *doing?*" Alice finally caught up with her runaway dog as he stopped short, staring at the sky and barking furiously. Alice looked up. The Slipskin was right overhead, her gigantic wings spread wide, and it looked like she was about to do battle with the escape pod. Her head was reared back, her beak open. Alice watched in horror as the creature readied herself to attack – and then Alice saw something even more terrible.

A shape, falling through the pod's hatch, tumbling to the ground. *Bastjan.*

"Crake!" she screamed. "*Crake!*"

The pod hadn't reached a very great height, but Bastjan was falling like a doll – he was floppy and uncoordinated, and he looked completely unconscious, or worse. Alice felt as though she was going to be sick. She turned and looked for Crake and there he was – getting unsteadily to his feet beside the airship, clutching at his chest. Blood poured between his fingers and as he staggered towards her, Alice could see the glint of metal, like a piece of armour buried in his flesh.

"Crake, he's falling!"

As if she'd heard Alice's cry, the Slipskin wheeled around, her body twisting in mid-air into something sinuous and quick, a creature thin as a ribbon yet wide as a river. She wrapped a fold of herself around Bastjan and turned her head to look at Crake, struggling across the snowy, rock-strewn ground. The Slipskin floated down from the sky, spinning gently in the air as though it were water and she some strange type of fish, uncurling herself once she was close enough to the ground for Bastjan to roll, unconscious, out of her grip. Her golden eyes met Alice's for the briefest moment. Then, enveloped in her glow, she resumed her former shape, her armoured wings and terrifying beak shining in the sunlight. She pushed away from the ground and flapped her wings, gaining height as she focused on the pod once again.

Crake ran to the spot where Bastjan lay. Alice wasn't far behind. The strongman's shirt was torn and his chest and arm were bleeding, but still he ran. He fell to his knees beside Bastjan, clutching the boy to his heart and sobbed, huge tears rolling down his cheeks.

"I've got you, darlin' boy," the strongman wept into Bastjan's hair. "I've got you now and I ain't never lettin' go."

Bastjan's head was gashed and his face was grey. He was out cold. Alice placed her hand in front of his mouth; his breaths were shallow and fast, but he was breathing.

A shriek from the sky overhead made Alice and Crake crane their heads back to look. The Slipskin was doing battle with the still-rising pod, trying to bat it out of the air with her wings. Alice could just see the figure of Cyrus Quinn standing in the open hatch, the harpoon gun in his hand.

The creature raised her massive talons and took the pod between them as though she were a bird of prey catching a mouse. Then, with a screech of metal and the noise of smashing glass the pod, and the ringmaster within it, were reduced to smithereens, crushed into nothing by the mighty, unstoppable power of the Slipskin.

Crake reached out to Alice and pulled her close, protecting both the children as debris began to rain from the sky, pieces of the smashed pod landing in the snow all around them. Alice whimpered as the gun, its harpoon still loaded, landed a few feet away.

The Slipskin gave one final cry, circling the airship one last time, and then she was gone over the mountaintops. Alice watched her disappear into the distance. Tears rolled down her face, pooling at her chin, where Wares licked them off. She buried her face in his soft fur and tried to breathe normally, her heart aching with every thud.

When she finally looked up, something shining and blue caught her eye, lying in the snow not far from where Bastjan had fallen. Her breath hitched as she realized what it was, and she pushed herself away from Crake, scrambling across the ground on her hands and knees.

As she got close she could see that she'd been right – it was a fragment of the lid of Bastjan's box, the fish mostly intact. She scanned the ground – here was the key and there the feather. A few feet further over were the tattered remains of his mother's notebook. Her eye was caught by a fluttering in the whiteness; it was the childhood sketch of the Slipskin girl and Alice hurried to catch it before it blew away.

She gathered as much as she could find, and by the time she made it back to Crake and Bastjan, she found they were no longer alone. Atwood and Clement were approaching, their faces contrite. Not far behind was Lahiri, looking dazed. Hubert was there too, being helped to walk by some of the other rousties.

Following them was a woman in a black-and-white robe, her face surrounded by a veil of stiff white linen, with a bulging bag in her hands. Beside her was another woman, dressed in the same fashion. The second woman stopped beside Crake and wordlessly asked for Bastjan to be placed into her arms while the first got to her knees in the snow and opened her bag. There looked to be bandages and medicines inside.

Alice slipped the remains of Bastjan's mother's belongings into her pocket and reached for Crake's hand. She didn't let go, not even when the women lifted Bastjan in their arms and took him away.

CHAPTER
FORTY

Silent snow fell all around the mountain hospital. Alice hadn't left Bastjan's bedside since the moment he'd been brought in. His head was tightly bandaged and his face was still drawn and pale. He hadn't yet woken up.

"There is someone to see you," said a dour voice. The words were English, but the accent was not. Wares, tucked beneath Bastjan's bed, gave a small *gruff* of irritation, but settled as soon as Alice reached her hand down for him to lick her fingers. She turned to see a starched-looking nurse peering at her disapprovingly. Alice knew how lucky they'd been to have landed so close to this mountain refuge, one which was more used to dealing with lost mountaineers and their broken legs than boys with injuries like Bastjan's. Still, sometimes she wished the quiet, forbidding women who ran it weren't quite so unfriendly.

"Someone to see me?" Alice asked, frowning. "Are you sure?"

"You were requested by name," the nurse replied.

"Who—" Alice said, but the nurse sniffed and turned away. As she left, a small well-dressed gentleman appeared in the doorway. He wore a tweed suit and held his hat in his hands. His moustache was brushed, his hair was oiled and his eyeglasses were polished to a sheen. His cheeks were red and his eyes were weary, and he wore an expression Alice had never seen on his face, not in all the years she'd known him – one of sorrow and joy and love, all mixed together. At the sight of him she began to tremble and her teeth clenched tight.

"Grandfather," Alice whispered. She squeezed Bastjan's fingers – she was, as always, holding his hand.

"Darling," Lord Patten said, stepping into the room. "I'm so glad to see you."

"What are you doing here?" Alice asked, recoiling slightly. Even if she wanted to leave Bastjan's side, she had nowhere to run.

"I've been looking for you since the moment you left, Alice," said her grandfather. He walked to the end of Bastjan's bed and placed his hat on it. Then he stood, flexing his hands as though he didn't know what to do with them. "I looked everywhere. I made inquiries with various –" he gestured vaguely – "*street* people, some of whom had seen you. I paid a large sum to a woman named Palmer in return for information about your whereabouts, to no avail. Then I received a telegram telling me you'd, somewhat unofficially, joined a circus, from someone purporting to be its ringmaster." He gave a quick, incredulous laugh. "And here you are, in a mountain hospital in the Italian Alps. And here I am, so grateful to have you back." He smiled, briefly, but Alice couldn't return it.

"You don't have me back, Grandfather," she told him. "I've found my people."

"Those circus folk encamped outside? They're keeping vigil, you know. For this boy." Lord Patten paused. "But they won't be allowed inside, Alice. The nuns will not permit it."

Alice's jaw clenched. One of the nuns spoke French and Alice had tried her hardest to explain how important Bastjan's family were to him, but the woman had been unmoved. It was lucky she'd allowed Alice to stay by his bedside. *I don't look like I belong in a circus, I suppose.* "I'm staying here until Bastjan gets better. We can go to them instead," Alice said, turning back to her friend. Bastjan was frowning in his sleep and Alice squeezed his hand a little more firmly.

"Come with me, Alice," Lord Patten said. "Come home."

"I won't go where I'm not wanted," Alice replied. "You

made your feelings very clear, Grandfather."

Lord Patten took a step or two towards his granddaughter and placed one hand on her shoulder. "I was wrong, Alice. I'm sorry." His voice wobbled a little. "You look so like your dear father, you know, and I was very fond of that boy. He would be extremely proud of you."

Alice swallowed hard. Her nose ran and she turned away to wipe it on her sleeve. "I'm not leaving him," she told her grandfather, looking up at him coldly. "I'm not leaving Bastjan. If you're going to make me come with you, then you're taking him too." She stared at her grandfather, hoping this condition would be enough to send him away forever.

"I've already settled his bill, darling," Lord Patten said. "The nuns are preparing his papers now, for discharge."

Alice's eyes widened, and her mouth fell open. "But what about his family? I can't take him away from them."

"I can pay for excellent medical treatment in England," Lord Patten said. "He needs expert care and he won't receive it here. But if he comes with me – if you both come with me – I'll see that he gets better, Alice. I swear it."

Alice turned back to Bastjan. His frown had become a definite wrinkle and, as she watched, his eyes fluttered open. "Bastjan?" she whispered. "Can you hear me?"

Bastjan blinked at her, confused. There was no recognition in his gaze. "Who're you?" he said, in a creaky voice.

Quickly, Alice fetched some water from the bedside locker and put the glass to his lips. He drank thirstily, then let his head fall back on the pillow.

"I'm Alice," she told him. "Do you remember me?"

Bastjan looked at her for a long moment, taking in every detail of her face. Finally, he shook his head. "All I remember is fallin'," he whispered, his eyes fluttering closed again.

"Bastjan?" Alice said, tears pricking her eyes. "Bastjan?" But there was no answer. Bastjan had fallen unconscious again, into that dark place where nobody could follow.

"I've already spoken to one of the men outside," Lord Patten said, his voice low. "Large, red-headed. He told me he knew the boy well. I've explained that I want to bring him to England, pay for his treatment, and he eventually gave his blessing."

"Crake," Alice whispered, her tears falling.

"That was his name," Lord Patten said. "Genial fellow. Ex-army. Showed me where the nuns had bandaged him up; he was lucky it was on the site of an old war wound. The metal plate he'd had inserted during his time in uniform saved his life the other day, it seems. Enjoyed his company very much. So does that convince you?" He paused before continuing. "Your choices are to stay here and watch your friend decline, my dear, or bring him home with me and watch him thrive. What will it be?"

There was a knock at the door and Lord Patten turned as one of the nuns entered. Alice heard some low, mumbled conversation, in a mixture of Italian and English. Then, out of the corner of her eye, she watched her grandfather take out a pen and sign his name on a piece of paper. The nun nodded and left the room.

"You promise to care for him," she said.

"Like a grandson," Lord Patten assured her. "My carriage is waiting outside to take us to the Paris train. We can be there by nightfall and on the first boat across the Channel in the morning."

"And Crake really has given his permission?"

"He told me to give you this." Lord Patten patted his pocket until he found what he was looking for. He drew out a tiny key, a delicate enamelled fish on its shaft. "He said you'd know what it was."

Alice nodded, taking the key from her grandfather's fingers. She slid it into her own pocket, where she'd been keeping the shards of Bastjan's treasure box, and the remnants of his mother's possessions, until she could give them back to him. She had the battered remains of the notebook, including the sketch of the Slipskin, the broken feather and the large key made of dark metal which unlocked a door that, one day, she hoped she'd help Bastjan find. Alice stroked some strands of stray hair away from his forehead and then looked up at her grandfather.

"I also promised Lieutenant Crake we would return the boy to his circus family as soon as he's made a full recovery. I intend to keep that promise," Lord Patten said, his gaze steady. "They plan to travel home once they've completed repairs to their airship and go back on their performing circuit, or whatever it's called, once they've found a new ringmaster. But my promise is on the condition that you stay with me from now on. No more running away, my dear."

Alice looked down at Bastjan's pallid face. She knew she had no choice, but she tried to pretend she was making one anyway – and she hoped it was one Bastjan would forgive her for.

"Let's go home," she whispered.

I don't know who they are, these folk. They keep callin' me by the wrong name too – *Bastjan*, they keep sayin', like I should know who that is. That ain't me. I ain't got no name like that. There's a hole where my name is, where everythin' is, everythin' except gettin' away. There's somethin' I got to look for, an' it ain't here.

They're kind – or at least, they're *tryin'* to be. The girl, Alice, keeps showin' me this pile of rubbish she keeps with 'er all the time. Keys, an' a feather, drawin's an' pictures an' a pile of scribbles I can't even read. She keeps talkin' about "Ducrow's Acre", an' how she wants to bring me there. I en't got a clue what she's on about. She looks so hopeful, an' I hate tellin' her it all means nothin' to me. So instead I smile a bit an' say things like "Yeah, I reckon I'm rememberin' – no doubt it'll all come back to me soon." An' then she smiles an' leaves me in peace, fer a while at least.

We're on a train. A fancy one. It's got shiny taps in the bathroom an' little curtains on the windows an' someone to hand you a plate of grub at mealtimes, but I know I don't belong. Alice's grandad, *he* belongs. He's forever wrinklin' up 'is nose when I slip Alice's dog, Wares, a bit of grub underneath the table, or when I forget which fork to use. I know, if 'e could, 'e'd like to see the back of me.

Sometimes, I do get flashes of ... *somethin'*. Memories? I don't know. But always, beneath it all, there's fallin'.

"Bastjan?" the girl says, in the mornin', when we arrive. We step out of the train station an' the day's bright. It hurts my eyes. The buildin's are tall and the streets are wide, with trees everywhere. Horses pull carriages. Men an' ladies walk, arm in arm. People play music on the street. Someone juggles and it feels like a jab in my brain. *I know that*, I think. *That's mine.* "Bastjan, we're here."

You stupid thing! The voice roars in my head, the one that's always there, the one I've got to listen to. I don't know who this Bastjan is. I know my name, an' it ain't Bastjan. *Thing. Thing. Thing.* That's all I know.

"Where?"

"Paris," she says. "We're getting the boat from here. The boat home."

She smiles at me, then, an' I smile back, but I got one thing absolutely sure. Wherever this girl's home is, it ain't mine. I don't remember where home is. Home is a nowhere place. I can never find it by standin' still, is all I know. Home moves.

An' then there's a boat right beside us, tall as a mountain, shinin' in the mornin' light. It floats in the water, up an' down an' up an' down, an' something else in my memory feels like a string bein' plucked. But before I can think about it, it's gone.

"The Northern Jewel line," says Alice's grandad, in 'is shiny shoes an' dapper coat. "This will see us home, you mark my words. And then we'll have you right as rain, young man."

He's booked us a suite on the ship, three cabins all stuck together. The door to mine is locked – at least, the door to the corridor is, the one that leads outside. But 'e forgot to lock the one that connects it to the room beside me. Alice's room, where she's asleep with Wares at 'er feet.

I get up sometime 'round two. Alice is sleepin' soundly. I tiptoe to the bed an' look down at 'er, sayin' goodbye inside my 'ead. She's keepin' the rubbish by 'er bedside – the lid of a broken box, looks a bit like a fish; the keys; the feather;

the sheets of paper, folded so many times that they're worn soft, includin' one that's got a picture of a boy in a shinin' suit on it, a boy flyin' in a silver hoop – an' it makes me smile. But it ain't enough to make me want to stay.

She stirs in 'er sleep an' I move away. The dog stirs too, an' I reach down to pat 'im. He gives my palm a lick an' I leave a treat beside 'im on the bed, a lump of steak I saved from dinner, wrapped up in a napkin. A gentle ol' fella, this little dog. I'll miss 'im.

By the time I make it to the door of Alice's cabin, I'm ready fer anythin'. I en't got a clue where I'm goin', but I do know this – wherever it is, I'll go there by myself, by my own choice. I got a full belly an' a smile on my face, an' I don't need much more.

I close the door behind me as gently as I can, an' slip away.

EPILOGUE

A girl – or a creature who looked, to the unwary, like a young girl in a plain linen dress – came walking through the grass between the Silent City and the town that lay in the shadow of its walls. Around her arm, a long narrow bracelet was wrapped in a complicated pattern, its clasp made of ancient bone. She raised her face to the sun, feeling the warmth on her skin, and closed her golden eyes for a moment or two, breathing deeply. Then, with a litheness more animal than human, Dawara moved on.

Every step brought her closer to the house. The memories of the human girl who had once lived there – all that was left of her now – filled Dawara's head as she walked and the Slipskin let them come. The threads of the Relic had held these memories for years and now it was time to release them. Dawara saw the key, large and dark, that had hung above the stove. A slender hand reaching up to take it. The sleeping mother who did not stir when her daughter, swallowing tears, kissed her goodbye. The door closing gently against the night.

Dawara remembered the journey to distant lands, the days and nights of hunger and sorrow, the terror of being alone. The handsome, brown eyed farmer's son and the baby who'd looked so like him. The work, the struggle, the pain of broken bones and sore muscles. All of this she remembered, as though it had happened to her. Then the human's memories of flight flooded Dawara's mind and she smiled. How strange it felt to fly in a body without wings.

The house came into view. Its door was open, the scrubby olive bush beside it throwing it into shade. A man with silver-grey in his dark hair came out through the door and something lit up in Dawara's borrowed mind as Ester remembered his name. *Nikola.* He had stayed to care for her mother, Ester realized, after Bastjan had been claimed by the sea and she by the air.

An old woman sat in a comfortable chair stuffed with bright cushions, in the sunniest corner of the small yard. Her hair was white and her clothes were black from head to toe, but she smiled at Nikola. Dawara watched the old woman as she drew near, and something slowed her steps until finally she stopped. It wasn't fear; Dawara didn't know what it was. Her hearts sped up and she blinked once, twice, wondering why her eyes were filled with tears. Somewhere deep inside her, Ester knew the reason.

Mrs Manduca looked up and her mouth fell open. She raised one hand. The other lay powerless upon her lap, and she tried to speak as she reached for Dawara. Her words wouldn't come – not now, not since the stroke had stolen them – but even if she had been able to say them, Dawara would not have understood.

Somehow, the Slipskin felt her mother in the woman's grief and she let her own tears roll.

For as long as she could Dawara stood there, looking exactly as Ester had looked on the day she fell from the wall. The man called Nikola stared at her, his cheeks wet, and he hurried to the old woman, who was trying to stand on feet that could not hold her, trying to call for her daughter. The last spark of Ester raised Dawara's hand to her mouth. The Slipskin blew a kiss and Ester vanished with it.

Then, in a golden whirlwind that kicked up the dust, the Slipskin rose into the air. She became a blackbird, soaring above the walls of the Silent City, until she landed on the crumbling stone to watch the sun set over the island of Melita.

Dawara perched there for a time, watching and thinking, before swooping down into the Silent City, resuming her own shape as she landed at the edge of her pool. Its waters ebbed with the tide of the sea below and Dawara smiled at her reflection.

She slipped into the pool and changed once more, into a creature built for water. Her tail was wide, her body strong, her lungs as great as a whale's. Down, down through the network of caves she swam, until finally she emerged from an underwater cavern into the sea. Her mother, Dawara remembered, had sung her songs of others just like them. Families of creatures who could slip their skin, lands where she would be among others of her kind, and she knew, one day, she would find them.

Now that she had her power back, a power she never intended to lose again, she would find her kin and they would welcome her. They would greet her like a long-lost sister and she would sing to them of her time among the humans. She would sing of her mother, and in her stories, she would live again.

On and on the Slipskin swam, and the ocean rang with her song.

ACKNOWLEDGEMENTS

This is a book which has had a long and twisting path, and thanks (as always) are due to the many who helped me to bring it this far.

Firstly, my family. To my husband Fergal and to our daughter, who grows more wonderful by the hour – thank you for your loving patience. Bucket, and Little Bucket. To my parents Tom and Doreen – thank you for every word you gave me, and the love with which each of them were given. I love you both endlessly. To my parents-in-law – thank you for the boundless, enthusiastic support and your pride in me. To my aunts and uncles and cousins – thank you for being there, particularly in a year which was so hard on us.

To my darling brother, Graham. Thank you for everything you are. This one is for you.

To my many dear friends – legends, all. Thanks, lads. To my fantastic neighbours, who became my second family in the very strange time during which this book was written, rewritten, and rewritten once more – thanks for getting me through.

To my agent, Polly Nolan, thank you for (mostly) stopping me from making an eejit of myself in public, and for always having my back.

To Katie Jennings, who was my editor at Stripes/Little Tiger Publishing for much of the writing of this book, and without whom it would never have existed – thank you, not only for your expert guidance, but also for your excited email asking me if I was serious about that idea I'd been discussing on Twitter… Your enthusiasm was infectious, and this book is the result.

To Ella Whiddett, who (brave lady) took over the job of editing me, and to the entire Stripes/Little Tiger team, for welcoming me into your midst – most grateful I am, chaps. Special hollers to Leilah Skelton, Charlie Morris and Lauren Ace for their PR/marketing/general wizardry and to Sarah Shaffi for her expertise and guidance.

To Sara Mulvanny (my super-talented cover artist), Sophie Bransby (my super-creative cover designer) and Susila Baybars (my super-patient copyeditor) – thanks for sending this story out into the world with its face washed and its hair neatly combed, and looking so irresistible (I hope!)

To Vashti Hardy, without whose wise counsel at a point of crisis this book might have foundered in its first draft – thank you, story-queen. I can't wait to thrash out more bookish puzzles with you.

To Delia Campbell Hijar and and my fellow author Tarsila Krüse, for their guidance regarding my 'Iberian'. *Gracias. Obrigada.*

To Dr Tine Defour, who helped (as she always does) with my French. *Merci, mon amie.*

To Francis Leneghan, for the soul-music.

And to Shannon Byrne Winter, who was the first person besides my editor and me to lay their eyes on this story. Thank you so much for your encouragement, and for almost two decades of treasured friendship.

To bloggers and Tweeters and booklovers innumerable, including Steph Elliott (@eenalol – and I double-checked this time, Steph, believe me!), Mr Ripley (@EnchantedBooks), Roachie's Reviews (@laurajroach), Kayleigh (@snailycanflyy), Faith and Laura (@272BookFaith), Scoobiesue (@scoobiesue2), Seawood (@seawoodwrites), Louise Nettleton (@Lou_Nettleton), Jo Clarke (@bookloverJo), Karen and O (@karen_wallee), Kerry Tonner (@KerryTonner), Laura Noakes (@lauranoakes), Mrs Tami Wylie (@twylie68), Lily Fae (@faeryartemis), Library Spider (@LibrarySpider), Sarah Loftus and her wonderful pair of readers (@SarahCLoftus),

Gavin Hetherington (@TheGavGav7), Theresa Kelly (the Librarian for Children and Young People at County Wexford Library Services) and so many more – I appreciate you all more than I can say.

To Liam James (@NotSoTweets), who deserves a mention of his own for his wonderful Lockdown #StorytimeWithLiam initiative, and for his tireless support for me and so many other authors. We all owe you a debt, Liam. Thank you.

To the community of teachers on Twitter, particularly Scott Evans, The Reader Teacher (@MrEPrimary), who have enriched my reading and writing world, thank you all. You're marvellous.

To the real Mrs Mythen, who taught me in Senior Infants and First Class a very long time ago – I'm so glad I got to name a heroic, kind, brave character after you. I'll never forget the time and effort you took over me when I was your pupil, and I'll always remember you with gratitude and love. Thank you.

To every child I have ever met on this strange and brilliant journey, my eternal gratitude. Thank you for the sparkle in your eyes, the enthusiasm in your voices and the warmth of your smiles as we've discussed ideas, stories, books, universes and creativity. Imagine yourselves extraordinary every day.

To the army of heroes who kept us all going during

the Covid-19 pandemic of 2020, and who continue (at time of writing) to be the powerhouse behind our survival – the doctors, nurses, care workers, factory workers, retail and supermarket staff, delivery drivers, childcare workers, teachers, TAs and SNAs, cleaners, and so many others – a simple 'thanks' doesn't go far enough, but my gratitude is heartfelt.

And to you, the reader, whose love for Thing in *The Eye of the North* led me to giving him a book of his own, my sincerest thanks. I hope it has been a story worthy of him, and worthy of you.

READ ON FOR AN
EXTRACT FROM

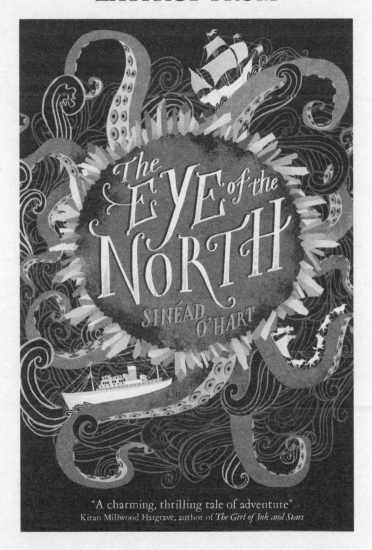

"A charming, thrilling tale of adventure"
Kiran Millwood Hargrave, author of *The Girl of Ink and Stars*

CHAPTER ONE

For as long as she could remember, Emmeline Widget had been *sure* her parents were trying to kill her.

Why else, she reasoned, would they choose to live in a creaky old house where, if she wasn't dodging random bits of collapsing masonry or avoiding the trick steps on the stairs, she had to be constantly on guard for booby-trapped floorboards or doors that liked to boom closed entirely by themselves? She'd lost count of the number of close calls she'd already clocked up, and so she never went anywhere inside her house – not even to the bathroom – without a torch, a ball of twine, and a short, stout stick, the latter to defend herself against whatever might come slithering up the drain. She'd started her fight for survival early. As a baby, she'd learned to walk mostly by avoiding the tentacles, tusks, and whiplike tongues of the various small, furry things in cages that would temporarily line the hallways after one of her parents' research trips. And she'd long ago grown used to shaking out her boots before she put them on in the morning – for, as Emmeline had learned, lots of quiet, dangerous, and very patient creatures liked to hide out in abandoned footwear.

Outside the house wasn't much better. The grounds were overgrown to the point that Widget Manor itself was invisible unless you managed to smack right into it, and that kind of lazy groundskeeping provided a haven for all sorts of things. The year Emmeline turned seven, for instance, her parents had come home from an expedition with a giant squirrel in tow, one with teeth as long as Emmeline's leg. It had wasted no time in getting loose and had spent three weeks destroying half the garden before finally being brought under control. Sometimes, particularly on windy nights, Emmeline wasn't entirely sure her parents were telling the truth when they said the squirrel had been sent back to its distant home. Even worse, a roaring river ran right at the end of their property, sweeping past with all the haughtiness of a diamond-encrusted duchess. Emmeline lived in fear of falling in, and so she never ventured outside without an inflatable life jacket (which, on its days off, doubled as a hot water bottle) and a catapult (to fight off any unexpected nasties she might find living amid the trees – or even, perhaps, the trees themselves).

As a result of all this, Emmeline spent more time in her room reading than did most young ladies of her age. However, she'd long ago dispensed with fiction, having digested everything that lived on the lower shelves of her parents' library (for Emmeline most assuredly did *not* climb, no matter how sturdy the footholds seemed, and so the higher volumes had to lurk, unread, amid the dust). Along with these literary efforts, she'd also worked her way through several tomes about such things as biology and anatomy, subjects that entranced her mother and father. This was unsurprising, considering the elder Widgets were scientists of some sort who had, in their daughter's opinion, a frankly unhygienic obsession with strange animals, but Emmeline herself had found them tiresome. Now she mostly read the sorts of books that would likely keep her alive in an emergency, either because of the survival tips they contained or because they were large enough to serve as a makeshift tent. She was never without at least one, if not two, sturdy books, hardback by preference.

All of these necessities, of course, meant that she was never without her large and rather bulky satchel, either, but she didn't let that stand in her way.

And, as will probably have become clear by now, Emmeline didn't have very many – or, indeed, *any* – friends. There was the household staff, comprising Watt (the butler) and Mrs Mitchell (who did everything else), but they didn't really count because they were always telling her what to do and where to go and *not* to put her dirty feet on that clean floor, thank you very much. Her parents were forever at work, or away, or off at conferences, or entertaining (which Emmeline hated because sometimes she'd be called upon to wear actual *ribbons* and smile and pretend to be something her mother called "lighthearted", which she could never see the point of). She spent a lot of time on her own, and this, if she were to be entirely truthful, suited her fine.

One day, then, when Emmeline came down to breakfast and found her parents absent, she didn't even blink. She just hauled her satchel up on to the chair next to her and rummaged through it for her book, glad to have a few moments of quiet reading time before she had to start ignoring the grown-ups in her life once again.

She was so engrossed in her book – *Knots and Their Uses,* by S. G. Twitchell – that at first she ignored Watt when he slipped into the room bearing in his neatly gloved hands a small silver platter, upon which sat a white envelope. He set it down in front of Emmeline without a word. She made sure to finish right to the end of the chapter (about the fascinating complexities of constrictor knots) before looking up and noticing that she had received a piece of Very Important Correspondence.

She fished around for her bookmark and slid it carefully

into place. Then, ever so gently, she closed the book and eased it back into the satchel, where it glared up at her reproachfully.

"I promise I'll be back to finish you later," she reassured it. "Once I figure out who could *possibly* want to write to me." She frowned at the envelope, which was very clearly addressed to a MISS EMMELINE WIDGET. PRIVATE AND CONFIDENTIAL, it added.

Just because it happened to be addressed to her, though, didn't mean she should be so silly as to actually *open* it. Not without taking the proper precautions, at least.

In the silence of the large, empty room, Emmeline flipped open her satchel again. From its depths she produced a tiny stoppered bottle, within which a viciously blue liquid was just about contained. She uncorked it as gently as possible, slowly tipping the bottle until one solitary drop hung on its lip, and then – very, *very* carefully – she let the drop fall on to the envelope.

"Hmm," she said after a moment or two, raising an eyebrow. "That's odd."

The liquid didn't smoke, or fizz, or explode in a cloud of sparkle, or indeed do anything at all. It just sat there, like a splodge of ink, partially obscuring her name.

"If you're not poisoned," murmured Emmeline, quickly putting away the bottle (for its fumes could cause dizziness in enclosed spaces, like breakfast rooms), "then *what* are you?"

In the side pocket of her satchel, Emmeline always carried a pair of thick gardening gloves. She put these on, and then she picked up – with some difficulty, it has to be pointed out – her butter knife. Suitably armed, she slowly slit the envelope open, keeping it at all times directed away from her face.

A thick sheet of creamy paper slid out on to the silver platter, followed by a stiff card. Emmeline, who'd been holding her breath in case the act of opening the envelope released some sort of brain-shredding gas, spluttered as the first line of the letter caught her eye. As quickly as she could, given that she was wearing gloves more suited to cutting down brambles than dealing with paperwork, she put aside the card and grabbed up the letter.

She stared at the words for ages, but they stayed exactly the same.

Dearest Emmeline, the letter began.

If you are reading this, then in all likelihood you are now an orphan.

Also by Sinéad O'Hart

ABOUT THE AUTHOR

Sinéad O'Hart lives in County Meath, near Dublin with her husband and their daughter. She has done many jobs in her life, including working as a butcher and a bookseller. She has a degree in English and History, a PhD in Old and Middle English Language and Literature and can read Middle English with perfect fluency. Sinéad is the author of *The Eye of the North*, *The Star-spun Web* and *Skyborn*.

@SJOHart

sjohart.wordpress.com